Stuck On Them

Maya Nicole

Edited by Karen Sanders Editing

Stuck On Them is a standalone why choose romance. That means the main character will have a happily ever after with three men. Recommended for readers 18+ for adult content and language.

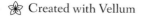 Created with Vellum

Dedication

To anyone who has ever been called vanilla—remember, vanilla is the essential ingredient in a banana split. You just need to find the right banana... or three.

Chapter 1

Rat Terror

Paige

I'd made a horrible mistake.

A blunder so big, it paled in comparison to all others I had made in my twenty-seven years.

Which was exactly how I ended up standing face-to-face with the biggest fucking rat I'd ever seen. And no, not one of those men with the pot bellies and thick gold chains pulling at their overgrown chest hair.

It was an actual rat in the flesh, with beady eyes and a tail so gross that even the bravest of exterminators would have simultaneously screamed bloody murder and pissed themselves. My bladder might have been as leakproof as a boat with Flex Seal, but boy did I scream.

I screamed so loud that the cat-sized varmint leapt right at me from its perch on top of my dorm-room-sized refrigerator. It was a fight-or-flight situation, and I was not in the mood to get rabies, so I ran.

In two strides, I was out the door, narrowly avoiding my neighbor's shoe rack in the process of fleeing from the clutches of the possessed Splinter.

I nearly jumped out of my skin as the door across the hall slammed open. A man who looked barely legal poked his head out with narrowed eyes and a tight-lipped expression. "What the actual fuck is going on out here?"

"Call the Turtles!" My foot caught on the edge of a neighbor's doormat, and I pitched forward, yelping as my elbow connected with the hard surface of the wall. Pain radiated up my arm in waves, and for a moment, my vision blurred.

"The Turtles? What are you smoking?" The man cocked his head to the side, examining me for any sign of what hallucinogen I might be on.

"I hate to break it to you, buddy, but this is me, au naturel." I leaned against the wall, rubbing my elbow.

"Well, keep it down. I'm trying to-" His gaze fell to the hallway floor. "Ah!" He slammed his door as the rat scurried past him and right for me.

What had I done to deserve such an unfortunate turn of events in my life?

With a high-pitched squeal that belonged in an opera house, not an apartment hallway, I nearly face-planted getting into the bathroom at the end of the hall. I slammed the door, turning the lock in hopes the rat didn't have any ninja skills.

My body shuddered, and I did the creepy creature dance, shaking out my body to rid it of any rat molecules that might have landed on me.

"Don't cry. Don't cry," I chanted as I paced the small, outdated space with a cracked sink and yellowing linoleum.

I wasn't equipped to deal with rats or any other type of bug. In fact, I was so emotionally fragile that a cockroach was liable to send me straight into a panic attack.

Turning on the sink, I bent over it, splashing cold water on my face. It immediately calmed me down but didn't stop the pounding of my heart.

It's just a rat. People have them as pets all the time. One is the Turtles' most trusted advisor.

I snorted water up my nose and coughed, shutting off the faucet. Water dripped down onto my shirt, and I lifted the hem to dry my face. I had left a towel on the towel bar the first day I moved in to dry my hands on and someone had used it and left it on the floor.

It wasn't that I wanted to live like a college student again, but getting into a decent apartment on such short notice and for my budget was impossible. As soon as I found a job, I'd start looking for a place where four micro-apartments didn't share a bathroom.

Straightening my spine, I flung open the door, ready to face the rat. Instead, I was met with an empty hallway and the faint smell of weed.

Cautiously, I walked back to my open door and peered inside. I'd completely lost my mind thinking a hundred-square-foot apartment was enough space.

Across from the door was a small kitchenette that had the tiniest of counters and a small sink with a microwave above it. Next to that was the minifridge, which was now missing the rat that had been chilling on top when I'd gotten back from the grocery store.

Leaving the door open, I grabbed the broom leaning in the corner and banged it on the small lift-top coffee table that also served as a desk and dining table for the small space. The likelihood the rat had come back in was small, but there were no guarantees.

I eyed the loveseat warily. "It's gone, Paige. Stop being- ah!" My cellphone buzzed on the table, and I flung the broom at it, narrowly missing it.

My heart hadn't seen this much action in a long time. Now I didn't feel so nervous about losing my health insurance in a few weeks because my heart was holding up better than expected given it had already been broken into pieces.

I grabbed my phone, inhaling sharply at the countless unanswered message notifications that were displayed on the bottom of the screen. That's exactly how they were going to stay until I was ready to deal with the fallout from my decisions.

I accepted the call from my best friend. "Thank God, Nora. You will not believe what just happened."

Nora hummed as if thinking. "You met a dashing young prince who made up for all the orgasms you've been missing out on?"

"I wish." I shut my door and locked it before staring at the loveseat and deciding to sit on one of the small stairs going up to the bed loft instead. "There was a rat in my apartment."

She laughed. "What I would pay to have seen your reaction."

"Hey, that's not nice." I cradled the phone against my ear and shoulder and leaned back on my elbows, my eyes scanning the room just in case my mortal enemy was back. "He almost ate my face off."

Nora and I laughed and then both fell silent. We'd been best friends since we'd been roommates in our freshmen year of college. My moving across the country had not only been a big decision but one I made rather impulsively. It was completely out of character for me, but I'd also never had my heart ripped out and put through a paper shredder before.

"You know you can always come back and live with me until you figure things out," she said softly.

My chin quivered, and I bit down on my lip. Enough tears had been shed over the past week to fill a small swimming pool, and I refused to cry anymore. "I can't be there right now. Maybe in a few months once this short-term lease is up."

"Well, if that's the case, then you'd better be living it up and not just stay holed up in that-"

I screamed, nearly dropping my phone as I scrambled up the steps. The rat was back, this time running across the small space and going under the couch. The broom was still on the floor where I'd left it, but I was too scared to step foot off the stairs.

Nora was laughing her ass off on the other end of the phone. "He's your new roommate. Or maybe it's a she and she's trying to find somewhere to have her little rat babies."

"Nora!" The tears I'd been holding back finally broke free. It figured I'd trade living with one rat for another.

"Hey... I was just teasing, Paige." Nora's voice softened, and I wished she was with me. "Pack a bag and I'll get you a hotel for the weekend, okay? It's Friday night, and even if the super was around, they probably wouldn't do anything right now."

I sniffled and wiped my tears, not taking my eyes off the couch. "You don't have to do that."

"I am. So go pack a bag and make sure to take a dress because you're going to go have some drinks and find yourself a man to hook up with." She spoke so nonchalantly that I had to laugh. "I know it's never been your thing for one-night stands, but a good orgasm from a man who knows what they're doing will help you relax and clear your head."

While considering her words of wisdom, I climbed the rest of the way up what could hardly be called stairs to my loft. Nowhere was safe from the rat, but there wasn't anywhere it could hide with my mattress taking up almost the entire space. In the corner, I had one of my suitcases still packed while the other lay open at the foot of the bed. I hadn't exactly figured out storage solutions just yet, and I was glad I hadn't spent the money. I was quickly realizing my mistake in running away to New York City and already wanted to go home.

Nora had gone silent besides the clicking of her typing. She'd tried to convince me to stay when she'd dropped me off at the airport just over a week ago, but I couldn't find it in me. Something inside me snapped when I found out what my now ex-fiancé had done. I'd thought he loved me, but boy was I wrong. Never again would I put myself in such a vulnerable position.

"Paige? You there?" Nora's voice snapped me back into action and I yanked my unopened suitcase onto the bed with one arm.

"Barely," I grunted. "I got this damn thing up here, but now I don't know how I'm going to get it down."

"You can just slide it down the stairs; maybe it will squish the rat at the bottom." She laughed as I gagged at the thought of having to deal with the aftermath of that.

Cradling my phone between my shoulder and ear again, I maneuvered the bag so it was lying flat on the stairs and let go. I flinched at the noise it produced.

"I probably just scared the shit out of my downstairs neighbor." I turned sideways and went down the stairs, leaping the last two steps to avoid the suitcase. "Phew, that was a workout."

"That can be your warmup for later. I booked you a room for three nights at The Bella Grand Hotel. They're sending a car to pick you up in fifteen minutes."

"That's way too expensive!" I kept my eye on the couch as I shoved a few pairs of shoes in a plastic bag and squeezed them into my suitcase.

"Only the best for you, babe. Just send a thank you note to my dad since I put it on his card." Nora's dad was a former hockey superstar who had traded in his stick for a whistle. To say he was generous to his daughter was an understatement.

"Nora," I admonished as I quickly grabbed my laptop

and charger from the table and put it in my tote along with my toiletry bag.

"He said I could use it for emergencies, and this is definitely an emergency. I can't have my best friend being eaten alive by rats." A car door slammed in the background. "I'm headed to work. Text me if you need to, okay?"

"Thank you. I don't know what I'd do without you."

We hung up, and I rolled my bag into the hall. At least all the excitement had made me forget why I was there, even if it was just for a minute.

Midtown Manhattan on a Friday night was nuts, and I'd never been so simultaneously giddy and anxious. There was something about all the different people and the noise that made me feel alive.

My driver skillfully navigated us through the streets, past hordes of pedestrians and vehicles. We turned into the entrance of the hotel and a man in a suit opened my door for me and got my bag out of the back.

I didn't know what Nora was thinking booking one of the most opulent hotels in the city for me.

When I made it into the lobby through the biggest glass and gold doors I'd ever seen, I stepped into a different world. There were so many twinkling chandeliers and golden columns that I almost needed my sunglasses.

It felt like everyone was staring at me as I walked to the check-in desk in my jeans and an oversized t-shirt. People were dressed in business attire, and I looked like something the cat dragged in.

After checking in, I found my room and immediately went to stare out the window at the city below. It was so much different from the view of a brick wall out of my apartment's tiny window that was just big enough to escape out of.

My phone buzzed for what felt like the hundredth time, and I sighed as I sat in an armchair and opened my messages. Daniel had called me at least ten times since last week and texted me ten times as much.

"Don't do it, Paige. Don't you dare," I muttered with my thumb poised over Daniel's name.

I'd packed my bags and left while he was at work. Most of the furniture in our shared house he had already, but I left a few things behind like my wall of books and things I never used. A few boxes went to the storage unit I had gotten before I'd moved in with him, and that was that.

He hadn't bothered to check on me when I no-showed to work and only cared when he got home to find me and my stuff gone.

The asshole should have cared the second I found out he was cheating, but instead, he'd taken my silence as acceptance.

What did he think would happen?

My willpower evaporated, and I pressed his name, pulling up the string of one-sided messages over the past week. I skimmed through them, most just repeating the same thing.

Daniel: *Where are you? Call me.*

Daniel: *You can't just leave and not tell me when you'll be back.*

Daniel: *Are you moving out?*

Daniel: *You quit? What the fuck, Paige? You're blowing this way out of proportion.*

Me: *I've moved. I didn't have time to pack my books. I will send Nora to get them at your earliest convenience.*

I didn't expect him to answer back immediately since he was most likely still working at the law firm he worked at with his father—the same law firm where I'd met him and fallen for his charms. There was no way I could show my face there again after breaking up with him.

Especially if the woman he cheated with was still working there.

My phone buzzed several times, and I was almost too scared to look. Daniel had always had a quiet calmness about him, but with all the texts and messages, I'd say his calmness was long gone.

Daniel: *We're getting married in two months.*

Me: *Definitely knot. Ha. Get it? We won't be tying the knot.*

Daniel: *Don't make jokes. Come home so we can deal with this like adults. People make mistakes.*

Me: *Should have thought about the consequences before you fucked someone else. Besides, what did you say? Oh, that's right, I'm too "vanilla." I'll show you vanilla.*

I stood, going to my bag and flinging it open. Things had been weird between us for the past few months, but I just thought it was a combination of wedding and work stress. It hurt to know it was because of his perceived boredom in the bedroom.

There had been no sign he was bored with our sex life. Granted, we had a total of three basic sex positions we rotated through, but he was the one that initiated them, and maybe if he'd been better with foreplay, it would have naturally progressed to more adventurous sex. Or he could have just *talked* to me.

Daniel: *What do you mean you'll show me vanilla? I shouldn't have said that... I was upset. We can fix it.*

Me: *It's over. I'm getting ready to go out. Have a lovely evening.*

He tried calling me, but I rejected the call. I didn't know how I could make it any clearer to him we were over. We had been the second he started sleeping with someone else. Who knew how many other women there'd been?

My stomach turned in disgust, and I grabbed a pair of underwear and a nightshirt from my bag. Staring down at them, I thought about what Nora had said about an orgasm relaxing and clearing my mind.

Shutting my eyes, I tried to relax my shoulders that were bunched up by my ears. Could I go on the prowl and find a man? I'd never been hit on in a bar or club before, but I also had never gone out alone or intending to find a one-night stand. I'd always gone with a group. If I was safe, it would be fine. Nora did it all the time.

The odds of me finding someone to hook up with were slim, but I dug to the bottom of my suitcase and pulled out a blush pink cap-sleeved dress with a purple and green floral design. It had a deep V neckline, an A-line skirt that went to just above the knee, and a fitted waist. It was the flirtiest thing I owned, and there was a small sliver of satisfaction knowing Daniel hated it.

With butterflies swirling in my stomach, I went into the bathroom to get ready. It might be a complete waste of time, but the alternative was moping in my hotel room and thinking every noise was a rat.

What trouble could come from a little fun?

Chapter 2

Lime Violation

Ryker

"The way you fingered that lime was not sexy." Luca leaned back in his chair, folding his hands behind his head as the final version of a social media marketing video ended.

A video that involved Garrett showcasing a new state-of-the-art air fryer by sexualizing the food he was cooking with. It took a lot of finesse to pull off, but with Garrett's acting skills and his camera-ready hands and forearms, it was a masterpiece. I expected the series of short videos to go viral.

Garrett smacked a hand on the table with a smirk. "I wasn't fingering it, asshole. I was teasing its little pucker, asking it to let me in." He demonstrated on the glossy wood of the tabletop. "See? A caress, not a finger. It was absolutely necessary before reaming it. You should know the importance of preparation."

I pulled off my glasses and pinched the bridge of my nose. The back and forth between Garrett and Luca was nothing new, but lately, it had done nothing but grate on my nerves. We were entering a whole new realm of clientele, and their expectations for success and professionalism were sky-high.

I cleared my throat, interrupting the banter between Garrett and Luca. "Let's talk standards. We're setting ourselves up to work with some big companies and we need to be sure we keep things professional. That includes in meetings, even if it is just us three."

Garrett crossed his arms over his chest, his playful smile disappearing, but said nothing.

Luca nodded slowly, finally understanding the seriousness of the situation. Or so I thought. "In my professional opinion, that lime didn't look like it was a consenting citrus. If we don't reshoot that, they're going to drop us for violating it. Do you really want that on your conscience? Hm?"

Was I the only one that could take things seriously anymore? We were one of the most successful marketing companies in New York, but that could all go away in an instant. Companies had collapsed for much less.

"For fuck's sake, Luca. Can you be professional for one minute so we can leave for the day?" I pushed my chair back and stood, leaning forward with my hands on the conference room table. "This is a business in case you've forgotten."

He held up his hands in mock surrender. "Woah, woah, woah! Calm down, old man. It's Friday and we're finally finished with this project. You should be smiling, not looking like someone used an unlubed citrus reamer on your ass."

"Old man?" I knew where this was going, and I straightened, smoothing a hand down the front buttons of my cardigan. Unlike him with his tailored three-piece suit, I preferred to dress down on Fridays. But he was right about calming down, and sometimes I needed the reminder. "You only wish you could pull this off."

"Atta boy!" Luca jumped to his feet and clapped his hands together. "Let's send all of this over for final approval and go celebrate."

"Celebrate by doing what exactly?" Garrett didn't look up from his laptop screen where he was sending our client an email with a link to all of the material we'd created.

This had been our biggest marketing project to date, but the easy part was over. Now we had to wait for the go-ahead to run the campaigns we'd spent every waking hour planning for the past few weeks.

Luca pushed in his chair and ran a hand across the back of it before picking at something invisible. "Well... I was thinking... it's been a while."

Garrett paused for a beat in the middle of typing, leaving the room silent besides the soft whir of the air conditioner. He was the reason we hadn't been out, and Luca and I both stared at him, waiting for his response.

He finally shrugged but didn't look up from his screen. "If it feels right, then sure. If not, I'm just going to head home."

"I think this is what both of you need. I'll have my

driver pick us up in ten unless you want to go home and change." Luca raised an eyebrow in my direction. "Might improve our chances."

Garrett shut his laptop and looked at me. "I think the Mr. Rogers look will actually improve our chances. It somewhat cancels out the semi-permanent scowl on his face."

I kept my expression neutral, even though I wanted to scowl. "Let's go before I change my mind."

Friday nights were both the best and worst nights to go out. On one hand, there were a lot of opportunities to find a woman, but that also increased our chances of being recognized.

As we walked into the Diamond Lounge at The Bella Grand Hotel, we split up—Luca and Garrett heading to the far end of the bar and me to the other. If any of us were going to be recognized and draw attention, it would be Luca since his family owned The Bella Grand along with other locations across the world.

The bar was busy, but there were still seats since there was a lull between the happy hour crowd and the late-night partiers. With dark wood and strategic lighting, the atmosphere was the perfect romantic backdrop.

I slid onto a barstool next to a pair of blondes who were both drinking something pink. I nodded to the bartender, who nodded back, acknowledging he was getting me my usual.

The two women looked over at me and then whispered to each other, giggling. Giggling wasn't really my thing, but they were both attractive.

Until the one next to me spoke.

"Hi, I'm Sarah. This is Megan." Her voice was nasally, and I knew without a doubt it would be an erection killer. "What's your name, daddy?"

The urge to roll my eyes was so strong I had to look away. Garrett met my gaze and subtly shook his head. Luca was laughing into his whiskey glass, obviously having heard her say the word *daddy*.

Fuck. The whole bar practically had.

I looked back at the women, who were both smiling at me. "I'm not your daddy." I grabbed the drink the bartender had just put down and slid over to the empty barstool next to me.

Both women scoffed and pinned me with dirty looks before the one named Sarah turned to give me her back.

Shaking my head, I picked up my bourbon and took a drink while scanning the room. I felt out of practice since I'd been using an exclusive dating app for hookups for the past year. In a way, it was cut and dry with what both parties wanted, and an added benefit was the non-disclosure agreement automatically in place.

It wasn't the same as meeting someone in the wild, though. On the app, there was very little flirting, no anticipation, and only physical attraction. So far, the bar wasn't much better thanks to the giggling blondes.

Someone gently touched my elbow, and I turned my head back in the direction of the blonde, ready to make it abundantly clear I wasn't interested. She might have been attractive, but I was bored with carbon copies of the same woman.

"Is this seat taken?" A woman with brown hair smiled sheepishly, her cheeks tinged pink.

"It's not." I glanced at her mouth, unable to resist as she bit into her bottom lip. "It's all yours."

Tucking her hair behind her ear, she scooted the stool out, turning her body toward me as she sat. Her knees brushed against my thigh as she swiveled forward, and my skin tingled with awareness.

She drummed her fingernails against the bar and then reached forward to grab the drink menu. "What's good?"

"You can't go wrong with any of the drinks here." I swiveled in her direction, one of my knees settling against the side of her leg.

She didn't move away from the touch, but her hands subtly tightened on the menu and she looked over at my glass. "What are you drinking?"

"Bourbon." She scrunched her nose, and I scooted my drink toward her and reached over the bar to grab a cocktail straw. "Try it."

"Out of your glass?" She took the straw from me and put it in the amber liquid. "What if you have cooties?"

"What if you do?" I put my hand on the back of her chair and leaned in to whisper in her ear. "If I have it my way, the last thing on your mind will be my cooties."

Her skin broke out in goosebumps as I brushed my lips just under her ear before returning to my space. It was a bold move, but if I wanted this to happen, I couldn't tiptoe around what I wanted.

She stayed silent and nodded as she swirled the straw. She put her finger over the end of it and lifted it from the glass, placing it in her mouth. My cock stirred as her pink lips closed around it, and she met my eyes as she removed her finger.

Her hazel eyes dilated, and she slowly pulled the straw out, her cheeks hollowing as she sucked the liquid from it. Heat spread down my spine as I imagined her doing that to me.

"Was that good for you?" I moved my hand off the back of her stool and trailed my knuckles down her bare arm.

"It was." Her face twisted a bit, and she coughed.

I chuckled and gestured for the bartender to bring me two more. "It gets smoother the more you drink it."

She brought a hand to her throat. "Wow. That's strong enough to grow some hair on your chest."

"Oh, yeah? You have experience with that?" The juxtaposition between what she'd just done to the straw and what came out of her mouth was amusing. I grabbed my glass and tried to hide my smile as I took a drink.

"And if I do? Body hair is natural. You wouldn't let a random nipple hair distract you from the goods, would you?"

I choked on my drink, and my eyes watered as the alcohol went down the wrong pipe. I didn't even have to look across the bar to know Luca and Garrett were laughing their asses off; I could hear them.

She slapped my back a few times before rubbing it in

circles. "Oh, God. I can't believe I said that. That is not cute. Not cute at all."

Sensing she was about to flee, I mustered up the strength to speak. "Do you have nipple hair?" I asked in a strangled voice.

Her hand left my back to my dismay, and she covered her face. "I'm horrible at this."

The bartender put our fresh drinks in front of us, including a glass of water. He even put ice in her bourbon to make it easier to drink. He was going to get an extra-large tip for being so observant.

I gulped down some water and braved a glance at my friends. Their eyes were on us, but they were whispering to each other like two schoolgirls discussing their crushes. I raised an eyebrow and both of them subtly nodded.

My attention returned to the woman next to me, who still had her face covered. "Hey." I trailed my fingers up her forearm to her wrist and gently circled it, pulling it away from her face. "You aren't horrible."

She leaned closer to me. "I just brought up nipple hair to a very attractive man that I want to um... you know," she whispered.

I didn't let go of her wrist and lowered her hand to my thigh. "Do I seem bothered by that?"

Her breath hitched and she squeezed lightly. "I've never done this before... I mean I've done *it*, but not with someone I don't know." She bit her lip again and I cupped her jaw, brushing my thumb across her lip to free it.

Her hand moved to my inner thigh, so close to my dick that I could feel the heat of her skin. She might have been too innocent for what I had in store for her, but if things didn't happen the way I wanted them to, I'd at least have her to myself for the night.

"What's your name?" I moved my hand to the side of her neck, resisting the urge to pull her closer and take her mouth with mine.

She was naturally a stunner with smooth skin and wavy brown hair that made me want to bury my fingers in it as I fucked her full lips. Her eyes were so expressive, and I could tell she was turned on but a little apprehensive.

"Paige." Her voice was lower as I stroked her throat. "What's yours?"

"Ryker, but you can call me Ry if you want." I hoped I didn't regret giving her my name. "Do you live here in the city, or are you just visiting?"

"Here on business." She shivered as I slowly removed my hand from her neck, my fingertips lingering.

"Me too." The lie felt bitter on my tongue, but the less she knew about me, the better. "Shall we?" I gestured to the drinks in front of us.

Her hand still on my thigh, she lifted her drink and watched me over the rim as she took a drink. For never having picked up a guy before, she was doing a damn good job of it.

I swirled my drink in my glass and then gulped it down, ready to get this show on the road. And what a show it would hopefully be.

Chapter 3

Cowabunga

Paige

I'd summoned up every single ounce of self-confidence I had buried deep inside and approached a man who was probably out of my league. In the thirty minutes I'd been in the bar, not one man had piqued my interest quite like he had.

He'd caught my eye when he walked past the table I'd been at having some liquid courage. My heart had nearly stopped as he strode through the dimly lit room.

He had a commanding presence about him, and his impeccably styled blond hair glowed under the lights. His intense blue eyes scanned the crowd quickly before settling on a seat next to a blonde at the bar.

At first, I'd been apprehensive when I saw him move away from the woman he sat next to, but the alcohol had loosened me up a bit and I took a chance.

And now there we were, after some flirting and not-so-subtle conversation, heading up to his room.

Was this how it was supposed to go? From the first moment of contact to now, it couldn't have been more than fifteen or twenty minutes.

There was maybe a one percent chance he was a serial killer, and I was just another one of his victims. He had an unwavering confidence and charisma I'd never encountered before. I didn't know how else to explain how I'd ended up on his arm so easily.

"I'm in one of the executive rooms on the fortieth floor." Ryker laced his fingers with mine as we walked toward the exit. His grip was strong but gentle, reassuring me as we made our way to the door.

I trailed behind slightly and tugged on his hand, looking back over my shoulder at the bar. "Don't we need to pay?"

"He'll charge it to my room." He fell into step beside me and let go of my hand, opting to put his hand around my waist and pull me against his side. I leaned into him, our strides syncing together in a comfortable rhythm.

There were so many questions I wanted to ask him, but we were headed upstairs to have sex and I didn't want to kill the mood. Although, if my nipple hair word vomit didn't scare him off, asking him what he did for a living and where he was from probably wouldn't.

I should have asked Nora what the typical protocol was for hookups. Was I supposed to give him my number when we finished? Did I spend the night? Were we supposed to discuss what we liked and didn't like first?

Even without those worries, I had the unease of wondering if there might be something wrong with me in the bedroom. I hadn't had sex with my ex for at least six weeks before I caught him with someone else, and even before then, it wasn't anything to shout about from the mountaintops.

We walked past the bank of elevators to a small reception area with a security guard at the desk. He smiled at me and Ryker and then a large ornate door next to him automatically opened.

The door led to a sitting area with leather couches and chairs, and a massive chandelier hanging in the center. We approached a bank of four elevators, their golden doors gleaming.

I gulped as my chest tightened and my palms started to sweat. "Wow, this is fancy." I looked at each of the elevators since the one he scanned his card for was taking its sweet time. "Can't we use one of the other ones?"

"The other three go to the penthouse floors. This goes to the two executive levels." He brushed his lips against the shell of my ear. "You're trembling."

I blew out a shaky breath. "What if-" I was saved from the embarrassment of confessing my worries by the elevator sliding open with a ding.

He led me inside and before I could get more nervous, he had me against the cool mirrored wall, his lips meeting mine for the first time.

His kiss was gentler than expected, and I slid my hands from where they'd landed on his biceps to his waist.

My touch was the catalyst he needed to dig his fingers

into my hair and tilt my head to deepen the kiss. I didn't think I'd ever been kissed with so much passion. I opened my mouth when his tongue pressed against my lips. There was no going back now.

All of my nerves went out the window, and I was left with a burning ache between my legs. If his kiss was any indication of his skills in the bedroom, by the end of the night I was going to forget all about my shit show of a life.

He broke the kiss and I groaned, not wanting to stop, but also grateful for the break to breathe. His lips traveled down my jaw to my neck, and my body thrummed in appreciation.

"The elevator." I gasped as he nipped at my sensitive skin. "Room."

"Mm." He didn't reach for the elevator button. Instead, he lifted me, my legs wrapping around him of their own accord. My purse slid off my shoulder and hit the floor, but all of my thoughts were on how soft his sweater felt on my thighs and his hands on my ass.

The elevator doors started to close but then popped back open as two men walked in. I attempted to unwrap myself from Ryker, but he held me tighter,

"What floor do you two need?" A man with tattoos covering his forearms and running under his rolled-up sleeves pressed a button and the doors slid closed.

"Forty." Ryker kissed me again, distracting me momentarily from the fact that we had an audience.

Heat raced across every inch of my skin, not just from feeling the warmth of his body through my increasingly wet panties, but from the eyes I knew were on us.

One of his hands let me go, but I didn't attempt to escape again. I was too far gone with my lust to care about our very blatant PDA. My thighs squeezed around him as he kneaded my breast through my dress.

He kissed down to my neck again, and I opened my eyes to find the two men watching us with lust-filled gazes. I'd never felt so uninhibited and desired in all my life.

Ryker moved up to suck my earlobe, his warm breath tickling my skin as he breathed heavily. "Do you want me to stop?" His fingers brushed the swell of my breast at the V of my neckline.

"Don't stop." The elevator was just about to its destination, so how much further could it really get?

I quickly got my answer when Ryker pulled the top of my dress and bra down and took my nipple into his mouth. The man without the tattoos on his arms brought his hand to his lips, rubbing his bottom one with his index finger as he watched.

Was I into this? My body certainly was as my hunger ratcheted up another notch, my core aching to be touched.

The elevator came to a stop and the doors slid open. Both men hesitated for a moment before stepping out. Tattoo man looked back over his shoulder and gave me a smoldering look and wink before the doors shut.

"Oh, God," I moaned. I'd been holding it in the whole minute we'd been in the elevator. "What just happened?"

The elevator ride to the next floor was short, and Ryker put my dress back in place and lowered my legs to the ground. "I hope that was okay. I couldn't wait to get my hands and mouth on you." He picked up my purse before guiding me out of the elevator with his hand on the small of my back and down the hall to his room.

I didn't speak because I wasn't sure how I felt about what had just transpired. I'd never been big on kissing and showing affection in public, but had that just been because of the men I'd been with?

"Paige?" Ryker opened his door, stepping to the side to let me enter. "That didn't cross a boundary for you, did it?"

I trailed my hand across his chest as I walked past. "No. I kind of liked it. We got lucky they didn't pull out their phones and record."

The room was double the size of a typical hotel room with a sitting area and a small dinette area. The king-sized bed looked like a dream, but that wasn't what caught my attention. Two sides of the room were floor-to-ceiling windows with views that made my heart flutter.

Momentarily forgetting the wetness between my thighs and the man who caused it, I went to a window overlooking Central Park. "This is breathtaking."

After growing up without a lot of money and then focusing on school and my career, I hadn't had the time or money to travel yet, but this was my sign to start. It was everything like the pictures I'd seen, yet nothing like them at the same time. I felt so small compared to the spread of lights reaching into the horizon.

Ryker stood behind me and wrapped one arm around my upper chest and the other around my waist, leaning his head against the side of mine. With heels, my five-foot-eight-inch frame was only a few inches shorter than his.

"You're breathtaking." His hand grabbed a handful of

my dress, slowly easing it up. "I want to see how wet you are for me." He slipped a finger under the side of my panties and groaned against my neck. "Fuck, Paige. You're soaked. Is all of this for me or is some of it for the two men in the elevator?"

At the mention of the onlookers, my thighs squeezed together, trapping his hand. I couldn't control it, and with this man, I didn't want to. "For all three."

His finger ran up and down my slit, teasing me with a promise of what was to come. "We could have stopped the elevator."

I bit my lip and put a hand against the window, bracing myself. "And then what?"

He peppered kisses underneath my ear. "I would have turned you just like this against the mirrored wall so they could watch me finger fuck you."

Two fingers plunged in, and I gasped, my legs squeezing even tighter as he bit down on my ear. There were no languid strokes or teasing; he thrust into me like he was using his cock. I could hear how wet I was, and that only turned me on more.

"Oh, God. Please, Ryker." I had to put my other hand on the window to steady myself.

He met my eyes in the reflection on the window. "Are you imagining them watching us? How turned on they'd be from hearing how wet you are?"

I could picture everything in my mind. The man with the tattoos leaning back against the wall and adjusting himself. The other man showed no emotion on his face besides his darkened eyes and the bulge in his pants. They couldn't take their eyes off us.

The tingling sensation of an orgasm rippled down my spine and my clit burned with the need for more stimulation than the occasional press of his palm. "I'm almost... there."

His fingers slowed and my knees nearly gave out. "Your orgasm belongs to them just as much as to me."

"What?" My chest heaved and I briefly considered reaching between my legs and rubbing my clit.

"Do you want them to watch you come on my hand?" He removed his hand that had been locked against my chest and turned my head, so I was looking at him. "Do you want to let them watch us fuck?"

Oh. My. God.

My lips parted but nothing came out. Was he for real? Was I actually considering the idea?

"But... what? How?" I craned my neck to look past him at the door where I could see a sliver of light from the hallway peeking in. He hadn't shut the door. "Ryker..."

"They're my two most trusted friends. You can say no, but..." He pulled his fingers from me and held them up for me to see before putting them in his mouth. As he sucked them, he groaned, his eyes shutting for a moment before opening with a renewed heat. "I think you want to say yes."

"They would just watch?" I whispered. "This is all so... you tricked me."

He turned me so I was facing him, backing me against

the window. "I can see how you'd think that, but I wanted you to feel what it might be like before I asked."

I bit my lip, wondering if the honesty in his blue eyes was real or a look perfected to bend women to his will. "And if I say no?"

He cupped my cheek, the scent of me strong and reminding me of how turned on I'd been at the prospect of sharing my body with three men. "Then I lock the door and I make you come over and over again."

I shut my eyes as he ran his thumb back and forth across my bottom lip. The escalation of events over the past thirty or so minutes was insane, and I was both terrified and excited. This could all go horribly wrong, but would it? Even if the two men joined in, I wasn't opposed to the idea, was I?

"I know it's a lot to take in." He kissed my cheek. "I completely understand if-"

"Yes."

His thumb stopped moving as if he was shocked. "Yes?"

I opened my eyes, meeting his. "Yes, they can watch. My safe word is cowabunga." The rat incident had affected my brain more than I thought. Who picks cowabunga as their safe word during an incredibly sexy sexual encounter?

A flash of confusion washed across his features, but then he threw his head back and laughed. It was the most beautiful sight seeing his wide grin and the amusement in his eyes. The tense moment we'd just had evaporated. "That cannot be your safe word."

"Why not? It's my word. It's either that or hairy nipple, and I don't think you want me saying that in front of your friends." *Shut up, Paige.* "I didn't grow any hairs from that bourbon, did I?"

His eyes twinkled in the dim light, and he ran a finger down to my cleavage. "I can check."

I batted his hand away. "Cowabunga!"

He captured my wrist and pinned it above my head against the window, his face turning serious. "Safe words aren't a joke, Paige. If you say it, I'll take it as my cue to stop what I'm doing to find out what you're uncomfortable with. Do you understand?"

My breath stuttered at his intensity, and I nodded.

He let go of my wrist, trailing his fingers down my arm. "I need to hear it."

"I understand." My skin broke out in goosebumps and my heart rate increased. This was actually happening.

"Do you have any limits?" He stroked back up my arm, entwining our fingers against the window above my head.

"I... I don't know. I'm vanilla." I cringed as the word left my lips and looked down. The less confident side of me threatened to take over, and I grasped at the woman I'd been only a minute ago.

"Look at me." Ryker sounded angry, and my head snapped up, taken aback at his tone. "Men who use the term vanilla think saltines are spicy. They're projecting their issue on someone else."

I snorted, even though he was dead serious. "I don't know what my limits are."

"Then I guess we'll have to test them." He let go of my hand.

My eyes widened as he backed toward the door, his eyes not leaving mine. Were they waiting in the hall? Oh, God. This was happening and my heart felt like it was trying to escape my chest cavity.

"Paige." He stopped next to the door, his rumbly voice both a threat and a promise. "On your knees."

It felt like my vision tunneled in on him as he opened the door and the light from the hallway bathed one side of his face in light and the other in shadow. I could hear footsteps in the hall, heading closer and closer.

With a deep breath and a silent prayer to the sex gods to protect me, I got on my knees.

Chapter 4

The Cannoli Gods Giveth

Luca

The anticipation was killing me to the point where I prayed to the cannoli gods that tonight was going to happen. It had been too long since we'd watched Ryker with a woman. One year and twelve days to be exact.

It wasn't from lack of me or Ryker suggesting it, but from Garrett refusing to partake. Sure, Ryker and I could have just done it between the two of us, but the one time we'd tried, it just hadn't felt right.

The first time Garrett and I had watched Ryker with a woman was our junior year in college. There had been alcohol involved, but not enough to forget how fucking alive I felt watching one of my best friends please a woman. It wasn't just that, though; it was the way Garrett reacted.

We were silent observers, but Garrett was anything but

silent. Not in a moaning and groaning way, but in the way his eyes tracked every movement and the way he palmed his cock through his pants.

Garrett scrolled on his phone, avoiding my stare as we waited in the hallway outside of room 4004. He'd been quiet ever since Ryker had led the curvy brunette out of the bar and to the elevator.

Clearing my throat, I pushed off the wall to move closer to him and kept my voice low. "You shouldn't have your phone out."

He looked at me from where he was leaning on the opposite wall without lifting his head. "I doubt this is happening. She had an innocent look about her."

"Did you see the way she sucked that straw?" I grabbed his phone, looking at the screen. "What the fuck is this?"

"Nothing." He snatched it back, turning it off and shoving it in his pocket. "Just research."

I balled my hands so tight my short nails bit into my palms. "Searching for marketing jobs on LinkedIn while we wait to see if we get to watch Ryker fuck someone isn't research, *Gary*."

He hated when I called him Gary, and his jaw ticked. "We'll probably need to hire more people for the social media marketing department soon. Things are blowing up."

I didn't believe him for one second since we didn't handle hiring for any department in our company. That was what we had a recruitment specialist for. "Why?"

"Why what?" He was playing dumb, but I didn't want to get into it in the hall. Not when we had a beautiful woman who'd looked so sexy with her legs wrapped around Ryker in the elevator, her eyes filled with need.

The door opened, and my cock—which Garrett had caused to deflate—tingled in anticipation. I turned on my heel so quickly my belt chain went flying and almost hit my dick.

Garrett sighed but was right behind me as I walked the short distance to the door where Ryker was standing. He looked over his shoulder, his dilated pupils retracting from the light, and stepped to the side.

The cannoli gods did not disappoint.

She was on her knees in front of the windows, her pink dress just long enough to touch the ground. I could see why Garrett would think she was innocent with her subtle makeup and tame dress. But there she was, on her knees for us.

I stopped just inside the door, stepping out of the way for Garrett to enter. The urge to tell the woman how beautiful she looked was strong, but there were rules, and Ryker would kick us out if we didn't follow them.

Ryker shut the door and the woman shuddered, squeezing her hands together in front of her. I'd hazard a guess she'd never done anything quite like this before.

He walked toward her, stopping a few feet away and leaving us a view of her. "What's your safe word?"

Her lips twitched and she looked over at us before whispering it so only Ryker could hear.

"Loud enough for them to hear it, Paige." Did he sound amused? That was a surprise.

She looked up at him, sighing heavily. "Cowabunga."

Garrett made a noise, trying not to laugh, and I couldn't help the grin that broke the indifferent expression I was supposed to be wearing.

He looked over his shoulder with a warning glance before tipping his chin toward the two swivel chairs strategically placed in the living room. They could easily be turned around to face any direction and were to the side of the bed.

"And what will happen when you use cowabunga?" I didn't know how Ryker could say it without laughing, but then again, he wasn't one to laugh very often.

"You'll stop and check in."

We'd never had someone use their word before, and I hoped tonight was no different. I wanted to see her come apart.

Ryker walked past us to the bed and sat down on the edge. Paige's nervousness and uncertainty peaked and she looked at the door, probably planning her escape.

"Come here." Ryker's voice had deepened to match his eyes, and when Paige started to stand, he growled, "Crawl."

Her eyes widened almost comically but she complied and started to crawl. The only problem was she was wearing a dress that went to her knees and had a lot of fabric. Every time she moved forward, it would get caught under her knees.

Tell her to take it off.

Ryker didn't, though.

About halfway to us, which was about ten feet away, she let out a frustrated huff and sat back on her heels. Her eyes closed as she toyed with the hem of her dress. I could understand her hesitation. There we were, three strangers, watching her crawl to us, and now she was faced with the choice of whether to take off her dress or not.

Come on, baby. You can do it.

When she finally opened her eyes, they were filled with tears and determination. I almost jumped up right then to go to her, but she whipped her dress over her head and crawled so fast I would have missed it if I had blinked.

She sat back on her heels again, her hands crossing over her stomach. I didn't like that she wasn't comfortable with us seeing her. Garrett must have had the same thoughts as me because he white-knuckled the arms of the chair as we swiveled to face the side of them. The view was absolutely perfect.

Ryker stood, towering over her, and he grabbed her chin, tilting it up. "You are fucking beautiful." He turned her head so she could look at us. "Show her how hard you are."

This wasn't part of our thing, but I could see what he was doing. I undid my pants and my hard cock sprang free, the tip glinting with my reverse Prince Albert piercing.

Her lips parted and her tongue darted out to wet her lips as I wrapped my hand around the base of my shaft. Since I couldn't tell her how turned on I was by her, I gave myself a few solid pumps.

Ryker released Paige's chin and unbuckled his belt, drawing her attention back to him. He freed his cock and grabbed a handful of her hair, causing her to whimper and get back up on her knees. "Open that sweet mouth of yours, so I can fuck it and show you just how much you turn me on."

She opened and took him all the way to the back of her throat, gagging when he went too far. Her hands wrapped around the back of his thighs as he pulled all the way out and traced her lips with the tip.

He smoothed back her hair. "Are you okay?"

"Yes." She took him in her mouth again and he groaned, his eyes never leaving hers.

"I was going to fuck your mouth, but I like this much better, don't you?" He flexed his hips. "That's it, Paige. Your mouth feels so good, just like I knew it would."

Garrett shifted in his seat, his cock jutting out from his pants. His fingers dug into his thighs as he watched the erotic display in front of us.

My attention was drawn back to the scene as Paige shoved Ryker's pants and boxers down to his ankles. Her hand went between his legs to massage his balls as she sucked and licked his dick like it was her dessert.

Gone was the shy woman who'd looked like she was ready to cry or bolt out the door, and in her place was a woman who wanted to be seen. It probably helped that she was performing the sexual act on Ryker instead of vice versa. Being watched by two strangers was a big leap of faith to take.

Ryker moaned, his eyes shutting and jaw clenching as if he were holding back. "Are you going to let me come down your throat, baby?"

She nodded and wrapped the hand not fondling his balls around the base of his cock and twisted while pumping. My balls tingled as I did the same to myself. I wanted to come at the same time and paint her back, but that was out of the question.

"Fuck, yes," Ryker said through clenched teeth, his ass muscles flexing as he spilled down her throat. "Take it all. That's it. Swallow it like a good girl."

I fucked my fist, gritting my teeth to stop any sounds from coming out every time my hand rubbed over my piercing. Garrett made a soft strangled sound, and I looked over right as his cum shot out in a stream all over his hand.

I was a goner.

My own orgasm hit me like a ton of cannoli, all the pressure that had been building up in my balls releasing in a rush. My hot cum spilled onto my hand, and I quickly placed my other under it so it wouldn't get all over the damn place.

She released Ryker's cock and he caressed her cheek. "Look at the mess they made because of how sexy you look."

Ryker backed up a step, his cock hanging half-mast against his thigh as he unbuttoned his sweater.

Her freshly fucked face turned toward us, her lips red and swollen and her cheeks flushed. A bead of sweat glistened on her forehead and she wiped it with the back of her hand. "I should um... get them towels."

Ryker's pants were still around his ankles so he couldn't stop her from standing and going to the bathroom where she promptly shut and locked the door.

"What the fuck just happened?" Garrett muttered to himself.

"It's been a while for us, and maybe that was a bit too far having you two take your dicks out." Ryker shuffled closer to us and threw his shirt and sweater onto the coffee table behind us before he toed off his shoes.

"Think she'll come back out?" I swiveled some to look at the bathroom door where I could hear water running. "Would be a shame if she wanted to stop."

"She was into it, but maybe she's nervous about what's next." Ryker kicked off his pants and left them in a pile on the floor with his shoes, which was unlike him, and started walking toward the bathroom. "I'll check on her."

I swiveled toward Garrett. "How are you doing?"

"Fine." He looked across the bed and out the window on the other side.

I looked down at myself and sighed. "The only thing that would have made that orgasm better is if she'd wrung it from me herself."

He tensed right before my eyes, and I smirked. I knew I was pushing his buttons, but it had been over a year since all of us had crossed the boundaries we'd set long ago. Ryker was the only one who got to touch and we never had the same woman twice.

The few times I tried to bring up our indiscretion and the fallout over the past year, he went all clammy and avoided me. Yet another reminder that we had rules for a reason.

I lowered my voice so only he could hear in case Ryker was listening while he waited outside the bathroom door. "It's okay if you want to leave."

He stood, cupping his dick like he was about to spill

40

the most precious liquid, and went around to the other side of the bed where there was a box of tissues. I sighed, slouching down and resting my neck on the back of the chair to stare at the ceiling.

From the second I laid eyes on him moving into the dorm room across the hall, I knew he was going to be my best friend. He was the nicest guy I'd ever met, and we'd become fast friends, along with Ryker, who he shared a room with.

To say I was surprised when Garrett was okay with watching Ryker was an understatement. He wasn't one to hook up with random girls, but he was okay with watching his buddy do it. It blew my mind.

"Here." Garrett put the box on my lap and sat back down, his pants back in place.

I quickly cleaned up, leaving my pants undone but tucking myself inside my boxers. "I'm sorry."

"Nothing to be sorry for." He finally looked over at me. "Our focus should be on her."

"Right. And then tomorrow we'll forget all about her."

He looked back at the bed, not saying another word. Maybe it had been a bad idea suggesting we revisit our favorite sextivity—which clearly wasn't his favorite anymore.

I turned just in time to see Paige step out, her head held high and her shoulders back.

Naked.

Chapter 5

The Perfect Seat

Paige

Six eyes raked over me as I stood naked as a freshly plucked chicken in the bathroom doorway. The temptation to put the towels I had in my hand in front of me was so strong I shoved them at Ryker's bare chest for him to take before I could act on it.

Ryker's eyes were practically on fire as he slowly looked down my body and then back up again. "I guess I have my visual confirmation that you're okay."

"Yes," I breathed as my eyes locked on the two other men eating me up with their eyes. "What are their names?"

Ryker made a tsking noise in his throat and pulled me against him, trapping the towels between us. "You don't get to know their names, sweetheart."

He kissed me and my knees grew weak at how commanding he was. It had been a surprise when he'd asked me to get to my knees and crawl to him. I'd been tempted to use my safe word the second I started stepping on my dress with my knees and needed to take it off so I didn't ruin it.

It was my worst nightmare come to life. Three hot as fuck men watching me crawl with my stomach jiggling in the most unattractive of ways. But it wasn't to them.

I'd never felt more attractive and that was exactly why I'd taken off my bra and panties and planned to walk boldly across the room, my head held high.

The towels fell to the floor and Ryker put his hands on the back of my thighs, lifting me to wrap my legs around him. There was a small bit of worry he'd drop me, but now that I had put my hands on his muscular ass and thighs, and seen him with no clothes on, my worries were gone.

His tongue moved against mine in a way that made me even slicker between my legs. Anticipation grew with each step he took toward the bed, but I didn't get my hopes up that it would be anything other than him fucking me. I'd lost that hope long ago.

And that was probably my first sign I deserved more.

He put me down on the edge of the bed and broke our kiss. He had a hold of my calves and bared me to my onlookers. "I want them to see how wet you are. Put your foot on the bed."

A shiver ran through me, but I did as he asked while he put my other leg up on his shoulder, moving slightly to the side so the two men could get a good view. I covered my eyes with my forearm as the silence only grew louder.

Not that they would have said anything anyway.

Ryker trailed his fingers down my calf to the back of my knee and slowly rubbed in circles. "There's no greater gift to a man than a woman's wet pussy."

I laughed, but it quickly died in my throat when he pinched my inner thigh. "No pinching."

He did it again, and I propped myself up on my elbows to glare at him. He paid me no mind, continuing his exploration of my exposed skin. "I wasn't planning on spanking you, but if you laugh again, I'll be forced to."

I purposely laughed again, and his nostrils flared as he knelt next to the bed, my leg now hanging over his shoulder. I liked getting a rise out of him, and I didn't think I'd mind a spanking. There was only one way to find out.

He plunged two fingers inside me without warning and all laughter and potential spankings were forgotten. I fell back onto the bed, and he stopped, causing me to pop right back up.

"Watch." He slowly slid his adept fingers back in, moving them in a way that hit a spot so sensitive I tried to close my legs. "I don't think so." He pushed the one leg he didn't already have captive back to where it had been.

He slid past the spot again and again, each time the knot forming in my stomach growing tighter and tighter. My clit throbbed with the need to be touched, but he avoided it, opting to switch hands to continue fingering me for a few more thrusts.

He dropped my leg and stood, staring down at me briefly before walking over to his friends. My mouth opened on a sharp inhale as he held his fingers out to his friends.

Both men kept their eyes on me as they took his fingers in their mouths and tasted me. I was going to store the imagery forever in my flick file.

I sat up, unsure what to do with myself as they finished sucking his fingers clean. Was he going to taste me? I squeezed my thighs together and brought a hand to one of my nipples.

Ryker turned back to face me, his eyes locking on where I was pinching my nipple. "Did I say you could touch yourself?"

My hand fell and I gaped at him as he prowled back toward me. But he passed right by, going around the end of the bed to the other side.

The man with the tattoos and penis piercing took his cock back out, playing with the ring on the end as his eyes went between me and Ryker who had lay down, his head facing them. The other man, who was much more serious, adjusted himself.

"Come here." Ryker was stroking his hard cock when I turned to look at him. "Sit on my face."

"Wh... what? Sit on it?" There was no way he wanted me to do that. Couldn't he just go down there and do his thing without that?

"Yes. Straddle my head, facing them so they can see." When I didn't move, his eyebrows furrowed. "Now, Paige."

"But..." I crawled over to him and turned to face our onlookers. "Sit on it?"

"Have you never sat on a man's face before?" His face softened the smallest amount. "It'll be fine. I wouldn't tell you to do it if I didn't want you to."

He was right. This man knew what he was doing and if he felt I'd squish him or suffocate him, he wouldn't have asked. Unless he was into that sort of thing, which was totally fine, but I didn't want to have someone's death on my hands... or my pussy.

I straddled him and then moved on my knees up to his face. His hands immediately grabbed my ass and pulled me closer. I practically squealed as his face went between my thighs, his stubble scraping the sensitive skin and his mouth... oh, God, his mouth.

My instinct was to fall forward, but he put a hand against my stomach, stopping me. He shook his head, but I couldn't tell if he was telling me no or if it was a move to get his tongue inside me.

"Ryker!" I grabbed onto his hair, my legs trembling to keep myself hovering over him. He grabbed my hips and pulled me down farther. "Yes," I hissed.

I didn't know what he was doing, but I didn't want him to stop. He was using his entire face, and my concerns over logistics went out the window, right along with all of my other insecurities.

My body wanted to rock into him, so I let it do just that, bringing one hand to my breasts to play with my nipples. He growled into my cunt, his tongue flicks and suction harder and more desperate.

"Oh, God. Right there." I pinched my nipple hard, my eyes finally returning to my onlookers. "Yes, yes, yes!"

The stoic one wasn't doing anything but watching, but there was no missing the erection in his pants. The other man was stroking himself, and when I met his heated gaze, he brought a finger to his mouth and sucked it.

"Fuck!" I leaned back, not caring that it made my thighs burn. I rolled my hips against Ryker's face, needing more friction, more everything.

He removed his hand from where it was trapped, thanks to me lying back, and attacked my clit with his thumb. There was nothing gentle about it. It was rough and purposeful and sent me right over the edge.

A strangled cry unlike anything I'd ever produced filled the room and my legs squeezed around his head. Every nerve ending went off at once, making me wonder if this was what death by orgasm felt like.

Ryker's ministrations slowed and stopped altogether when I shoved his hand away and attempted to free myself. I was practically lying backwards on him now, and my legs were at an unnatural angle that was difficult to move from, especially when they felt numb and tingly.

He chuckled when I didn't move. He rolled me off him with superhuman strength and I settled onto my stomach. I groaned into the comforter as my legs unfurled, the numbness turning into full-on leg tingles.

I was aware he moved off the bed and I turned my head to watch him grab a condom off the nightstand and slide it on his cock. My body was still recovering so I didn't move, not sure if I could.

He went to where my feet were hanging off the bed,

his hand wrapping around my ankle. "We're not done yet, Paige."

"Five more minutes," I muttered, closing my eyes.

His hand suddenly cracked across my ass and I yelped, scrambling to my hands and knees. He caught me around the waist and flipped me over. My cheeks flooded with heat and my stomach clenched in need. I wanted him to spank me again but he grabbed a pillow and shoved it under my ass to lift me.

We were still angled in a way where his friends could see both of us and he put my legs on one of his shoulders, the head of his cock teasing my entrance.

"I can feel your pussy throbbing for my cock, Paige." The way my name rolled off his tongue was like a caress to my clit. "Whose pussy is this?"

He pushed the tip in.

"Yours," I panted. "It's your pussy. Now fuck it like you own it."

He filled me with one smooth thrust, taking my breath away. "You're so fucking tight." He stilled for a moment, giving me time to adjust to his size. "You good?"

I nodded enthusiastically as he pulled out, leaving just his cockhead inside. I lifted my ass a little and he groaned before thrusting back in. His pace was borderline brutal, but it felt beyond amazing.

"More." I gripped the comforter, glad there was something to hold onto. "Please, give me more."

"You want more?" *Thrust. Thrust.* "This wet pussy wants me to own it?"

"Yes!" My breaths were coming hard even though I

was doing minimal work, and sweat beaded on my brow and between my breasts.

He held my legs tighter to him and leaned his body back, hitting a new angle so his cock rubbed directly against my G-spot. "Pinch those sexy little nipples."

I released the comforter, my fingers aching from squeezing so tight. "It feels so good, Ry." I played with my nipples, zings of electricity going straight to my clit.

His thrusts were deep and fast, our skin slapping together, and the sounds of my wet pussy making me even more turned on.

"Pinch them hard," he said through clenched teeth, reaching around my legs and sliding two along my clit.

"I'm so close." I thought coming on his face was the best orgasm I'd ever had, but what was building in my core was about to knock that out of the water.

I pinched my nipples, and he squeezed his fingers on either side of my clit, moving his hand with impressive speed. Sparkling lights danced across my vision and then my orgasm slammed through my body. My mouth opened but no sound came out.

"Fuck, yes." He groaned loudly, his cock slamming into me one last time before he joined me on the orgasm train, his hips moving in small circles and thrusts as he filled the condom.

I wished it was filling me.

My orgasm ebbed, and although my ears rang and my extremities tingled, I managed to prop myself onto my forearms to watch tattoo man come for a second time. The other man stared back at me, his hand covering his crotch.

Ryker was still, and I found him staring down at me. "Your pussy is perfect."

I fell back onto the bed, throwing my arm over my eyes. "No. I think that was all your dick's doing."

He pulled out, and I whimpered at the sudden loss of contact. My legs were lowered, but I didn't move, not ready to face the awkward aftermath.

There was movement from the three of them and I wondered what the heck they were doing until I heard the door open and then click shut. He wouldn't just leave me without saying goodbye, would he?

I was too scared to look, but after a minute, I heard the sound of a light switch and then running water. It turned off and I listened closely for the sound of his feet against the carpet.

"How are you doing?" He pushed my knees apart and ran the warm washcloth over my sensitive flesh.

"Good." I bit my lip, slightly embarrassed he was cleaning my nether region.

"Just good?" He finished cleaning me and then pulled back the covers, climbing into the bed. "Come here."

His foot kicked my arm from under the covers and I groaned, rolling over and crawling next to him. He pulled me close to him and we sank into the pillows, my head resting on his shoulder as he stroked my arm.

"When can we do that again?" I yawned, and for the first time in what felt like forever, my body felt completely relaxed.

He didn't speak for a moment, and I craned my neck to

look up at him. "We'll talk about it in the morning. Get some sleep."

"Thank you." I settled back in against him and pulled the sheet to cover me to my chest.

"You're welcome." He kissed the top of my head, wedging his leg under mine.

When I woke up the next morning, he was gone.

Chapter 6

Perky Squirrel

Paige

I stared up at Caponetti Tower, in awe of yet another New York City high-rise. I'd been around plenty of tall buildings in my life, but they were nothing like what I'd seen over the month since I'd been there. While I still resisted the urge to go back to Los Angeles, the city was growing on me.

Someone bumped into me, nearly knocking me off the curb.

Okay, maybe it wasn't growing on me quite as much as I thought.

Adjusting my bag on my shoulder, I walked toward the front entrance of the Caponetti Tower. It was part of a trio of buildings that shared a plaza with a large fountain with geometric shapes stacked on top of one another, benches, and pristine landscaping.

I stopped just past the fountain, digging my hand in

the front pocket of my bag for the sticky note I'd written where I needed to go. "Where the fuck is it?"

Just as the tips of my fingers clasped the note wedged into the bowels of the pocket, someone slammed into me from behind. I stumbled forward, my arms flailing like a deranged chicken's wings to keep my balance. My bag slid off my arm and the contents spilled onto the ground.

Why was everyone in such a damn hurry all the time?

Not even bothering to look to see the culprit—there was no point really—I squatted down to collect the pens, sticky note pads, and a package of googly eyes that had spilled out. The sight of the adhesive eyes instantly made me feel better about how my morning was going so far.

"I'm sorry. Here, let me help." A man put a drink carrier down on the ground that had three coffee cups in it. The cups had a fully clothed squirrel wearing a fanny pack overflowing with nuts printed on them. He grabbed a few pens and handed them out for me to take.

"It's okay. I shouldn't have stopped right in the..." My voice trailed off as I looked up and met light brown eyes I was very, *very* familiar with because they'd been all over me just three weeks ago as his friend fucked me silly. "Way," I whispered.

His eyes widened, and he dropped the pens into my bag before grabbing the drink carrier. All of the drinks had those little stoppers in them, which explained how they didn't end up all over us. "Again, I'm sorry."

I didn't even have time to form a coherent thought before he was rushing away, his strides practically a run as he disappeared around the side of the building.

My eyes brimmed with tears, and I sniffled them back as I picked up the last few items. I'd been over that night a hundred times since it happened, and it still stung that I'd woken up alone. Nora assured me that it was typical of one-night stands, but after how good it was, I thought they'd want to do it again.

What were the odds of me running into one of them again in a city so large? Did that mean he worked in the area?

I needed to get it together; I had an interview in fifteen minutes. Not that I was hopeful since I'd submitted over a hundred applications and resumes and had ten interviews in the last few weeks. None had led to a job offer. I barely even knew what I was applying to anymore, just going through the motions.

Maybe it's time to go home.

The thought made my stomach churn, and I stood up, reshouldering my bag. I couldn't afford to go back, not without borrowing money from Nora or my parents. My credit cards and student loan debt were already up to my eyeballs; I didn't need to pile more debt on top of that.

At least my apartment had been rat-free since reporting it to the super. It didn't change the fact that in two months my short-term lease was up, and I prayed on my collection of sticky notes and pens that I could afford somewhere nicer... and bigger.

The doors automatically slid open as I walked up to them, and I entered the lobby. It reminded me of a hotel with its high ceilings, sitting areas, and reception desk.

I stepped up to the large, curved desk that had four

people evenly spaced on the other side. "Good morning. I'm here for an interview at nine with LRG Marketing."

The man didn't look up from his computer screen. "Name?"

"Paige."

He sighed and finally looked at me. "Your last name too."

"Oh." I laughed nervously, still flustered from my encounter in the plaza. "Paige Harper."

His fingers flew across the keys. "You're to go directly to the sixty-fifth floor and the receptionist will direct you to your interview." He handed me a visitor pass and returned his attention to the computer screen.

I'd once worked in reception and knew his coldness was nothing against me but probably whoever had been rude to him. "Thank you. Have a great morning."

That caught his attention, and he looked up again. "Thanks. Good luck."

I smiled, happy I could reset his grumpiness meter.

Clipping the badge to the lapel of my suit jacket, I went through the security turnstile that counted people coming and going before stopping at the bank of elevators to wait for the next one.

A memory flashed through my mind, and I shut my eyes, taking a calming breath. Elevators were forever ruined for me.

In a matter of minutes, I was whisked to the sixty-fifth floor and nervousness took over again. I hadn't bothered to prepare for the interview in any way. It was unlike me, but after so many failed ones and rejection after rejection no matter how much I knew about a company, it didn't seem worth my efforts.

I probably just needed to take a few days off and regroup. It was discouraging to have such a glowing resume and struggle to find work.

After my interview, I'd go grab a slice of pizza, a six-pack of seltzers, and binge-watch something on Netflix.

The receptionist led me down a short hallway to a grouping of chairs outside a closed office door. Now all I had to do was wait.

By some miracle, I'd impressed the recruitment specialist and my day was looking brighter by the minute. I'd inter-viewed for a data entry position since I'd pretty much been applying for anything and everything clerical, ready for a slower and less stressful pace, but the recruitment specialist had decided I would be the perfect fit for an assistant position.

While I wasn't too keen on it at first because it included assisting the owners of the company with emails and scheduling, but also with *anything* they might need. I thought my days of running errands and doing bottom-of-the-fishbowl-type tasks were behind me, but once I saw the salary and benefits, I pushed those thoughts aside. It was nearly twice as much as I had expected.

After I signed paperwork and had gotten my computer login, Sue, the head of recruitment, walked me from human resources and to the elevators.

"Mr. St. James, Wilson, and Caponetti are in a big marketing meeting right now, but I forwarded your new email a list of tasks that need to be done. You can get settled in your office while you wait for them to be finished. They'll want to meet with you before you get going on anything of importance." She pressed the up button. "Ethan will be at the reception area on the seventieth floor and show you to your office on the executive floor. Congratulations. I think you are going to be a perfect fit for those three."

I looked over my shoulder as she started to walk away. "Wait... Caponetti? Isn't that the name on the building?"

"It is. Luca Caponetti is one of the CEOs of LRG. His family owns several properties here and has luxury hotels across the globe. The one here in the city is The Bella Grand."

"The Bella Grand?" My face scrunched inadvertently. Was everyone and everything going to remind me of that night?

"Oh, no. What's that face for?" Sue suddenly looked concerned.

"Nothing. Just didn't have a good experience there." I shrugged, even though I felt like doing anything but. "Thank you again for this opportunity. You don't know how badly I needed a win."

She smiled warmly. "I knew the second you walked into my office you had something special about you."

I wanted to know what she meant by that because in my own eyes, I was just... me.

The elevator dinged and, with a final goodbye, I got on

and pressed seventy. What if there was a windstorm? Would the building sway?

As soon as I stepped off the elevator a tall man—I'm talking at least six foot six—rushed toward me from around a large, curved desk. "Oh, praise baby Gaga, you're here."

I laughed. "Baby Gaga?" I assumed this was Ethan.

"I'm sorry! I'm just so excited." He put his elbow out for me to take and cleared his throat. "Hello. I'm Ethan, executive receptionist of this fine establishment. Let me show you to your office."

I took his arm. "Nice to meet you. I'm Paige, newly hired executive slash personal assistant."

"You're the answer to all my prayers. It's been *hell* around here since Audrey was fired last week."

I gasped. "You're giving me the gossip already?"

"You have to know what you're walking into, my dear." He led me past the reception desk and into a larger hallway. "This is the heart of the floor where you'll be most of the time. To the left of the reception area is the entrance to the other half of the floor which houses the top-tier marketing teams."

"How many marketing teams are there?" I felt a little guilty that I knew nothing about the company I was now employed by.

"Four if you count the owners themselves. The lower tiers have more employees, but with the recent growth, the mid and top tiers have been growing." He stopped in front of an office with an open door. "Here's your office. You have a direct view to the main conference room and two of the executive offices. They expect you to have your door open so they can get your attention if needed, but most of the time they text or email."

I walked in and was surprised at how nice the furniture was. There was a fancy office chair, a desk with plenty of space, and a wall of cabinets and shelves. "Wow."

"What are we talking about in here?" A woman popped her head into the office. "Please tell me you aren't already scaring the new girl."

Ethan put his hand over his chest. "I would never."

"He was just about to tell me about Audrey." I put my bag on my new desk and sat down in my chair. "I'm Paige."

"Ophelia." She looked down the hall, walked in, and shut the door. "The bosses have been on a warpath lately."

Ethan sat on the edge of my desk, crossing his ankles. "The tension has been almost unbearable, but Audrey was late a few too many times and-" He made a slicing motion across his throat. "She wasn't even that bad at her job."

"And just yesterday they fired one of the project managers." Ophelia shook her head in disapproval. "I just don't get why they are such assholes lately."

"Luca isn't." Ethan stood up and adjusted his tie. "It's probably all the pressure they're under with the new clients. Bigger names. Bigger demands. Bigger assholes."

"Ethan. She's been here like two minutes."

"It's better she has some warning." He looked apologetic. "I'm sorry."

"Don't be." I smiled up at him. "Don't worry about me. This should be like my average Tuesday." They both raised their eyebrows. "At my previous job, I was executive

assistant to the top partner of a law firm. He had his days."
I didn't add that he was the father of my ex-fiancé.

"You'll be just fine then. The legal department scares
the bejeezus out of me when they come up here with their
scowls and stacks of papers." Ethan shuddered. "I've been
doing a lot of things over the past week so if you need any
help, just let me know. It sounds like Sue has full confidence in your abilities after your interview if she hired you
on the spot and sent you right up to the wolves."

"Sue is the best at what she does. I'm in the office right
off the reception area. I edit and proofread anything and
everything for anyone that needs it." Ophelia opened the
door and both of them walked out, leaving me to finally
catch my breath.

It had all happened so fast, and my head was spinning.
Speaking of which... I spun toward the window and was
met with a tall building, but I could also see around it,
giving me a spectacular view of the city.

"So much for a job with less stress." I sighed and spun
back around, looking down the hall where I had a direct
view of the conference room my new bosses were in.

I opened the laptop sitting in the middle of the desk
and logged in with the temporary password I was given.
After changing my password to a permanent one, the
laptop loaded, and I pulled up my new work email.

The normal executive assistant duties were on the list
Sue had sent me like checking and responding to emails,
maintaining their schedule, and keeping records. But it was
the list of everything personal that had piled up over the
last week that caught me off guard.

"Take Garrett's plant to the doctor? What the..." I scrolled down the list. "Take Ryker's sweater to PBS..."

My heart beat hard as I scrolled through, seeing Ryker's name a few times. But it couldn't be that Ryker, could it? He said he was here on a business trip just like I had. He'd had a hotel room—although I didn't remember seeing any luggage.

There was no way.

You saw one of them outside.

I scrolled back up to the top where it mentioned coffee and I was pretty sure I was going to throw up all over my new desk and laptop. "One green tea, one black coffee light roast, one latte from Perky Squirrel when we'll be in the office."

It had to be just a coincidence the man I bumped into had three cups with a squirrel on them, right? A CEO wouldn't have gone to get his own coffee, let alone two others.

I was freaking out over nothing. What had I done to warrant such karma?

Looking around the office, I found the printer and turned it on, grateful it was already connected to the laptop Bluetooth. I'd need to ask them about a few of the items on their to-do list because they were ridiculous. Picking up dry cleaning and arranging tickets to a movie I could understand, but who asks their assistant to line up miniature gnomes on their desk when they are out of the office?

I wasn't an investigator by any means, but I did notice that all of the weird requests were for Ryker and Garrett.

I was just about to Google the LRG, which I was kicking myself for not doing in the first place, when the conference room door opened at the end of the hall. A man and woman stepped out, the man stopping to shake someone's hand just inside the doorway. Some laughter filtered down the hall, and then the man and woman went toward the reception area.

It's not them. It can't be.

Feeling reassured I was just having first day jitters, I grabbed the list I'd printed along with my favorite pen from my bag and walked down the hall.

Time to meet my new bosses.

Chapter 7

Someone Better Call HR

Garrett

"**G**arrett, were you even listening?" Ryker dropped into his office chair rather aggressively after seeing our new clients out. It had been a great meeting and was yet another big marketing account we had made a deal on.

"What? Of course I was." I was listening to bits and pieces, but I was sure he would fill me in since he tended to micromanage nearly everything we did. With this new client, he would be even more up our asses since they'd paid a premium for us to handle most of the creative work.

I grabbed my latte and took a sip, the drink reminding me who I ran into a few short hours before. Was it awkward as fuck? Yes. What do you say to the woman you're still jerking off to daily?

"You know what we need... well mainly you two, not

me." Luca leaned back and put his feet on the table, crossing them at the ankles. "You need-"

He didn't finish his thought thankfully—it was probably about getting laid—because there was a soft knock on the open conference room door.

Paige stood there with just as much surprise on her face as I felt. She met my eyes briefly before lifting a white sheet of paper and staring down at it.

My hand squeezed around my nearly empty cup, just hard enough to dent it. Ryker stiffened next to me, and Luca's feet flew off the table as he sat up straight in his chair.

"Paige?" It was the first time I'd ever heard Ryker sound confused.

He'd told us she was in town on a business trip, but clearly that wasn't the case since it was three weeks later and there she was, standing in our conference room doorway looking like a hot secretary from a fantasy.

She was dressed in a black business suit that hugged her curves in all the right places. The neckline of her white blouse wasn't by any means low cut, but if I just reached over and unbuttoned one button, it would give the perfect amount of cleavage.

I set my drink down and ran my hand down my face. There was a reason I hadn't wanted to watch Ryker fuck again and it was because of shit like this. Gone were the days of hit it and quit it.

"Hi." She didn't look up from the piece of paper she had in her hand, her cheeks tinted pink. "I'm your new assistant. I just needed clarification on a few of the items on the list I received and to check in to see if you needed anything before I get started on it," she said in one breath.

No one knew what to say, not even Luca, who usually had enough to say for all of us. What were we supposed to do with this? With her?

I already couldn't stop thinking about her and the way she had morphed from self-conscious and unsure to confident and bold. But the woman in front of us right then was anything but those things.

Her hand shook slightly as she looked up through long lashes right at me and then quickly looked back at the paper.

"Absolutely not." Ryker took his glasses off and put them on top of his closed laptop. "What are you doing here? What do you want from us?"

Her fingers tightened on the paper. "I want to know if I really need to take Garrett's plant to the doctor, take your sweater to PBS, and... line up miniature gnomes on your desk when you're not in there."

Luca couldn't hide his smile. "Those items are a priority. Did they get you a card yet?"

Ryker glared at him. "Can't you take anything seriously? This is a business."

"Oh, lighten up, Rykie. I didn't know we'd have a new assistant today or I wouldn't have put them on there. They were solely for Ethan's amusement." Luca's smile was gone as he met Ryker's disapproval head-on. "Life isn't all about work. Maybe you'd be happier if you had a little fun... with gnomes."

"That's easy to say when you have Daddy's money."

Ryker stood, walking around the conference table and snatching the paper from Paige's hand. "We need a minute to discuss this. Sue did not consult us."

She sucked in a sharp breath, the wrath only a woman could carry all over her face. "You're an asshole." She turned on her heel and pulled the door shut behind her, the loud click feeling like a slap.

"What's there to discuss?" Luca stood, going to the door and stopping with his hand on the handle. "I'd rather go enjoy my daddy's money."

"Luca." Ryker put his hand on the door so he couldn't open it. "Sit down."

"Move your hand before I move it for you." Luca was pissed, which made me uneasy since it took a lot for him to get that way.

Ryker let him out and the door slammed so hard the painting on the wall shook.

I leaned forward, putting my cheek on my fist. "That was uncalled for."

"How did she find out where we work?" He threw the paper onto the table, ignoring my statement, and started pacing. "She was supposed to be here on a business trip."

"But you told her the same thing about yourself, so the lie doesn't matter." I crossed my arms over my chest. "Either way, she can't work here."

"Well, at least we fucking agree about something." He ran his fingers through his hair, making a mess of it. "I knew we shouldn't have done it again, and now that we're more well known, it's a big risk. Case in point." He gestured to the door. "She probably figured out who we were and got a job here on purpose."

He was so full of shit it was almost comedic. "You like her." I'd seen how he'd looked at her and treated her that night with my very own eyes. He had known her all of maybe thirty minutes and yet he cared.

He didn't confirm or deny my observation, but his jaw ticked. "This is why it's once and that's it."

I knew this better than they did. The last time we found someone to have some fun with, we made the mistake of making it a frequent thing with her. That turned into me taking her out on a few dates behind Ryker's and Luca's backs. And then I found out she just wanted to find a way to get to Luca.

We all had money, but Luca had *money,* and everyone knew it.

The door opened and Luca came back in, his face devoid of any emotion. This was the scary Luca that made me wonder if he was hiding that he was in the mafia or some shit.

He sat down next to me, mimicking my posture. "We can't fire her."

"Sure we can. Out of all the jobs in the city, she ends up here? Aren't you worried that she's about to pull a Kristy?" Ryker reached across the table and picked up his laptop, glasses, and phone.

Luca shuddered at the name. "It was a one-off occurrence. I have a little more faith in humanity than that. You should try it sometime."

"I'll email HR."

"On what grounds are you going to terminate her? She hasn't been here more than an hour. What if she's the best assistant in the history of assistants?" Luca scoffed.

"She called me an asshole." Ryker might as well have stuck out his bottom lip and pouted for how uncharacteristically whiney he sounded.

Luca rolled his eyes. "That just shows us that she holds honesty in the highest regard."

Ryker's neck started to turn red, which meant he was about ready to throw his shit down and lunge across the table at Luca. We might have all been in our early thirties and owners of a multimillion-dollar business, but we acted like teenage brothers half the time.

Someone needed to be the adult, so I stood, getting their attention. "Let's just wait until a replacement is found. Ethan has been working over twelve-hour days for the last week. He can't keep doing that. Tell Sue that Paige isn't a good fit and to find someone else." That was entirely reasonable to me, and it would only take a week or two to find someone with the salary and benefits we offered. "The job market is tough right now. Maybe she can just move to another position we never interact with."

Luca put his feet on the table, pulling his phone from his pocket. "She'll probably quit with the way you treated her. She wasn't in her office when I went to find her, so maybe she already did. I would."

Ryker practically growled like a territorial wolf. "You went to find her?"

"I'm not a heartless bastard like you are." Luca

shrugged. "We had a good time with her. That's that. I'm not the one who has an issue with her working here."

"Because you're a certified man whore." I ruffled his hair as I walked past, and he swatted at me. "I'm leaving for the day. Text me if you need something."

Getting away from the situation was the only way I was going to stop myself from doing something rash, like resigning. Could an owner even quit their own company?

I was tired of the pressure and the constant need to expand the company. We made good money the size we were; adding more marketing teams and offering more services wasn't something I was keen on.

Neither of them said anything as I left the conference room. They knew I was unhappy, yet they ignored why. It was just easier that way, especially when we'd worked together for so long and loved each other like brothers. Well, most of the time.

I shut the door because they were probably going to continue bickering and no one needed to be subjected to that.

I glanced down the hall at Paige's closed door. Luca had said she wasn't in there, but maybe she just didn't answer or had been elsewhere.

You do not need to check on her.

Ignoring the warning voice inside my head, I walked to her office and knocked lightly on her door. She probably wasn't even there.

"Come in!" She didn't sound upset or flustered, so I opened the door and stepped inside, shutting it behind me.

Was it the best idea in the world to shut the door?

Probably not, but I wasn't about to have Ryker see me. "I'm sorry for Ryker's behavior."

"I don't accept your apology for him. But I appreciate your concern." She didn't look up from her computer screen. "Did you need something? I'm currently working on getting emails sorted. I took it upon myself to decide that was the highest priority from the list."

"I'm taking off for the day, so you can skip mine and I'll go through them later." I leaned back against the door, watching her.

"Is he really that much of an ass?" She was still avoiding looking up.

I sighed and moved to the chair in front of her desk. "He's complicated. It's no excuse for how he treated you, but he goes all alpha businessman when a lot is on the line. We're expanding into more social media content creation and, so far, our results have brought us several new clients who are willing to spend a lot of money."

She seemed to consider that for a few moments. "Listen, Garrett, if me working here is going to be an issue..."

"I never told you my name."

She finally looked up, her eyes a little puffy. Fuck, had she been crying, or did she have an allergy? "It wasn't hard to figure out."

"Are you okay?"

She waved her hand in dismissal, returning her attention to her computer. I reached forward and shut it so she'd talk to me. I was treading in dangerous waters, but it was too late to turn back now.

"I've never felt so... so..." She looked down at her hands

in her lap and a tear slid down her cheek. "I'll finish out the day, but you'll have to find a new assistant." She laughed sadly. "I didn't even apply for this job. I just wanted a nice easy job in a cubicle doing data entry or something. If I'd looked up information before applying, I wouldn't have."

My stomach did some strange twisty action. "But Sue offered you this job instead? And you just know how to go through our emails without training?"

She wiped her tears and sat up straight, grabbing the laptop and lining it up with the edge of the desk in front of her. "I was an executive assistant before I moved here. Going through emails and labeling them is easy."

I hated dealing with emails, and Ethan wasn't exactly accurate at sorting through them. "When did you move here?"

"A month ago. A week before we..." She didn't need to finish that statement.

"Why'd you move? Clearly not for a job if you're just now getting one. Or did you have one and quit? Fired?" The smallest part of me did have concern over whether or not she'd purposely tracked us down. It wasn't entirely out of the realm of possibilities.

"Does it matter?" she snapped. "I applied to over a hundred jobs and even with being overqualified, no one wanted me."

She sounded so dejected and... sad.

"That's their loss." My stomach decided at that moment to growl. "Let's go get lunch," I blurted, my stomach ruling over any warnings that were floating through my brain.

She looked a little taken aback, and she touched her phone to see the time. "It's not even lunchtime."

"Tell that to my stomach. My favorite deli is practically always open." I was already getting too comfortable around her, but I couldn't exactly pinpoint why.

This was bad. Very bad.

Was it because I'd seen how trusting she was with her vulnerability? How she blossomed under our stares? It's not like it was the first time we'd ever done it, but it was the first time Ryker hadn't seemed detached and didn't want us to be either.

That was exactly why we needed to fire her.

She stared back at me, uncertainty in her eyes. "What about Ryker and Luca?"

"What about them? They're probably still down the hall taking cheap shots at each other. Then they need time to kiss and make-up." I stood and went to the door. "Bring that list and I'll mark off what Luca put on there for Ethan's benefit. It can be a working lunch."

That was what I was telling myself anyway.

Chapter 8

Mustard Boob

Paige

Instead of going to lunch with Garrett, I should have been running for the hills, or at the very least calling Nora to have some sense knocked into me. Why was I even bothering to have lunch with the guy when I was either going to be fired or be forced to quit?

They'd all seen me naked and not just that, they'd seen me have multiple orgasms. How could I look any of them in the eye when every time I did, I thought about that night?

And then there was Ryker.

I'd say I was surprised, but I'd be lying. He had said we'd talk in the morning but had left me alone after a night that was anything but ordinary. If we'd just slept together that would have been fine, but we hadn't, had we? It was a whole event.

Garrett walked next to me as we headed out of a

73

special exit for executives at the side of the building. We went in the opposite direction I'd entered the plaza from, which took us away from a lot of the noise.

We walked a few blocks in companionable silence before Garrett looked over at me after we crossed a street. "So...where are you from?"

"Los Angeles area. Are you from here?" I couldn't imagine growing up in a place this busy. It never seemed to be quiet.

"Ah, well." He rubbed the back of his neck and looked back ahead. "I moved around a lot as a kid but ended up in a suburb outside of Boston when my dad stopped being traded."

"That must have been rough as a kid. What sport did he play, if you don't mind me asking?" While I didn't religiously follow any sports, I did have a sports-obsessed best friend.

He sighed and stopped in front of Pastrami Palace. We hadn't been walking that long, but it felt like we were in a whole different neighborhood. "NHL."

"That's crazy! My best friend's dad used to play and is now a coach for the Pacific Storm."

He paused with his hand on the door. "No shit. Brett Hastings?"

"Yup. He's a great guy. Did you play hockey?" I did a quick perusal of his body as he opened the door. It was hard to tell in a suit, but his ass looked like he frequently did squats.

Stop checking him out. This is a business lunch.

"To the disappointment of my father, I didn't play

74

any sports seriously enough to get on a college team. I played hockey for a bit, but it wasn't my thing." He let me walk in ahead of him and I stifled a moan at the smell.

I never knew a deli could smell so mouthwatering. The rye bread and the pastrami met in a swirl of nose orgasm-inducing harmony. "I've never actually had a pastrami sandwich."

"Excuse me. Repeat that?" Garrett put his hand on the small of my back and guided me to the short line. "You've never had it? How on earth have you survived until now without having a pastrami experience?"

"They have a turkey bacon sandwich. Is that good?" I looked over at him to find his eyes locked on me. "Uh... I don't want to waste food if I don't like it."

"Jay will let you taste a slice, won't you?" He raised his voice, drawing the attention of one of the men behind the counter along with everyone in line.

"Anything for you, my man." Jay held out a slice over the counter.

I stepped forward to grab it. "Thank you."

"Prepare for a culinary experience that transcends reality." Garrett put his hand on the small of my back as I returned to my place next to him. I didn't mind his touch at all.

I took a bite of the pastrami, and it unleashed a chain reaction of flavors in my mouth. It was unlike anything I'd ever tasted before. It was like the most tender beef had crashed into a melting pot of spices. "Oh my God, this is amazing!"

Garrett laughed. "I told you. When I'm having a bad day, a pastrami sandwich from here can turn it all around."

It was so good that I almost forgot why we were there. Almost.

We ordered our sandwiches and found a semi-private table near the back of the deli.

Garrett looked across the small table at me with concern in his brown eyes. "About this morning..."

I knew what he was going to say. He was going to tell me that they were going to have to let me go. "I'd like to have a chance at this job."

As much as I wanted to quit and run far, far away, I needed a job, at least until I could find another one. The bills weren't going to pay themselves, and I was running low on funds. New York was more expensive than I'd anticipated. That was what I got for jumping into something headfirst.

Garrett shook his head. "I just want to make sure you're okay. That was a lot to take in all at once... for all of us."

Warmth spread through me, and it settled in my chest. I almost hoped it was acid reflux from the sample slice of pastrami and not because I was growing heart eyes.

"I feel like there's a but coming." I twisted my hands in my lap. Maybe he'd been tasked to get me away from the office and fire me so I wouldn't make a scene.

"Why would you even want to stay? Won't it be awkward?" Garrett looked past me and then a tray with our food was put on the table.

Jay clapped Garrett on the shoulder. "I hope this fella

is treating you right. He usually comes alone; you must be one special woman."

My cheeks flushed at his words, and I felt a mix of emotions wash over me. Garrett was bringing me to a place he clearly didn't share with anyone else, but the entire situation we were involved in was so... inappropriate.

Jay winked at me before he left us to our sandwiches.

"Well... I can see what you mean by awkward, but this job is the first opportunity I've had in weeks. I don't really have a choice and I'd prefer not to have to stay where a rat could potentially gnaw my toe off in the middle of the night."

"Rats?" He looked concerned. "Where exactly are you sleeping?"

I waved his question off and took a bite of my sandwich, stifling a moan. It looked like I had a new favorite sandwich.

Garrett's gaze never left mine. "I understand you need a job, but I want to make sure you know that what happened that night... it was a mistake. Ryker let it get out of hand and he's not going to be able to handle seeing you every day."

I frowned, feeling a pang of hurt at his words. "And what about you and Luca? It didn't feel like something special to you? Even if it was just for one night?"

Why did I just say that? I sound like a needy puppy.

The way the three of them had made me feel was indescribable, and two of them hadn't even laid a hand on me. What if they had, though?

I shifted in my seat, squeezing my thighs together to

squash the ache that immediately started at the thought of the three of them taking me to a place I'd never even considered. It couldn't happen. It *wouldn't* happen.

Garrett watched me closely, his brows slightly furrowed and his mouth in a set line. There was a war going on inside his head, and I could see the conflict in his eyes.

To my dismay, he shook his head slowly. "I'm sorry, but it didn't. I know it's not what you want to hear, but it's the truth."

I nodded, feeling the sting of tears at the back of my eyes. I didn't want his apology because what we had shared that night had been anything but a mistake. It had felt right to me, even if it was just a one-night stand.

"I would never want to put you in a situation where you felt uncomfortable or taken advantage of. That's why this isn't a good idea. I can try to help you find another job, or Sue can put you in another position that works on another floor."

A lump formed in my throat, and I blinked back the tears that threatened to spill over. "No, it's fine. I under-stand. I'll find another job, no problem." Now I sounded like a wounded puppy. *Get it together, Paige.*

Garrett's eyes were filled with concern and hesitation as he slowly extended his hand across the table. I took it without question, even though it was a terrible idea to touch him.

He sighed before speaking again. "I really am sorry."

I pulled my hand away, feeling like a fool. All of the words he'd spoken were well-intended, but at the same time, I was the only one facing the consequences of that night.

We started eating our sandwiches in awkward silence. I wasn't sure how things would be when we returned to the office, but that worry could wait a little longer. Finishing my sandwich was more important at that moment because the pastrami was fucking amazing.

I wasn't going to let this ruin the rest of my day. The sandwich was making me feel better and I could just lock myself in my temporary office until it was time to leave. The alternative was running away with my tail between my legs, and I refused to let any of them chase me off. I agreed it wasn't best for me to work with them, but a solution to my employment status needed to be considered too.

While chewing a bite, I reached into my bag and pulled out the email I had printed out. We were supposed to be having a working lunch anyway, and I needed to break the silence since he wasn't.

"What should be my top priorities today besides situating the email sorting?"

"That will take you most of the day." He put his sandwich down and took the paper, his eyes skimming down it. "What you do depends on if you're moving to a new department or leaving altogether."

"I honestly don't mind doing most of it. I just need to know what's a priority since it's a pretty long list." Plus, I didn't know what the rest of the day was going to bring and if I would find myself crying in the bathroom, so prioritizing was going to save me... and them.

Garrett looked up from the paper, his gaze lingering on

me for a moment before his eyes darted away. "I'll talk to Sue and see what she thinks is best. I don't want to put any unnecessary pressure on you."

"Thanks, Garrett. I appreciate it."

We finished our sandwiches in comfortable silence, but the tension between us was still palpable. And unfortunately, I couldn't help but wonder what would have happened if things had gone differently that night and Ryker had stayed.

I needed to have a good long conversation with Nora over some wine to flesh out all my feelings. She was the one who had encouraged me to experience life outside my comfort zone, and now look at the mess it had made.

Garrett and I left the deli and headed back in the direction of the office. We were about to turn right at the edge of a building when someone on a motorized skateboard came out of nowhere right in front of us.

I stumbled back, gasping in surprise as a blur of black and silver whipped past us.

Garrett caught my arm, steadying me before I fell. "Are you okay?" he asked, his voice laced with concern.

"Yeah, I'm fine." I took a deep breath to calm my racing heart and leaned against the building. "That was just unexpected and the third time today I've been run into. It's probably a sign to stay inside."

Garrett's hand was still on my arm, and I looked down at it. Even through my suit jacket, his warm hand sent shivers down my spine. I knew I needed to pull away, but I found myself frozen in place, not wanting to break the contact.

His eyes locked on my lips and my breath hitched. We were in our own little bubble; the sounds of cars honking, buses huffing, and people chattering fell away.

"You've got mustard," he said in a husky voice.

I started to open my mouth to ask him what the hell he was talking about when he cupped my cheek and moved his thumb across the corner of my mouth before pushing his thumb between my lips.

I sucked on instinct—and okay, maybe because I wanted to—the faint hint of tangy mustard hitting my tongue. His breaths came quicker, and his eyes fell to my barely visible cleavage.

Releasing his thumb, I looked down. "Oh, oops. Glad that didn't get on my shirt."

I moved my hand toward where there was a small smudge of mustard right where my skin was visible. Garrett's hand was faster than mine, and he grabbed my wrist, using his other hand to undo the button on my shirt that took my top from professional to one button too far.

"Garrett," I whispered, looking around but finding no one paying us any attention. "Someone's going to see."

He made a strangled noise in the back of his throat, and he pulled my shirt apart just enough before he lowered his head to the spot.

Holy rat on a cracker.

Heat gathered in my belly as his tongue swiped across the mustard right at the start of my breast. My skin erupted in goosebumps and my nipples hardened, rubbing against my bra.

Oh, dear God.

I drew in a sharp breath as he licked me right in the middle of Manhattan.

His tongue was light, almost teasing, and I squeezed my thighs together for the second time around him, trying to ease the growing ache between them. When his head moved away, I almost whimpered at the loss.

And then he leaned forward and kissed me.

He swallowed my gasp as his tongue pushed through my lips and explored my mouth. I moved my hands to his waist under his suit jacket, but as soon as I made contact, he took a step back, his eyes hooded as he looked at me.

My hands fell to my sides and my stomach clenched at the loss of his lips against mine.

Had I lost my damn mind? Had *he*?

His hand raked through his hair. "I'm sorry, I shouldn't have done that."

"No, you shouldn't have." I hadn't moved an inch from where I was against the wall. "I thought I was a mistake." It wasn't a question; I was just repeating what he'd said in the deli.

"It was out of line. *I* was out of line." He didn't look like he'd convinced himself of that. In fact, he looked like he was about to have a panic attack.

I finally was able to move and buttoned the button he'd undone. "Look," I said quietly, trying to break the tension. "We both had a rush of adrenaline and what happened, happened. It's not like I stopped you. We don't even have to talk about it. Okay?"

He cleared his throat. "No, I mean... yes. We should talk about it." He ran a hand over his face. "I knew that mustard wasn't going to stay on your boob, and I guess I just wanted a chance to touch you since I didn't get to before."

My heart thumped in my ears as I met his gaze again. His expression was vulnerable and honest, and for some reason, that made me even more attracted to him than before.

"I can understand that," I said quietly, my cheeks heating up as a blush spread across them. "Besides, mustard boob is a delicacy in some countries."

Garrett nodded slowly and breathed out a sigh of relief before looking away from me with a sheepish smile on his face. "I should walk you back."

He gestured in the direction of the building, and we started walking, both of us silent. What the hell was in that pastrami sandwich and why did I want more?

Chapter 9

Mr. Spiky Sea Urchin

Ryker

Everything felt out of control, and it came back to one reason: her.

It was my own damn fault. I'd let my carefully constructed guard down and broke the rules Luca, Garrett, and I had come up with long ago. Not only that, but I'd let myself feel something other than just sexual need.

And now she was employed by our company.

The ramifications of reconnecting with a one-night stand were one thing, but it hadn't just been simple sex. Luca and Garrett had watched.

Sue hadn't stopped glaring at me since I'd called her and the heads of both human resources and our legal team into my office. We didn't have a fraternization policy, but this was unchartered territory.

My mind was racing, trying to figure out how to

contain the fallout. If I didn't handle this the right way, it could be catastrophic for our business. The papers would latch onto a story like this like a hungry infant.

Everyone was staring at me expectantly. It was up to me to come up with a plan that would protect us. I just wished Luca and Garrett were taking things as seriously as I was.

I tapped my pen on the table, feeling the most on edge I had in a while. "Out of all the jobs in the city, she ends up here as our assistant? It's just too much of a coincidence for me to be comfortable with her remaining employed here."

Sue rolled her eyes, not even bothering to hide her annoyance with me. "She applied for a data entry position, Ryker. I was the one who decided her resume and interview were too strong. She has the experience and the personality to do a great job."

"Did you check her references? Didn't you just interview her today?" I looked down at Paige's resume and the interview notes Sue had given me. "Why did she leave her last job? What did they say when you called?"

Sue had worked for us for years, and while I usually trusted her judgment, a person with bad intentions could easily worm their way into her good graces. Maybe I needed to reassess not sitting in on interviews.

Javier, the human resources director, cleared his throat. "Regardless of her employment history, your connection to her on an intimate level is the issue. You openly admitted to sleeping with her, and even though it was before she worked here, it's a precarious situation."

"We can't just fire the girl. I'll just move her to the data entry position she applied for, although the pay is almost half." Sue's frown deepened like she knew the damn woman personally. "She's an adult. You're an adult. I just don't understand why you're so worked up about this."

She didn't understand because I'd left out the part about Luca and Garrett being involved. None of our employees knew about that side of our personal lives and they never would.

Fatima, the company's chief legal counsel, stopped typing on her laptop. "He's worked up about it because he wants to do it again." She went back to typing.

I resisted the urge to tell her to get the hell out of my office. She unfortunately was partially correct, but I also couldn't help but feel like there was a bigger plot here.

As much as I wanted to deny Fatima's statement, there was a truth to it that I couldn't ignore. The thrill of that night still lingered in the back of my mind, and the thought of seeing Paige every day at work only made it worse. But there was something more than just a physical attraction; there was a connection that I couldn't explain.

I closed my eyes and exhaled, trying to push away the unwanted memories of her lips against mine and the soft noises she made for me.

Clearly, it wasn't working.

"Regardless of my personal feelings, we need to think about the potential consequences for the company. If word gets out about this or she has ulterior motives, I don't even want to think about what could happen."

Javier nodded in agreement. "We could face legal action from other employees for preferential treatment.

How many in-house applications did we have for the assistant position?"

Sue hesitated, flicking the edge of the small stack of papers she had in front of her. "A few, but none were a good fit. The only employee here that I'd even seriously consider is Ethan Roberts."

I snorted. "We'd kill each other."

Sue's mouth quirked with a hint of a smile. "That's exactly what he said the last time I asked him."

Ethan was a phenomenal receptionist, magnetic and hard-working, but he was like Luca on steroids.

I leaned back in my chair, rubbing my temples. "Regardless of the reasons she's here and how she got into the position, I want her gone; not just moved to another position on another floor. Can we give her a termination contract with a non-disclosure agreement and a severance package?"

Sue shook her head, her black hair with streaks of silver emphasizing her rejection of the idea. "We can't just fire her without cause, Ryker. It's a legal minefield, not to mention a dick move."

Fatima coughed to cover her laugh and closed her laptop. "The goal here is to protect the company. Both parties didn't do their due diligence in regard to her hiring, but she has only been employed for mere hours. She isn't protected by a union, and if you're willing to pay her severance, this should not be an issue. There's also no legal precedence in the state of New York for something like this, but I can continue to search."

"No. I tried Googling the situation earlier and all I got

were romance novel recommendations." I'd immediately deleted my search history.

Javier stood, stretching like he'd been sitting for hours. "Fatima and I will start working on the paperwork and have it on your desk within the hour. How many weeks of severance?"

I looked at Sue, even though she had just called me a dick. "Will two weeks suffice?"

"Absolutely not. Make it six." Sue crossed her arms over her chest. "This isn't her fault. I know you might not believe it, but she has a pure soul."

"Fine. Six weeks." I got to my feet, walking to the door as they gathered their belongings. "Thank you for meeting with me on such short notice. As always, I expect the utmost discretion in handling this matter."

Fatima and Javier left, but Sue lingered in the doorway. The last thing I needed was for her to lecture me. I only allowed her to pop off at me because most of the time she was right, and I respected her hiring capabilities. So much so that when we disagreed, I listened and considered what she said before I made a final decision.

Except this time.

"Sue. Don't start."

She gave me a long, sorrowful look as she put her hand on my arm and squeezed. "I wasn't going to. I can tell you're already beating yourself up over this." She paused for a moment before adding, "I just wish you would give her a chance. When have I ever steered you wrong?"

I couldn't help but feel a twinge of guilt. It felt like a sharp needle poking through my heart, digging deeper and deeper as I tried to ignore it. I had let my personal feelings cloud my judgment once before when it came to this sort of thing, and I wouldn't do it again. Feelings needed to stay the fuck away from my choices.

"My decision is final."

Her lips tightened and she nodded before she turned away and left me standing in the doorway of my office, alone.

There was a heavy sensation of regret that seemed to weigh on my chest, making it hard to breathe.

Garrett had the right idea leaving for the day, but I had too much to do.

I closed my door, and just as I sat back down at my desk, the door opened, and Ethan walked in. "Ethan. To what do I owe the pleasure?"

"What was that about?" He sure did cut right to the chase.

"We're going to be letting Paige go as soon as the paperwork is drawn up." I looked at my computer screen, avoiding his stare. A stare that had quickly turned from curious to downright vicious.

"Why?"

"That's none of your concern. She'll be gone by this afternoon, so you should probably get started on the things we need done today." I clicked around on my computer, doing nothing in particular.

He put his hands on his hips. "Did you know she already has all of your email sorted? It took her probably thirty minutes tops."

That caught my attention, and I clicked open my

email. "That's impossible."

"Go see for yourself. I don't know why we never thought to use a mail sorter plugin or program of some kind. I didn't even know such a thing existed beyond what's offered by the email provider. At her last job, she worked with a computer programmer to have one made. It apparently sorts based on frequency of emails from the person, key phrases, that kind of stuff. Super fancy and beyond what my geriatric brain can handle."

"You're twenty-five, not eighty-five. How do you know all of this?" I wasn't surprised he had all this information. He saw and heard a lot sitting in the reception area for our floor.

"Well, when she came out of the bathroom after crying, we were talking about the ongoing email issues. It doesn't solve the problem entirely, but it at least correctly sorts most of it to make it more manageable."

"She was crying?" My stomach churned at that. I figured she'd probably be upset after what happened earlier, but not crying upset.

Jesus, I had the emotional intelligence of a sea urchin and was just as spiky.

A knowing grin slowly spread across his face. "I see."

"You see nothing, Ethan. Go do your job." I went back to opening random files and closing them. I couldn't even think about what I needed to do, but maybe Ethan would see I was busy and leave.

"I wonder how Garrett will feel about her unfair and untimely termination seeing as he took her out to lunch... to Pastrami Palace."

"Garrett. Did. What?" It was common knowledge that when Garrett went to Pastrami Palace he wanted to be left alone. I'd eaten there plenty of times with Luca or grabbed a sandwich to go, but never with Garrett. "Wait. How do you even know this?"

"I heard them talking on the way to the elevator." I wouldn't have put it past Ethan to make shit up. If he wasn't my sister's best friend, I'd have fired him already.

Stop firing people, asshole.

It wasn't my own voice in my head. Now, apparently Paige's voice had wormed its way into my conscious thought.

I picked up my cell phone and scowled at Ethan, sending him scurrying out of my office. Garrett taking Paige out to lunch complicated things a bit, and I needed to find out what exactly he was thinking.

The phone rang once before Garrett answered with a loud sigh. There were muffled sounds of traffic in the background and the click-click of a turn signal.

"No hello?" My voice was calm even though I was anything but.

Out of the three of us, Garrett was the last one who needed to be taking one of our hookups out. We'd been down this road before, and it had been a clusterfuck.

The only difference this time was I was feeling some kind of way too.

Fuck.

"I told you I was leaving for the day." He sounded as tired as I felt. "What is it?"

"I heard you took Paige to lunch." It annoyed me more

than it should have, or was that jealousy? No, I wasn't jealous. Why the hell would I be jealous? I barely knew her.

You know her better than you think.

"Uh... Yeah, so?" His tone was dismissive and made me want to throw my phone across my office.

I looked at the time on my computer. "It's barely eleven."

"Again, yeah. So?" Garrett's words were sharp and clipped.

"You took her to Pastrami Palace."

He was silent.

"Garrett." My voice was low and rough, my agitation starting to get the better of me. "You aren't denying it? I thought Pastrami Palace was your sacred place of solitude or some bullshit."

"Have you looked in the mirror lately?" he snapped.

"What the fuck does that have to do with pastrami?"

"You might want to take a look. You might be turning green." Where was his attitude coming from? He was usually the calm one out of the three of us.

His words hit me like a wave. Why did I have the urge to jump through the phone and put him in a headlock? That type of behavior was completely beneath me, so I swallowed down my indignation and kept calm.

You forget where you came from.

"I just got out of a meeting with Sue, Javier, and Fatima. They're drawing up termination paperwork and a severance package. Is there anything that we legally need to be concerned about?"

"Uh..."

"Uh? Uh, what? You just had lunch together, right?" My hand was starting to hurt from how hard I was clutching it.

He cleared his throat. "I may have kissed her."

It was my turn to be silent.

"And I may have licked her cleavage in broad daylight. In my defense, I couldn't let perfectly good mustard go to waste."

"Have you lost your ever-loving mind? What are we supposed to do now? That's sexual harassment!"

"You're ridiculous. Go ahead and fire her if you want. I'll just pick up the pieces you leave in your miserable wake." He hung up.

I tried to call him back and went straight to voicemail.

All-consuming heat flooded my body. How could he be so careless? He'd taken a huge risk with his actions.

A chat box popped open on my computer, distracting me from the spiral I was inevitably headed down.

Fatima: *Here is the paperwork. It has what we discussed.*

I quickly double-clicked on the attachment and skimmed through it. It was the same we gave every employee except for the glaringly craptastic reason for termination.

Me: *Looks good. Go ahead and send it. Once she e-signs let me know and I'll have security escort her out of the building.*

I wanted to be done with this even if, somewhere deep inside, I didn't really want to be done with her.

Chapter 10

Blue Alien Cock

Paige

"**Y**ou hussy!" Nora squealed in my ear after I recounted my lunch date with Garrett. I'd just gotten back to my office and promptly shut the door to call my best friend.

"And then he walked me back to the office, waved me goodbye, and disappeared. I feel like I'm on some kind of gotcha show and at any moment a camera crew is going to pop up with John Quiñones. So, the question is, what would you do?" I knew what I *should* do, but I kept looking at my bank account.

"Enjoy the ride... or should I say rides? How does the penis piercing guy feel about all of this?"

"His name is Luca, and I don't know. He seemed unfazed after the initial shock wore off." I logged into my laptop. "Well, fuck. Looks like I don't need to worry about it. I'm being fired." With a heavy sigh, I clicked on the email with the subject line 'Termination of Employment' and opened the DocuSign.

"They can't do that! Can they?"

"I've only been employed here for a few hours. They can do anything they want. I should have known it was too good to be true. Being hired for a position I didn't apply for and to have an immediate start? Red flags. Red flags everywhere."

"Sometimes the best experiences come from ignoring the red flags. What does the email say?"

"We are writing to inform you of the termination of your employment with LRG Marketing, effective immediately. This decision has been made due to a conflict of interest that has arisen, which was unknown at the time of your hiring. Specifically, it has come to our attention that you have had a personal relationship with your direct supervisor, Ryker St. James.

"As an employee of LRG Marketing, it is important to maintain a professional environment and avoid any conflicts of interest that may compromise the integrity of our company. Your previous relationship with your supervisor creates a potential bias and may lead to concerns regarding fair treatment and objectivity in the workplace. To ensure the best interests of the company, we have made the difficult decision to terminate your employment."

The document on the page began to blur as hot tears threatened to fall. I blinked a few times, trying to clear them away, but the words remained nothing more than a jumbled mess.

"Those fuckers! I'm getting on a plane right now to

come kick their asses." She was trying to lighten the mood, but her declaration on my behalf made the tears fall.

My eyes latched onto the word severance pay. "They're giving me six weeks' pay. That's..."

"Hush money! The nerve!" If Nora was in my place, she would have already been down the hall yelling at them.

It was weird to say the least and made me feel like a toy. This could have all been avoided if I had just used my brain and looked up the company. Their business photos were right at the bottom of the main page.

I scrolled down further to a non-disclosure agreement. I'd signed one in regard to the company with my hiring paperwork, but this one was about that night. It was vague and only mentioned Ryker, but it was clear as day to me.

My lunch turned in my stomach. It was one thing to fire me because they were uncomfortable having me as their employee, but something else to legally bind me to never speaking of it.

"I don't want their money." I closed out of everything and shut down the laptop. My decision was made. There was no way I was going to sign my rights away.

"Technically it's LRG Marketing's money. It's normal to get a severance package. Either way, they're going to fire you, aren't they? Might as well get paid."

"They want me to sign an NDA about my one-night stand. I believe the verbiage it used was 'the previous relationship between Ryker St. James and Paige Harper'. Who does that?" I grabbed a pad of sticky notes from my purse and a pen. "I'd rather eat rice and pasta for the immediate future than give them the satisfaction of treating me like I'm dirt beneath their shoes."

On one sticky note I wrote "fuck you" and on another "I quit." I put them right in the middle of the desk and stood with my bag.

"Rich people do that, that's who. Maybe they just don't want it to get out that they like to watch and be watched? What are you planning on doing?" Nora sounded suspicious, as if she just watched me quit via sticky notes.

"Quitting." I peeked out the door to find the hall empty and made a mad dash for the stairwell. If I went to the elevator, I'd have to pass by their offices, the conference room, and Ethan.

"But-"

Our call was cut short as I lost reception in the stairwell. It was just as well because I didn't want to doubt or regret my decision. Was it stupid to not take the severance package?

I was the one that had to live with my decision, and being forced to never say anything about it in exchange for money was where I drew the line—even if I never planned to do so. There was an icky feeling that came with even thinking about accepting it. Had I just been a random hire, it would have been a different story.

I stopped on the next floor down and had my hand on the door handle before reconsidering going through another floor. People would wonder who I was and possibly call security, but the other option was going down sixty-nine more flights of stairs.

"Fuck!" My voice echoed in the stairwell, and I slipped off my heels. They weren't that high, but my feet would be dead if I wore them.

Going down wouldn't be so bad. I needed the time to think.

"Does catching your fiancé cheating kill your brain cells?" I typed into Google on my phone as I sat on my couch with my feet propped on the coffee table. My legs and feet were killing me, and I didn't know what the hell I'd been thinking going down all those stairs.

You weren't. That's the problem.

I tossed my cell phone away from me and watched it slide between the arm of the loveseat and the cushion. Good. Now I wouldn't have to see Daniel's name come up at five-minute intervals as he tried to text and call me.

He'd been relentless over the past hour, and I'd chosen to ignore him. I probably should have turned my phone on silent before chucking it.

We were a month out from what would have been our wedding day and he said he needed to know what I planned on doing. I thought I'd made it blatantly clear, but apparently, he thought each time he asked I'd change my mind.

In hindsight, there were a lot of issues with our relationship that I'd ignored, and I felt like such an idiot for almost marrying him. So much time wasted on a man who gaslit me and treated me like a doormat.

I grabbed an Oreo from the package next to me and shoved the whole cookie in my mouth. I'd made my life infinitely worse by making an unplanned decision to move to New York.

The sticky notes of my debts lining one edge of my coffee table reminded me as much.

37,000 *student loans*
3600 *credit card one*
5900 *credit card two*
7200 *credit card three*
2000 *dental bill*

Yup. I was fucked right in the ass with an unlubed blue alien cock, but for now, I'd eat another Oreo.

There was a firm knock on my door and I nearly choked. Coughing, I gingerly got to my feet and shuffled to the door. A peephole was too much to ask, and I couldn't afford a doorbell camera. I felt safe on my floor and building, but was it really safe anywhere in a gigantic city?

"Who is it?" I spluttered out, swallowing the last bit of cookie in my mouth.

"Ryker."

Ryker! What the hell was he doing at my apartment?

"I don't know a Ryker." I croaked, letting the wayward cookie crumbs coating my throat work for me.

"I see the heels you wore today right outside the door, Paige. Open up." God, that voice made my entire body react, and so did the fact he remembered what shoes I'd worn.

"Paige is currently closed for business. Please find your way to the exit," I said in a mechanical voice.

"You aren't a business. Just open the door." I couldn't pick up on what kind of mood he was in, but he sounded calm despite his attitude toward me when I saw him in the conference room.

"I'm not? Oh, I'm sorry. I thought being paid for sex was a business. Hey! Maybe that's what I'll do now." There was good money in selling feet pictures. No shame in utilizing the assets. Unfortunately, those assets were currently swollen.

"That's not what... just open the damn door." Did he just *growl* at me?

I whipped open the door, ready to give my neighbors their prime-time drama for the night but was greeted by a man who had stress radiating from his every pore.

His blond hair looked like he'd run his fingers through it countless times and his suit jacket and tie were missing. In one hand, he was gripping a manila envelope, and I didn't need to ask what was inside.

His tired blue eyes took me in, stopping at my chest on his way back up. "Jesus Christ. You shouldn't be wearing that."

My cheeks heated and I looked down at my biker shorts and thin camisole. He was right, I shouldn't have been wearing it, but I also hadn't expected anyone to see me.

"You didn't have a problem with it when I was naked." I started to close the door and he jutted his foot out to stop it from closing. "What part of go away do you not get?"

"That's not what I meant." He pushed his way inside

and I was too weak to stop him. "Your neighbors are going to see your nipples and thighs and get ideas."

"My neighbors are harmless." I didn't need to tell him I had an oversized shirt for when I went to the bathroom.

He looked around my barely-there apartment as I shut the door. "You live here?"

"No. I turn tricks from here." I winced as I walked the five steps to the kitchen to lean against the counter.

"Stop talking like that." He turned to face me and held out the envelope.

I stared at it with a frown. "I'm not signing anything."

His hand dropped to his side, and he turned to look up at my loft and then my sitting area. "Is this even legal?"

"What are you going to do, report my building to code enforcement? The loft counts as space." Why was I defending my apartment that I hated? It had looked a lot bigger in the pictures, but then again, it didn't have anything in it besides the couch.

Without asking, Ryker went and sat on the couch. "I have all night to wait."

"Making someone sign legal documents under duress won't look good." I crossed my arms over my chest because his eyes kept falling to my nipples. "Why would you think it's even okay to show up here unannounced and barge your way in?"

"When it comes to my business, I'll stop at nothing to protect it." He held out the envelope again. "Sign them."

With a defeated sigh, I stepped forward and snatched it from him. I could faintly hear the buzzing of my phone which he was right next to.

I opened the prongs and pulled out the printed papers, ready to throw them in the sink and turn on the water. Two smaller pieces of paper fluttered to the ground, and I bent with a groan to pick them up.

There was no way I was going to be able to walk or even get up the next day with how sore I was.

"Why are there two checks?" One was for six weeks' pay, just over ten thousand dollars, and the other was a check from Ryker for another ten thousand. "What is this?"

My hand shook as I read and reread it. How could something be so amazing yet so heartbreaking at the same time?

"It's for the inconvenience I've caused you." There was genuine concern in his voice. "What are these? More love notes?"

Love notes? I looked up at him just as he reached for one of my sticky notes. "Don't!"

But I was too late. He'd of course grabbed the one with my student loan debt. "What is this?"

My phone buzzing just added to the whole ambiance in the room as he picked up each sticky note, stacking them on top of each other.

"What does it look like?" I looked at checks and papers in my hand and shoved them back in the envelope. "You should really go."

He didn't speak, only stared at the brightly colored squares in his hands. My legs trembled, but as badly as I wanted to sit down, I didn't dare move.

He finally cleared his throat. "Did you know who I was?"

"What do you mean?"

"That night at the bar. Did you know who I was?" He looked up at me, his eyes sad.

"No. Why would I? I was just..." Being brave. Being stupid. Being impulsive.

My phone buzzed again.

"Who the hell keeps calling you?" He reached down into the bowels of the couch to locate the buzzing and pulled out my phone. "Who's Daniel?"

The phone stopped buzzing, thank fuck.

"No one. Give it here." I dropped the envelope on the table and held out my hand just as it started to ring again.

He stood, moving away from me and bringing the phone to his ear. "Hello?"

I sat down in defeat, sucking in a breath as my body radiated with pain. The likelihood of getting my phone back was slim to none. Ryker was strong, and I was about to pass out from the pain in my hamstrings and quads.

"Who the hell is this?" Daniel's voice was easy to hear from where I was since I always had the volume all the way up. I hated the way speakerphone sounded, and max volume was perfectly loud enough.

"Who the hell is *this*?" Ryker echoed. "Why do you keep calling?"

"I'm her fucking fiancé trying to make arrangements for our wedding. Put her on the phone."

I grabbed my package of Oreos, avoiding Ryker's glare,

and put them in my lap. It was much more of an ice cream situation, but it was too expensive, and the tiny freezer didn't work very well.

"Fiancé?" Ryker started pacing, a hand sweeping through his hair. "What do you mean you're her fiancé?"

"Ex," I muttered through a mouthful of Oreo.

"Paige's mouth is full right now so she can't talk to you." There wasn't even a hint of humor in Ryker's voice.

"Listen, asshole. I don't know who you think you are-"

Ryker hung up on him. "You have a fiancé?"

I pointed an Oreo at him. "An ex-fiancé who was cheating on me."

"Is that why you're living here?" He looked around the apartment again, his brows furrowed.

What I wouldn't give to hear his train of thought. One second, he seemed like he cared, the next he was asking me to sign paperwork again and insinuating I was after money.

I threw the package on the table, and it slid off the side and onto the floor, spilling cookies. Oops.

"I live here because I lost my damn mind, packed my bags, and moved here with enough for three months' rent and expenses. I used all my money on wedding deposits because my parents couldn't help, and Daniel's family is traditional in the fact that the woman's family should pay for the wedding. Of course, since I'm fucking broke anyway, Daniel said if I put all my extra money into it, he'd cover the rest." I laughed because if I didn't, I was going to cry.

"He doesn't deserve you." His hand tightened on my phone, and I worried for its safety.

"Yeah. I know that now." I looked at the envelope on the table. "Taking that money will only make me feel like shit. As much as I need it and it would make my life easier... it would make it ten times worse because it makes me feel..." A lump in my throat stopped me from speaking.

Ryker set my phone on the table and sat down next to me, clasping his hands as he leaned his arms on his knees. "What would it mean? Help me understand because right now I don't."

"That I'm not good enough. That I screwed up. Guilt." I tried explaining it the best I could since I didn't even entirely understand it. "Cheap."

He scrubbed his hands over his face and turned his head to look at me. "It wasn't my intention to hurt you."

"You did the second I woke up and you were gone." I wanted to look away because, damn, his eyes were intense. "I know it was a one-night stand, but it felt like... I don't know. Just forget it." I looked away and movement caught my eye. "Rat! He's returned!" My squeal probably scared him more than my revelation about my feelings.

Without so much as a second thought, Ryker got to his feet, grabbed my throw blanket off the back of the couch, and grabbed the rat from where it had started to chow down on my Oreos. What a bold move from both the rat and Ryker.

"Do you have a trash chute?" He went to the door, the rat making a sound like it was being murdered.

"At the end of the hall by the bathroom." I was frozen in place, not sure what to do besides dance around like I had bugs all over my body.

He seemed to have everything handled on his own, the blanket now a sack to hold the rat. "I'll have to buy you a new blanket. Get your bags packed. You aren't staying here."

Then where the hell was I going to stay?

Chapter 11

Rat Whisperer

Ryker

Dealing with the rat in Paige's apartment brought up way too many memories for me. I'd been struggling all day to keep my demons at bay and the rat was just the icing on the cake.

Or in the rat's case, on the Oreo.

If rats were coming out when people were in the room and so boldly chowing down, that meant there was a bigger problem lurking behind the walls. I would bet if I listened carefully, I'd be able to hear them.

Paige was right where I left her on the couch when I came back without the rat or the blanket. I knew she was going to try to argue with me, but I couldn't leave her in such a place in good conscience.

Yet you'd try to fire her and pay her off.

"I can't let you stay here with this rat problem. Where there's one, there are many. It's not safe," I said firmly, trying to ignore the way her curves looked in the tight clothes she had on. Her top was practically sheer and seeing her nipples poke at the fabric made me remember how she'd gasped when I took one in my mouth in that elevator.

She huffed and crossed her arms, clearly not happy with my interference in her life. "I've been living here for over a month and have only seen a rat one other time. The super said he took care of the issue."

"Well, clearly he didn't." I picked up the package of Oreos and the few that had spilled onto the floor. "Go put some clothes on and pack a bag for a few days until we can get you moved."

Paige rolled her eyes, but I could see the fear in them. "Fine, but I'm not leaving my apartment for good. I can't afford to."

I nodded to pacify her for now. "I understand. Let's just get you out of here, and we'll figure something else out."

She winced as she grabbed onto the armrest of the couch with one hand and pulled herself to her feet. I guess I now knew why she hadn't immediately jumped up when she saw the rat.

"What's wrong?" I located her trashcan and threw away the cookies before tying off the bag.

"Hm?" She moved to the bottom of the ladder to the loft and looked up.

"You sound like you're in pain and moving like you're the Tin Man in need of some grease."

"Just a little sore." She sighed and tried lifting her leg.

"A little? What did you do? Run a marathon?" I went to her and put my hand on the small of her back to guide her away.

She stiffened. "Seventy flights of stairs."

I turned her to face me, which was a mistake because now she was practically pressed against my body. "What do you mean seventy flights of stairs?"

"I went down them, okay? I'm a glutton for punishment." She traced her finger around one of my shirt buttons. "I made it up into my loft earlier, but I hurt a lot more now."

I grabbed her hand, stopping the torturous touch. "Is it okay for me to go up there and pack for you then?"

She nodded. "It's kind of a mess. Whatever you grab is fine."

"Why don't you go throw the trash out." I gave her a small smile and made my way up the ladder. The loft was small but cozy, with a mattress shoved against the wall and piles of clothes scattered everywhere like she'd been trying to organize them. There was no way to stand so I crawled onto the bed.

I didn't know why I cared about this woman so much. It had killed me to leave her in that hotel room and killed me even more to fire her. But it wasn't like I really had a choice.

"You have a choice to be happy, Rykie. You just choose not to be because that's easier for you and your heart." Luca's lecture from earlier had been playing in my mind all day and it took me seeing this place and the rat for it to make sense.

I had the choice to leave Paige in this dump and be miserable thinking about it or take her out of the situation. I got to work packing, ready to go home and sleep off all the conflicting feelings I was having with every single decision when it came to this woman.

Paige already had a half-filled suitcase, so I just piled essentials into it to fill it the rest of the way. Was this all she had?

"Everything okay up there? You aren't doing something gross like rubbing your dick all over my panties are you?" Paige said from downstairs. She didn't even have to yell for me to hear her; that's how small the space was.

"No, but that's a good idea." I smiled as I zipped up the suitcase. "Anything else besides your clothes you need? Vibrator? A special blankie or plushie?"

It had been a long time since I'd dated a woman—not that I was dating Paige—and there was usually at least one stuffed animal somewhere.

Paige laughed. "No, I'm good. Just get your ass down here so we can get out of here. I think I heard a scratching sound under the sink."

As I climbed back down the ladder, I couldn't help but feel a sense of relief that I was getting her out of this place. It was too cramped, and she deserved better.

She deserves better than you.

I shook the thought from my head. Did this woman have some kind of pheromone that was making me and Garrett think stupid thoughts? He wouldn't have kissed her if he wasn't having them too. And Luca? Who knew with him?

"Do you need anything else?" I rolled her bag to the door. "What about stuff from the bathroom?"

"It's kind of like living in a dorm here." She grabbed a plastic bag and came toward me. "My bathroom stuff is right behind you."

I moved out of the way, and she uncovered a three-tiered rolling cart. She put a shower caddy in the bag and filled a large cosmetic pouch with other bits and pieces that were scattered on the top shelf.

"Do you mind if I ask how much you pay for this place?" The city was expensive, so I couldn't exactly blame her for picking a shared bathroom arrangement.

She brushed past me and pushed open a curtain under her stairs that hid storage. "Fourteen."

"Hundred?" Her barely touching me must have short-circuited my brain.

She pulled out an overnight bag and put all of her bathroom items in it. "No, thousand."

"For the year?" I was about to go to prison if she said a month. It wouldn't be the first time I'd heard about land-lords taking advantage of new residents.

What was wrong with me? There was no way she meant for one month.

"I was joking. Fourteen hundred a month." She glanced up at me. "How much do *you* pay?"

"Too much, that's for damn sure." It killed me to watch so much money leave my account every month for taxes and common fees. I didn't even want to imagine what it would be if I had a loan on it.

She looked around and grabbed a t-shirt that was over the arm of the couch, pulling it over her head. "Ready."

"I'm a little surprised you aren't fighting more with me about leaving." I opened the door and stepped into the hall, immediately getting hit with the smell of marijuana. "Jesus, do Cheech and Chong live here?"

"It's not that bad. I've gotten used to the aroma. I'm not arguing with you because I wouldn't have been able to sleep here tonight anyway. That night I met you was the first time I encountered a rat." She slipped on a pair of Crocs and locked her door. "So you should be thanking them."

I did indeed need to thank them. As I walked toward the stairs with her at my side, I couldn't help but notice how right it felt.

For once, I didn't feel a twinge of guilt at the added expense of using a private car service. It was a luxury that had taken me a long time to even consider, but as life had gotten busier, I couldn't deny the convenience.

The ride was silent at first and I rested my head against the cool window. I was fucking exhausted from all of the emotions that had been swirling through me all day. I didn't know how I'd make it through the rest of the week if I kept it up.

I was just about to nod off for a power nap when Paige broke the silence. "You were pretty impressive with that rat. What are you? A rat whisperer?"

I kept my eyes shut. I needed to give her some kind of explanation; if not for my exceptional rat-catching abilities, then for my attitude toward her. "I caught a lot when I was younger."

She made a gagging noise. "For fun?"

"No, not for fun." I sighed, opening my eyes and looking over at her. "I grew up in a pretty rough neighborhood. Rats were just a fact of life. It was either catch and get rid of them or let them take over."

"But you had to catch them? What about a pest control service or a trap?" She shuddered, probably imagining the scenario.

"You have to be able to pay for those things. We couldn't."

Paige shook her head, a thoughtful expression on her face. "That's insane. My family didn't have a lot growing up, but it was never that bad."

"It's not something I like to talk about." I leaned my head back against the headrest, feeling the weight of the memories settling on my shoulders.

"I'm sorry," she said softly. "I didn't mean to pry."

"Don't be. What's in the past is in the past." I only wished that were true. Despite Luca reminding me earlier that I'm never going back to that situation again, the fear crept up now and again.

Paige's hand reached for mine and gently squeezed it, surprising me. "You don't have to be ashamed of where you came from, Ryker. It's a part of you and it made you who you are today."

I turned my head to look at her and our eyes met. It

was like she could see right through me, removing the bricks I had spent years building up to protect myself. "Thank you," I whispered, surprised at the lump in my throat. "No one's ever said that to me before, especially when I've been such an ass to them."

"I mean it," she replied, her thumb rubbing circles over the back of my hand. "Asshole or not."

It was strange how someone I hadn't known for very long could have such an effect on me. But there was something about Paige that made me want to let her in. Maybe it was the way she looked at me like I was worth something. Or maybe it was her unwillingness to back down, even when I was being difficult.

I cleared my throat, pulling my hand away from hers before I lifted it to my lips. "We're here."

"Where is here exactly?" She was behind the driver's seat and couldn't see the building out of the passenger side.

"My place. You'll stay with me until we figure out your living situation."

"That's not a good idea."

"Why is that?" I unhooked my belt and opened my door. "I promise it's rat free."

Paige gripped the handle on her door, eyes focused on her lap. "It's just that we, um... well, we slept together, and you've been pretty adamant you never want to see me again. And now I'm crashing at your place?"

I paused midway through getting out of the car. "Would you prefer I take you to a hotel?"

"It's just you've been all *rawr* and now you're going to let me stay with you? Why the change of heart? I'm still not signing anything." She'd made that very clear, and her reasons were all valid. They made me feel a bit guilty for how I'd handled the whole situation.

"I've been inside you, the least I could do is let you stay in my guest room." I got out, leaving the door open for her.

Real smooth.

The driver was already opening the trunk and pulling out Paige's bags, so I busied myself with helping him. I could separate what happened in the past from helping out a woman in distress, couldn't I? Besides, it was just for a few days until we found her another place to stay.

There is no we.

She eventually got out of the car, her lips pressed into a tight line. I didn't want to risk her demanding me to take her to a hotel or back to her place, so I stayed quiet as we made our way up to my condo on the thirty-eighth floor.

As I opened my door, Paige gasped in amazement. I couldn't blame her; my condo was like something out of a magazine. The modern, sleek design blended seamlessly with the warm, inviting furniture. When I'd first moved in, it had felt cold and uninviting with all of the white and chrome.

"Wow," she breathed out, looking around the space with wide eyes before walking toward the large windows with a view of Central Park and the Hudson River. "This is incredible."

A weird feeling of déjà vu passed through me as I left her stuff at the end of the hallway and walked toward her. This time, though, I didn't wrap my arms around her.

As we both stood in silence, our arms pressed together,

I couldn't help but notice how beautiful she looked in the soft glow of the city lights. I was struck by how badly I wanted to take her in my arms and kiss her again.

"I'm going to show you to your room." I stepped away from her before I did something stupid. "It's just down the hall."

Paige followed me, her footsteps echoing in the silence. I stopped in front of the guest room, gesturing for her to enter. The room was comfortable, with a queen-sized bed and its own bathroom. It didn't have the same view as the living room and my room, but it was still a nice one none-theless.

"I hope it's comfortable enough." I stepped into the room behind her.

"It's perfect. Bigger than my whole apartment." She turned to face me, and I could see the hesitation in her eyes. "Are you sure this is okay?"

I moved closer, my eyes locked on hers, holding steady for a beat longer than necessary. "Why wouldn't it be?"

My heart pounded in my ears, and my lower back prickled with sweat. She backed up a few steps, right into the wall.

"Ryker," she whimpered as I cupped her cheek. "Wow. Your hand is really hot."

"I've never had someone compliment my hand before. Usually, Garrett gets all the hand and arm compliments." My words were just the reminder I needed to snap out of it, and I took a step back. "Sorry. I don't know what's gotten into me."

She reached for my face, putting the back of her hand

against my cheek. "You're burning up. Are you feeling okay?"

I felt my forehead. Shit. "I've felt a little off today, but I just thought..."

"You thought it was me." She turned her hand over and the contrast between our skin's temperatures was noticeable. "You should go take your temperature and get some sleep. You do look tired."

I nodded, not really wanting to leave her presence. "Yeah, I think I will. Goodnight, Paige."

She smiled softly at me as I backed toward the door, not taking my eyes off her. "Goodnight, Ryker."

I closed the door behind me and leaned against it for a moment, feeling like a lovesick teenager. Maybe I did have a fever and it was making me delusional.

As I trudged to my room, my thoughts were consumed with her. The way she looked at me, the softness of her skin, the sound of her voice. Everything about her was making me crazy. It was like she had cast a spell on me, and I couldn't shake it off.

Apparently, neither could my dick.

I went into my bathroom, turning on my shower before stripping down. A cold shower would hopefully fix the need that was burning inside me.

At least for now.

Chapter 12

Ice, Ice Baby

Luca

I stood outside Ryker's door, wondering if I should knock or just use my passcode. Ryker not showing up to the office by nine o'clock was unheard of and I was worried. He hadn't called and his phone went straight to voicemail. After our conversation the day before, he wasn't in a good headspace, even though we ended our little spat with a hug.

Was I still angry he'd thrown my family's money in my face? Not really. I couldn't deny that my life had been a whole hell of a lot easier than his because of said money. I wasn't so far up my own ass that I didn't recognize the extreme privilege I had.

I raised my hand to knock and thought better of it. If he wasn't answering his phone, it was doubtful he'd answer his door.

I keyed in the code to enter, and the door beeped, granting me access. The first thing I noticed was the pair of pink Crocs in the entryway.

Ryker did not bring chicks back to his place and the type usually up for a tryst didn't wear Crocs to meet a hookup.

The living room and kitchen side of the condo were quiet, but the unmistakable sound of a moan was coming from Ryker's bedroom down the hall.

My heart raced with a mixture of adrenaline and jealousy. Was he really with someone when he should have been at work? Maybe he'd been seeing someone on the sly.

I kicked my shoes off so I could move stealthily down the hall to his slightly open bedroom door.

"Uh." That was definitely Ryker moaning, but he sounded... pained?

"Just a little bit farther," a woman directed in a strained voice. "That's it. Now open your mouth."

"I can't," Ryker croaked. What the fuck was she doing to him?

"Yes, you can," she cooed. "Now, drink."

I tried to see what was happening, but the angle of the door didn't let me see anything. I didn't want to just barge in there and interrupt. If anything, I wanted to stand and listen.

Adjusting myself in my slacks, I put my ear to the crack, trying to take in every sound. There should be the sound of skin smacking or bodily fluids, but I was met with silence.

"Is that good enough?" Ryker coughed. "Fuck, that burned."

My brows furrowed. I really needed to see what was going on in the room. Maybe if I just pushed the door a little farther...

The door flew open, and I stumbled back as the woman screamed. But it wasn't just any woman, it was Paige.

"What the hell, Luca?" Ryker was right behind Paige now, dressed only in his boxers.

I put one hand on the wall and another on my chest. "I think my heart just shifted positions."

"Were you spying on us?" Paige was holding a coffee mug with enough white-knuckle force she was going to break the handle off.

"I... well..." I looked to Ryker for help.

"He thought we were having sex." Ryker coughed and turned back to his bed. "Even though he *knows* I don't bring women back here."

"Well, obviously you do." I looked Paige up and down. She was wearing an oversized shirt and her legs were bare. "Did you *sleep* here?"

"In the guest room." She stood taller, making the shirt rise on her thighs a fraction of an inch. "Do you make it a habit of listening to people having sex?"

"Not on purpose. If they're loud enough... wouldn't you listen?" I backed up as she walked out of the room, softly shutting the door behind her. "Is he okay?"

"He has a fever and a sore throat." She brushed past me, and I followed.

"And he called you to come take care of him and you came of your own free will?" That didn't make any sense considering what an asshole he'd been and the fact he'd fired her. Or did she quit first?

"He came to my apartment last night with the paperwork and a check, there was a rat, he brought me here, and I woke up to his groaning." She walked into the kitchen and rinsed out the coffee mug. "Is he always a big baby when he's sick?"

"He doesn't get sick." I propped my hip against the island, staring at her legs.

Paige looked at me with a raised eyebrow and smirked. "But when he does, he really milks it, doesn't he?"

I nodded, still stuck on the image of her bare skin and wondering if she had on anything besides the shirt. "Yeah, he does."

She pulled at the hem of her shirt, trying to make it longer. "I should go change."

"No, no. You're fine." I pushed off the counter and stalked toward her.

She backed up right into the refrigerator, her face turning a pretty shade of pink. "What are you doing?"

I grabbed onto the top edge of the door, leaning toward her but not touching her. She smelled divine, like fresh strawberries and a hint of coconut.

"I'm just curious," I said, my voice low and playful. "Are you wearing anything under this shirt?"

She swallowed hard, her eyes flickering down to where my other hand was hovering right at the hem of it. "Luca, we can't."

"Ah, so you want to?" I took the fabric between my thumb and forefinger, my eyes never leaving hers.

"That's not why I'm here. There are rats in my apartment building. Splinter-sized ones." She wasn't pushing me away, but she wasn't giving me permission either.

"Is that where cowabunga came from?"

"Maybe." She looked down at my lips. "Shouldn't you, uh... be at work?"

"Shouldn't you?" I reached out my pinky and brushed her outer thigh.

She trembled and put her head back against the door, shutting her eyes. "I don't think this is a good idea. I'm sore."

Had Ryker fucked her last night? I wouldn't be surprised with as much as he was going on about her working for us. He didn't want her there because he couldn't control himself, and Ryker liked control.

"Where?" Since she wasn't pushing my hand away, I moved my hand under her shirt and onto her hip. "You naughty girl, walking around with no shorts under here."

She moaned, her breath becoming staggered. "This is a bad idea."

"I don't think it is. You like bad ideas, don't you?" I squeezed her hip, digging my fingers into her soft flesh.

She opened her eyes. "My legs are sore from stairs... and... and... Garrett kissed me."

"Then it's only fair I get to." I didn't give her any chance to protest. I brought my lips to hers and poured all the pent-up need for her into our kiss.

Our tongues met and tangled in a wild dance, and my hand moved up the curve of her waist, pulling her closer to me. She melted against me, her body pressing against mine, begging for more.

Who was I to deny her more?

I spun us around and backed her against the island, my lips leaving hers to kiss down her jaw to the sensitive part just below her ear. "Now's your one chance to stop me."

"Don't stop." She ran her fingers through my hair, and I groaned. Fuck, I loved my hair played with.

With every ounce of restraint I had left, I backed up two steps, loosening my tie to remove it. "Take off your shirt. I need to see those perfect tits while I have breakfast."

"Are you all bossy like this?" She cringed. "God, that makes me sound like a-"

I shoved my Prada tie in her mouth, her eyes widening as I grabbed her chin. "It makes you sound like a woman who knows what she wants and has three men willing to give it to her."

Her soft whimper went right to my cock, stoking my need even higher. I'd never wanted someone as much as I wanted her.

"Now, take off your shirt." I removed my suit jacket, laying it on the counter as she pulled off her shirt and held it against her chest.

I needed the bold woman from that night to come out to play. Rolling up my sleeves, I stepped into her space, my lips trailing along her neck and across her collarbone.

"I'm not going to stop until I have you begging for it," I murmured against her skin, my hand bypassing the shirt and cupping her between the legs. "I haven't been able to stop thinking about how good you tasted."

She said something, made an annoyed sound, and reached for the tie in her mouth.

"Don't touch it." I smacked her pussy, making her simultaneously jump and squeal.

Her chest heaved as she grabbed onto the end hanging from her mouth and gave it a little pull, her eyes not leaving mine.

I smacked her again. She pulled again.

"Oh, someone likes that, doesn't she?" I rubbed her through her panties to ease the sting. "I want to hear you scream for me, but now is not the time."

She nodded, shoving the small bit of tie she'd tugged free back into her mouth. But she was still holding her damn shirt against her.

I grabbed her by the back of her thighs and lifted her onto the counter. "Since you can't speak, if you want to tap out, just smack the counter three times, okay?"

She nodded, her body prickling with goosebumps. There was uncertainty in her eyes.

I ran my hands up and down the fronts of her thighs. "You said you were sore from stairs? I can help with that. Lie back."

She didn't hesitate, despite the apprehension written in her body language. She was tense, like a rubber band wound up too tight and waiting to snap.

I'd let her hold onto the shirt for now, but her underwear needed to go. Hooking my fingers under the waist-band, I pulled them off, throwing them to the side.

"So beautiful." I spread her legs more and ran my fingertip along her glistening seam. "Pink and perfect."

I turned, opening the cabinet next to the refrigerator and pulling out a cup. She made a noise that I took as asking me what the hell I was doing.

"When your muscles are sore you should rotate between hot and cold." I filled up the cup with ice and turned back to see her propped on her elbows, her brows furrowed.

I put the cup far enough away from her so she wouldn't knock it off the counter and grabbed a cube, placing it just above her knee. "We'll ice right now and then switch to heat."

She nodded, her eyes on the ice cube as I trailed it up and down her quad.

"You're all tensed up." I moved the ice to her inner thigh, and she lay back against the counter, clutching the shirt against her. "I can't wait to eat this pussy." I smacked it again. "Probably need some ice on that too, don't you, baby?"

I ran the cube up her slit, pressing it in when I got to her clit. She writhed on the counter, her legs trying to shut.

I popped the ice in my mouth, groaning as her taste hit my tongue. I wanted to take things slow, but my resolve was slipping.

Knowing her legs were sore, I carefully pushed each one up so her feet were flat on the counter. She adjusted her body until she was comfortable, and then I dove in.

I'd had a grand plan of torturing her with the ice, but I needed my mouth on her cunt like I needed air. She cried out around my tie as my cold tongue plunged into her.

"Mm, so hot and tight," I purred as I spread her wider and pushed my tongue farther in.

My hands found her hips and I tugged her closer, burying my tongue deeper. Her hips lifted off the counter, grinding against my face.

"There's my girl." I kissed her inner thigh and reached for the cup. "Now, move that shirt so I can look at those beautiful tits as I make you come."

There was no hesitation; she threw the shirt right at my face. She had a feisty side to her that I was going to enjoy punishing. I slapped her cunt twice and her legs fell open even more.

I buried my face once more, my mouth finding her clit and sucking as I grabbed a piece of ice from the cup. She rocked against my face and then squealed as I pushed a piece of ice into her.

Water dripped onto the counter as I moved it in and out, never letting up on her clit. She was close. I could feel her body tensing.

Throwing the ice to the side, I plunged two fingers in, then three. Fuck, she could have taken even more, but I didn't want to push it.

She was so pliant, so wet, and she began to thrash against me, her hands reaching for my hair.

I scraped my teeth against her tight bundle of nerves while I pressed into her G-spot, and she detonated just like

I knew she would. Her movements were desperate, and her hips lifted, begging for more.

I kept going until she came down from her high and collapsed against the counter.

I stood up straight, pulling my fingers from her and bringing them to my mouth to suck them clean.

"Good girl. You did amazing." I kissed her inner thigh before reaching for my belt buckle and pausing. "Do you want me to stop?"

She made a sound of protest and shook her head. I undid my pants but didn't pull them down, needing them to remain up so I could move.

"Sit up." As soon as she did, I pulled the tie from her mouth and kissed her.

She'd done so beautifully, and I'd hazard a guess that was her first time being gagged with something other than a cock.

I wrapped her legs around me and carried her into the dining room, right in line with a view of the building a block away. I broke our kiss, gently lowering her to the ground.

She looked behind her at the window and her head snapped back to me. "Someone will see."

"Maybe. Maybe not." I pulled out my wallet and grabbed a condom.

She looked down with wide eyes as I pushed my pants and boxers down and rolled on the condom. "I've never been with someone who had a piercing."

"It's going to feel amazing." At least I hoped it would.

Every once in a while, a woman would complain about it. "Turn around."

She tilted her head, confused, but did as I asked. Holy fucking chocolate chip cannoli, her ass was amazing, and I couldn't help myself from leaning forward and biting into it.

Her gasp unraveled the last thread of control I had, and I pushed her against the table, standing up just enough to line up, and then slammed into her. She cried out, but I didn't care if Ryker heard and came storming out. She was mine right then and he'd have to cut my dick off to get me to stop.

I hooked my foot around the chair, pulling it closer, before pulling her backward onto my lap as I sat. I was so deep inside her, and it felt so good I nearly came.

"Ride my cock, Paige. Ride it like it's yours to keep." I bit her shoulder blade, and she began to move.

She was slow at first, getting the hang of how to move in the direction she was facing, but with each torturous thrust, I could feel her relaxing.

"Does that feel good? It's hitting that spot inside of you, isn't it?" I kissed along her shoulder. "I bet you look magnificent from across the table... or from the building."

Her pussy squeezed around me. "Nobody is watching."

"Mm." I licked the shell of her ear. "You can't know that. They wouldn't want to be caught watching."

She whimpered, her body lifting farther off me each time she moved. "They can't see much."

"They can see enough." I reached around her and

dragged the table closer. "Now, fuck me, Paige. Fuck me like you hate me for letting them watch."

She leaned forward slightly, her forearms on the table, and looked back over her shoulder at me. "Like this?" She lifted almost all the way off my cock and sat her ass back down.

"Fuuuuuck, yes. Just like that." I held onto her hips to keep her steady. "Let them see your tits bounce."

She began moving, using the table as leverage. "You feel so good."

"So do you." I reached around, cupping one of her breasts. "I bet whoever is watching right now is touching themselves."

Her pace increased. She liked the idea of someone watching, or at least me talking about it.

"If it were a couple, she'd want him to take her just like this." I ran my hand up and down her spine. "Or maybe he'd let her watch as he knelt in front of her and spread her legs."

The sensations grew and grew as she bounced harder on me, and I couldn't continue my play-by-play of the hypothetical onlookers.

It wasn't long until I was on the edge. "Goddamn it, Paige! You are fucking perfect," I roared and thrust up to meet her each time.

With one last grinding thrust, I spilled inside her, my orgasm hitting me so hard I couldn't inhale for a moment.

She pushed back, grinding her pussy against me as I wrapped my arm around her and rubbed her clit.

With nails digging into my legs, she tightened around me. "Luca! Oh, God. Yes! Yes!"

Her body tried to move forward, but I pulled her back against me as she trembled from her release.

I kissed the center of her back. "Any regrets?"

Her breaths were still coming in hard pants, but she managed to say the one word I wanted. "None."

I was screwed.

Chapter 13

Bosom Buddies

Paige

It seemed that rats were a precursor to me having epic orgasms. If I got one as a pet, I'd probably be catatonic from all the pleasure.

"What's that about rats?" Luca was still inside me and my legs were too unsteady to try to stand.

"Nothing." I sighed, covering my nipples with one arm. Removing my shirt was completely unnecessary considering he hadn't even taken off his pants.

Now that the endorphins were settling down, my reality was crashing down on me. Anyone could have seen us if they had good eyesight or binoculars. And then there was Ryker who was right down the hall.

His apartment wasn't massive like I'd suspected it would be, and his room was right at the end of the long hallway. He definitely would have heard us at the end.

"We should get cleaned up." Luca kissed my shoulder

as he removed his arm from around my waist. "Are you okay to stand?"

"Yeah, I think so." I stood gingerly, a shudder running through me as he slipped out and wetness dribbled down my leg. "I should, uh..."

"Stay right there." Luca got up and waddled to the kitchen where he removed the condom, tied it up, and threw it in the trash under the sink. He pulled up his pants, leaving them undone.

Watching him made my body flush with heat, and not because I was turned on. There I was standing naked in the dining room that didn't even belong to the man I'd just fucked.

Before I'd moved to New York, I'd only slept with three men, and in a month, I'd slept with not one but two men. Not to mention the kiss with Garrett.

What was I doing?

Luca came back to me with a clean hand towel, concern furrowing his brows. "What's wrong? Did I hurt you?"

I sniffled back my tears. *Don't you dare cry after this man just gave you two mind-blowing orgasms.*

He gently put the folded-up towel between my legs and then pulled me into his arms, rubbing my back. "I'm sorry if I hurt you."

I shook my head, burying my face in his shirt. This had been a horrible idea, just like the hotel had been. My quarter-life crisis was turning into just that. "I don't think I'm cut out for casual sex."

With his hands still on my back, he pulled away just

enough to look me in the eyes. "What just happened here was nothing casual."

Then what exactly was it? I didn't want to think that they were meaningless words, but they defied logic. I'd barely spoken to this man and what we just did wasn't casual?

"It doesn't matter." I shrugged and stepped back, confused not only by my actions but all of theirs. It had just been one night and yet there was this weird pull I felt toward all three.

"It does matter." Luca sighed and ran his fingers through his hair. "I know this is in the wrong order, but let me take you out."

"But why?" I removed the towel from between my legs and found my shirt barely hanging onto one of the barstools. "My pussy isn't that magical, is it?"

"Oh, it's magical all right." He grabbed my panties before I could and shoved them into his pocket.

I scrunched my nose. "That's-"

"Nothing is acceptable coming out of your mouth, but that's incredibly sexy." He took the towel I'd left on the counter and threw it in the sink. "Don't yuck someone's yum."

I bit my lip, stifling a laugh. "Yum? You're going to eat them? Or maybe you'll boil them and make a soup. Maybe that will help Ryker feel better."

"Zuppa di figa is a delicacy in Italy. People travel from around the world to sample the savory pussy soup that takes hours to make." He shook out his tie before he rolled it up and handed it to me. "For you. Since I'm keeping your panties."

I looked down at the blue piece of fabric he'd shoved in my mouth, my face heating at what he'd just done to me. "Thanks?"

"You should wear that and only that the next time you get off." He grabbed his suit jacket, putting it over his arm, and my heart sank that he was going to leave. It was the complete opposite of the reaction I should have been having.

"You never told me why you want to take me out." I watched my hand as I traced a circle on the counter.

"Why?" he asked softly as he lifted my chin. "You brought Ry back to life... you made him smile, laugh, care about something other than work. And then when he cares too much about work, you call him an asshole and write him a 'fuck you' sticky note."

Tears stung my eyes, but I couldn't look away from his. "But... why ask me out?"

I could have sworn he clenched his jaw, but my eyes were too blurry. "Nothing brings me more joy than seeing my best friend lose his shit over a woman for the first time ever."

My eyebrows nearly shot clear to my hairline. "I see." I stepped back. "I think you should go."

I wasn't going to be used as a pawn in whatever fucked up game these three were playing. My feelings for them were already messing with my head and I didn't need to add going on dates to the pile.

"Paige." He reached for me. "That's not how I meant-"

"That's exactly how you meant it, Luca. I won't allow you to turn me into some kind of laughing stock." This was exactly why I'd run away from California, yet there I was again, putting myself in a situation where I'd inevitably be water cooler gossip. "I deserve better."

It hadn't escaped my notice that my termination papers had been sent to me by someone other than Ryker and had clearly stated I had a personal intimate relationship with him. People at their company knew I'd slept with him, and it was only a matter of time before word of that spread. Even though it wasn't like I'd be there to know, it was inevitable.

"A laughing stock? What are you even talking about? I want to take you on a date and get to know you better." He reached for me, but I moved to the other side of the island, leaving his tie in front of him. "You misunderstood me."

"I don't think I did. I'm one woman and there are three of you. Don't you have rules in place for a reason? To avoid this?" The fact I even had to remind him of this was enough of a deterrent to stay away from all of them. "I'm not going to cause a company to crumble or friendships to be ruined. That's not fair to me."

"No one is asking you to choose." He scrubbed his hand over his face, his shoulders sagging in defeat.

"That's exactly the position you're putting me in... that I put myself in." I needed to run and run fast before he could put any weirder feelings in my chest. "I need to go get dressed and start looking for a job and a place to live. Maybe I'll just go back to California."

"Paige." He anticipated my retreat and cut me off

before I got to the entryway that led to the hallway. "I'm bad at this. We all are."

"I can't be your practice." I crossed my arms over my chest and quickly uncrossed them once I realized it made the hem of my shirt rise. "Are you going to move or am I going to have to scream for Ryker?"

"Hang out with me on Saturday. As friends." Luca gave the phrase *puppy-dog eyes* a whole new meaning, and I felt myself soften just a smidge. "I'll invite some people to hang out with us too."

Damn it, Paige.

"I don't know, Luca..." I looked past him as the door at the end of the hall opened and Ryker leaned against the doorframe. My stomach twisted at the frown on his face.

"What can it hurt? If you're uncomfortable, you can just leave." He pulled me into a hug and my resolve to run away crumbled.

"Fine. I'll go." I would just plan several escape strategies beforehand.

"Perfect! I'll text you." He was grinning when he pulled away. "Do you have any food allergies?"

"No, I don't." I waited for him to pull out his phone but instead, he slipped on his jacket. "Don't you need my number?"

"Already have it." He gave me a quick peck on the lips and then was out the door, a bounce in his step.

Ryker didn't move from where he was leaning in his doorway as I went to the guestroom door. "Did you just agree to go on a date with him?" He sounded like he looked —like shit.

I felt a pang of guilt, which was ridiculous. "Not on a date. We're going to hang out. You should come."

He pushed off the door frame and shuffled toward me, a look in his eyes so heated it scared me. "To hang out?"

"Yeah, just as friends. We can be friends, right? Me and Luca, I mean. Well, and you too. I want to be friends with you. I think. Do you want to be friends?" My mouth wouldn't stop running, but every other part of me was frozen until he was close enough to touch me.

"Friends?" He grabbed my hand to stop me as I started to back into the room. "Does it feel like we're just friends, Paige?" He placed my hand over his crotch.

I think I stopped breathing as my hand inadvertently wrapped partly around his thick erection. "Yes," I squeaked. "The bestest of friends. Bosom buddies even. Chums. Amigos."

He smiled as he brought my hand to his lips and kissed my palm, which put me at a loss for more ways to say friends. His lips were hotter than they should have been temperature-wise. "Sisters from another mister?"

"Well, no. That would be incest."

He laughed and it lit up his entire face. The deep throaty sound of it, the way his blue eyes sparkled, the brightness of his smile. I wanted to make him laugh like that again and again.

His hand yanked away suddenly, covering his mouth as he coughed. It didn't sound like it was coming from his chest, so that was good.

"You should be in bed." I grabbed his elbow and

steered him back toward his room. "I'm sorry if we woke you."

"I have work I need to get done." Despite his sluggish movements, he ended up turning toward another door and opening it. "And don't worry about me. I'm a big boy."

You sure are.

I gasped as he entered a large room with a desk in front of the windows and floor-to-ceiling bookshelves surrounding the rest of the room. The wall with the door had cabinets on the bottom and shelves on the top displaying all kinds of pictures and trinkets. The other two walls on either side of the room were all books and both had sliding ladders.

"May I?" I walked to one of the ladders and was about to lift my foot when I remembered I didn't have on any panties. "Never mind."

Tugging on the shirt, I turned to find his eyes right where my ass would have been. He looked up and cleared his throat. "It's probably best that your Belle moment happen some other time."

"Of course." I patted a rung of the ladder. "I should probably go get dressed."

He went around his desk and sat down heavily in his office chair. "I'll order some breakfast. I don't have much in my fridge since Garrett usually cooks for us, or I grab something on the way to and from work."

"Garrett cooks for you?" I wanted to bang my head against the ladder, which I couldn't seem to stop touching.

"Honestly, he should have gone to culinary school." Ryker opened a laptop that was on his desk. "What do you want to eat? There's this really good bagel place that makes amazing egg and bacon sandwiches. Or pastrami and egg..." His lips twitched. Was he teasing me?

"You could get one of each and we could split." I scanned his books, surprised it was mostly fiction. Even more surprising were the bottom shelves full of manga. "Do they have soup? You should get some for later."

He made a noncommittal noise and focused on his computer screen while I walked to the other side of the room. There were so many books he had doubled them up in some places. I slid one out and he coughed so loud I jumped.

"I don't like people touching my books." He barely got the words out before coughing some more.

I slid the book back on the shelf, which didn't have a speck of dust in sight. "Sorry. I just miss my books. I didn't have quite this many since print copies are so expensive, but it was a few shelves worth."

"You didn't bring them with you?" He went back to clicking on his computer.

"I brought three big suitcases and put everything else in storage until I figured things out." I moved toward the door, sensing he wanted to be left alone.

He looked up. "Why didn't you just kick him out? He's the one who cheated."

"It was his house. I just paid him rent-"

"He made you pay him rent?" Rent came out a little higher pitched and he roughly cleared his throat. "Was this guy a deadbeat?"

I looked down and ran my big toe along the edge of the area rug on the floor. "No. He was a lawyer... a partner."

"And he was making you pay for the wedding?" I could hear the fury in his voice.

Hearing it from someone other than Nora and my parents really ripped at the last piece of dignity I had where that relationship was concerned. I'd been so naïve and in love with the idea of marriage and a life with someone that I had brushed aside all the negatives. And there were a lot. More and more, I was realizing, with each passing day.

"Let me know when the food is almost here." I turned and sped out of the office.

My name being coughed was the last thing I heard before shutting and locking myself in the guest bedroom. The last thing I needed was his pity.

Chapter 14

Puzzle Pieces

Garrett

What a fucking day. I was having a lot of them lately, and I was about to the point where I was going to throw in the towel. There was no reason any of us should have been working as hard as we did and putting more work on our plates by expanding.

We'd been working practically nonstop since we decided during our freshman year in college to go into business together. It had taken a while to figure out exactly *what* we wanted to do, but once we did, we were all in. It was made substantially easier with Luca's money for an interest-free loan for startup costs and free use of his family's property.

I was one lucky son of a bitch to be in the financial situation I was in, but I wanted more than long and stressful days. The only thing that kept me coming back lately was

141

my involvement in starring in marketing videos, but even those were bound to end sooner or later. There were only so many campaigns we could use my arms and chest for before it got old, and then what would keep me there?

I'd have loved to be able to say Ryker and Luca would be my reason to stay, but we'd grown apart over the last year. I still cooked for their lazy asses, but it wasn't like we sat down and ate together. I prepackaged their meals a few times a week by making a lot for my own dinner.

Cooking was one of my favorite things in the world to do, but I'd never had much interest in making it a career. I just loved cooking for other people and making something boring into something delicious.

My stomach growled at the thought of the steak waiting for me when I got home. I was just about to head out for the day when a text came through from Ryker.

Ryker: *Hey. What are you doing?*

Me: *Getting ready to go home. Why? How are you feeling?*

Ryker: *Like shit.*

Me: *I heard you have a new roommate who is playing nursemaid.*

Ryker: *Not a very good one. She burned canned soup. Nearly burned the place down.*

Me: *Do you want me to come by and make you soup?*

Ryker: *You'd do that?*

Me: *Isn't that why you texted me out of nowhere to see what I was doing?*

Ryker: *I texted you because we're bosom buddies... or would it be penis pals?*

Me: *What now?*

Ryker: *Nothing. If you want to come over and make us tomato soup with grilled cheese sandwiches for dinner, I'm not going to say no...*

Me: *Anything you need from the store?*

Ryker: *Oreos for Paige. A rat ate hers. Well, he tried to, and I karate chopped him.*

Me: *Are you drunk?*

The text conversation left me a little confused and quite amused. Ryker was always so serious and rarely joked around like he used to in college or the first few years after. It was like the more successful we got, the more he was like a stick in the mud.

When I left the office, it was still warm out for it being late September. The temperature had been in the eighties all week, which was nice, but I was ready for colder weather and hockey season to start. I might not have wanted to play professionally, but I grew up around the sport and my younger brother played for the Tri-State Titans.

I wondered if Paige would want to go to an NHL game. She'd mentioned her best friend being the daughter of a coach, but she'd never said if she enjoyed watching. Maybe I'd ask her to an exhibition game that was coming up.

None of us lived too far from the office, with Ryker

living the closest. It took a solid fifteen-minute walk to get there and there was a grocery store on the way.

Forty minutes later, I stepped off the elevator on Ryker's floor. Shifting the grocery bags into one hand, I keyed in his door code and let myself in. It was quiet and there was a pair of women's Crocs and tennis shoes right next to the door.

I kicked off my own shoes and made my way to the kitchen, stopping short when I saw Paige sitting on the couch staring out the windows. "Hey."

She jumped, her head whipping around. "Shit. You scared me!"

"Sorry. I thought you would have heard the door. What are you doing?" I placed the bags on the counter and turned on the oven to preheat.

She turned back to face the window. "Just watching the sky. I didn't think anything could beat a Pacific Ocean sunset, but there's something about the buildings coming alive for the evening and the sky that's just magical."

"It really is. Especially with this view." I walked around the island and stood behind where she was sitting, putting my hands on her shoulders.

Now that I'd had a taste of her lips and felt her body pressed against mine, I wanted more. I'd gone over all the reasons why I should or shouldn't pursue something with her, and one of the only reasons I could think against it was her working for us. That was no longer an issue.

She was tense under my touch but quickly relaxed as I gently kneaded her muscles. "Do you have a view like this?"

"No. I live in a brownstone. What it lacks in a view is made up for by the private outdoor space." I slid one of my hands to her throat and she inhaled sharply. I pushed up so she'd tilt her head back. "Can I have a kiss?"

She pulled away suddenly, standing up. "Did Luca not tell you?"

"Tell me what?" Feeling dejected, I loosened my tie and went back into the kitchen to keep myself busy. "He said you're staying here until your rat situation is figured out."

"That's all he told you?" She wrung her hands and walked over to the island separating us.

I couldn't help but let my eyes wander down from her tank top to her jeans that melded to her hips and thighs. "It is. Did he forget something?"

"He, uh... we, um..." She sighed and ran a hand over her head to her bun, which she fiddled with.

I raised an eyebrow, watching how she shifted her weight from one foot to the other. She was nervous and I didn't need to read minds to connect the dots. "You kissed."

She looked down at the counter, her cheeks turning crimson. "And other stuff."

I paused with the bag of tomatoes in my hand. "Other stuff? What did that other stuff entail?"

"We got carried away."

I put the tomatoes down before I did something like chuck them across the room. "Spit it out, Paige. It's not like you cheated."

She cringed, but it was the truth. I'd kissed her and that

145

was that. We hadn't talked about anything else, and it wasn't like I was in love with the woman.

"I slept with him, but I told him I didn't want to go on a date with him." She shook her head and covered her face with her hands. "Fuck, all of this makes me sound like such a whore."

"You aren't a whore." I was going to kill Luca for sleeping with her. He knew I'd kissed her and that I had a big enough crush on her that I was ready to say fuck it and break another one of our rules.

Clearly, with this woman, there were no more rules.

"Then what else would you call me?" She removed her hands and, thankfully, there weren't any tears. She wasn't looking at me, though. She'd turned to stare at the dining area. "I can't believe I did that."

I busied myself getting out a sheet pan and cutting board while I thought of how to respond. This was uncharted territory for me. She'd slept with my two best friends and yet I still had this need burning in my stomach to ask her out.

But no, I couldn't. I didn't want to complicate things with Ryker and Luca even more than they already were.

"Does Ryker know?" I took the tomatoes to the sink and put them in a colander to rinse. "Or did he join in?"

I didn't look back at her, but she made a small noise in her throat that sounded a lot like a whimper and a moan combined. "He knows. He didn't, um... join. Is that, uh... something you guys do?"

"No." Had I thought about what it would be like to

share a woman in the bedroom? Sure. But to date the same one? That was a mess with a capital M, especially since we were in business together.

It was quiet while I finished washing the tomatoes and brought them to the island to cut up along with an onion and garlic. Paige was standing at one of the windows now, her shoulders drawn forward like she was trying to make herself disappear.

I didn't want to make this awkward, but it was hard not to. "You turning into a turtle? That could explain why the rats are visiting your apartment."

She straightened so she was no longer hunched over. "Do you believe in fate?"

"I can't say I do." I wasn't sure where she was going with her question, but I hoped it wasn't in the direction of wolf shifters... or rat shifters. I could get on board with aliens walking among us but drew the line at shapeshifting.

But if she wanted to stick a wolf tail butt plug in and growl at me, I wouldn't have been opposed.

Man, I really needed to stop listening to my sister babbling on about the books she read.

"There's never been a time in your life where you've thought, oh, shit, all the stars aligned to make this unbelievable occurrence happen?" She finally turned around, and I was glad I had my fingers curled under as I brought the knife through a tomato. Otherwise, I would have chopped off a finger.

She was breathtaking with the glow of fading light behind her. Was this what she meant by fate? Because I felt like I was exactly where I needed to be even though the whole situation was messy as hell.

"I don't know if I'd call it fate, but I've had moments where everything seemed to fall into place like puzzle pieces. Why do you ask?"

Her eyes were fixed on mine as she walked to me in the kitchen. It felt like she was trying to see inside my soul. "Sometimes it feels like the universe is trying to tell me something, you know? Like there's this pull towards something or someone, and no matter what I do, I can't fight it."

She took the knife from my hand, her fingers brushing against mine, and set it down on the counter. Her touch sent a flurry of desire and emotion through me. My God, what would it feel like to be buried inside her?

There was no explanation for why I felt such a strong urge to make her mine. Was this what Luca felt? Like he was under her spell and there was no way to stop it?

"Paige..." I turned toward her, bringing the hand without tomato all over it to her cheek.

She leaned into my touch, closing her eyes with a resigned sigh. "It was just one night. You didn't even speak."

"I know." I was fighting the urge to brush my thumb across her bottom lip. If I did that, I was done for.

Paige opened her eyes and looked at me with a hint of sadness. "Then why do I feel like I can't stay away from you?"

I couldn't help but feel a sense of relief wash over me as her words confirmed that I wasn't alone in the way I felt. "I don't know, but I feel it too. Maybe it's fate, or maybe it's just our own messed up version of attraction fueled by loneliness."

"It's only messed up if we define it that way." She stepped back, clearing her throat. "Sorry, I'm being ridiculous."

But she wasn't being ridiculous; I knew exactly what she meant. There was something about her that drew me in, and I couldn't resist it... none of us apparently could. It wasn't just physical attraction, although that was a part of it. It was something deeper, something that felt like it had been a long time coming and all I needed to do was reach out and seize it.

I didn't know anything about her, but in a weird way, I felt like I knew everything. Talk about a mind fuck. "Maybe we're both coming down with whatever Ryker has. His texts were really strange today, like his brain had been hijacked."

"Oh, the penis pals thing?" She laughed and shook her head. "I think he double-dosed on the cough medicine by accident."

The oven beeped that it was preheated, and I quickly turned back to the cutting board. "Why don't you grab a knife and finish cutting these up while I get the onion and garlic done. That doesn't require using the stove."

"You know, I'm not a complete lost cause in the kitchen. I only burned the soup because I was rescheduling some meetings Ryker had for tomorrow and Friday." She grabbed a tomato and cut it in quarters just like I'd been doing.

"Why would you reschedule them?" I got started on cutting up onion and garlic.

She shrugged. "He's not going to work. There are a couple you or Luca are also involved in too and trying to find a new time with how you currently have things set up is nearly impossible. Your previous assistant must have spent a solid ten to fifteen minutes each time she had to schedule one with you all."

"So, you're our assistant again? I thought you were let go, but then quit."

"I don't know what I am. The whole point of me applying for the position I did was to have a low-stress job that didn't require a lot of brain power."

I could tell there was more to her story than she was letting on, but I didn't want to push her. Why take a lower-paying job when she had the skills she had? Was she really that messed up over her ex-fiancé?

Instead of asking twenty questions, I finished putting everything on the pan and popped it in the oven. I could feel the unresolved tension between us, but neither of us seemed to want to make the first move. Or in our case, I suppose it would be the second move.

"This will take about fifteen minutes. Would you like a glass of wine?" I pulled a bottle of Chardonnay from one of the bags. "Just because Ryker is sick, doesn't mean we can't enjoy ourselves."

"I'll take a glass." Ryker's scratchy voice came from the entryway like I'd summoned him, and then he appeared, looking like he'd just rolled out of bed. His t-shirt was wrinkled, and his hair was sticking up in all directions.

It had been a long time since I'd seen him looking so out of it. Hopefully, none of us got whatever crud he had going on.

"How are you feeling?" Concern was etched on Paige's face as Ryker walked towards us, rubbing the sleep from his eyes.

"I've been better."

I couldn't help but feel a pang of jealousy as I watched her reach out and touch his arm in concern as he opened a cupboard where he kept wine glasses. There was absolutely no reason for me to be jealous.

Yanking open the drawer with the wine opener, I tried not to think about that night and how he was the one who fucked her mouth. She had been on his tongue. His name had fallen from her lips.

Ryker put three wine glasses on the counter and reached around me to grab the opener from the drawer I'd been staring in to.

"You aren't having wine." Paige's scolding tone brought me back to the present, and I shut the drawer a little too hard.

"Break my shit, why don't you," Ryker muttered, leaving the wine and walking around to a barstool. "My entire body hurts."

"That's what happens when you don't take care of yourself." I uncorked the bottle. "Maybe this time off will be good for you."

He grumbled something under his breath as he sat down, laying his cheek on the cool surface. "I don't need time off. I'll take time off when I retire."

"You could retire right now if you wanted to." I poured the wine into two glasses and handed one to Paige. "We all could."

Paige took a small sip and made a contented noise in her throat. "Then what would you do? Play video games all day?"

"What if it isn't enough?" Ryker's eyes were closed, and he yawned, his cheek still on the counter, his arms dangling limply at his sides.

"It's enough." I didn't know what his portfolio of assets and investments looked like, but I was approaching thirty million and he was way more frugal with his spending. "Well, unless your goal is to own a yacht or a Hampton vacation house like Luca."

Paige spluttered into her wine glass. "He has a yacht?"

"Mm. Nice big yacht. Goes out to feed the fishies and sharkies." Ryker's eyes fluttered, trying to open them. He was fighting the urge to fall back asleep. "Paigey Waigey, do you like baby sharkies?"

"You are so fucked up man." I laughed and took a long drink of wine.

"Maybe you should go back to bed, sweetheart." Paige put her wine down and went to him, putting her hand on his back and rubbing circles. "Come on."

"But soup and grilled cheese." He slid off the barstool like he weighed three times as much as he did and surprisingly didn't stagger. "I'm a growing boy. I need to eat."

"It will be about thirty or forty minutes, Ry. Go lay down and we'll come wake you up when it's done, or we can reheat it later." I turned to the oven and checked on how the tomatoes were roasting. They were cooking perfectly, and the aroma made my mouth water.

Paige guided Ryker toward his room, leaving me wondering if maybe she was the puzzle piece I'd been missing.

Chapter 15

Just Friends

Paige

Sneaking out Friday morning before Ryker was awake, was much more difficult than I thought it would be. Not because of the fear of waking him up, but because it felt worse than when I'd left Daniel.

The two situations weren't even close to being the same, yet the whole time I'd packed my suitcase and made sure I grabbed all of my stuff that had slowly spread out in the bathroom and bedroom, I felt like throwing up.

Staying would be worse, though, especially with all the feelings that were floating around in my head. Who wants to pursue something with three men she barely knows? I suppose that would be how I'd get to know them, but all three? At once?

Maybe if their lives weren't intertwined, I'd be singing a different tune. There was no way I could just pick one to start dating. They all appealed to me for different reasons.

Ryker had a tough exterior, but I'd seen his softness on multiple occasions whether he wanted me to or not. A coldhearted man doesn't just move someone in with them because of a silly rat. He was fiercely protective of the life he'd built, and I couldn't fault him in his overreaction to me showing up at his company.

Garrett tried to keep his guard up where his heart was concerned, but also wore it on his sleeve for all to see. There was a quiet sadness about him that spoke to me. He cared deeply about his friends, but I couldn't help but wonder if they were partly the cause of his sadness after watching them interact.

And then there was Luca. Luca put on the appearance of not having a care in the world but cared more than he let on. He was adventurous and seized moments as they came at him. He was the hardest to get a read on, but I'd spent the least amount of time with him.

The last thing I needed to be doing was spending more time with any of them, which was why I ran.

I'd been running away from things a lot lately, which was a newer development in my life. It was easier than dealing with the pain that came with staying and letting events unfold. Of course, I'd never experienced someone cheating on me before.

I dragged my suitcase up three flights of stairs to my floor and stopped to catch my breath. The super had messaged me the night before that the rat problem was actually someone's pet from the second floor that had escaped.

I wasn't one-hundred percent convinced that was true,

but he'd at least sealed the gap between my sink pipe and the drywall.

Cautiously, I opened my door and jumped back, finding a piece of white paper with a color picture of the rat in question on it.

"How is this my life?" I picked up the paper and rolled my suitcase in, shutting the door behind me.

Sitting down on the couch, I stared at the picture of the rat, feeling overwhelmed with everything that had happened in the past several weeks. My love life was a mess, and I was still trying to process the fact that I wanted all three of the men that had stumbled into it. It was impossible and ridiculous, but my heart didn't seem to care.

I sighed heavily and pulled out my phone. Maybe distracting myself with some mindless scrolling would help ease my thoughts.

My heart fluttered as a text came through right as I was about to engage in some social media self-soothing.

Unknown number: *Good morning, sunshine! This is Luca. Are we still on to hang out tomorrow?*

I saved his number to my contacts, giving myself time to think about my response. It was barely seven in the morning. What was he doing texting me so early? Had he woken up thinking about me?

Me: *I don't think that's a good idea.*

Luca: *Why? Are you sick?*

I could have lied, but that wouldn't solve my problem. I needed to put an end to this right now. I took a deep breath and typed my response, trying to make it sound as polite as possible.

Me: *No, I'm not sick. I just don't think it's a good idea for us to hang out. It's too complicated and not fair to any of you. Trying to be friends after everything would be nearly impossible.*

I hit send and turned off my phone, feeling both relieved and guilty at the same time. I couldn't continue to lead any of them on.

Finding a job was rough. I spent all day Friday and half the day Saturday submitting resumes. It took time for employers to go through applicants, but I was starting to really worry if I'd made the right decision by jumping on a plane and coming to one of the most expensive cities in the country.

Los Angeles County wasn't cheap, but my rent to Daniel had been reasonable. I'd underestimated how long my money would last me and thought I'd at least get a few wedding deposits back. Turns out, I was wrong.

Just thinking about all the money I'd put into the wedding made me sick to my stomach. How could I have been so stupid to let Daniel convince me that I needed to put all my extra money toward the wedding?

I was going to have to get a job at a fast-food place while I waited to find a better-paying job. There was no other choice.

You could have accepted the money from Ryker.

That ship had sailed, right along with whatever had been brewing between us. Ryker had sent me a single text Friday morning when he'd woken up. "Take care of yourself."

That seemed pretty final to me and was exactly what I wanted, right?

Closing my laptop, I lay down on my small couch, my feet hanging over the arm.

I should have just gone to my parents' house. They would have accepted me home with loving arms and let me get my life in order. People my age moved home all the time during transitional periods, but usually their house had the space.

My family had never had much money growing up, but I'd been raised by two loving parents who were just trying to make it day by day. They lived in a very modest two-bedroom, one-bathroom house—the same one I'd grown up in—and never had the luxuries of new cars or vacations.

There had been a few times when I'd heard them discussing foreclosure, but that never came to pass. They'd put so much money and energy into making the little bungalow a home when they weren't working.

I'd hoped that one day, I'd be able to make their financial situation better, but there I was fucking up my own.

Daniel had painted such a rosy picture of our married future together that I didn't even think twice about what would happen if the rug was yanked out from under me.

But does anyone ever?

My phone buzzed on the coffee table with a call, and I sighed when I saw the name.

Luca.

He'd been quiet most of the day Friday after I told him I couldn't be friends with him, but then he'd decided he wasn't going to listen to me.

Hearing it from my mouth might get through to him, so I answered. "Hello?"

"Paige!" There was traffic noise in the background. "How do I get into your building?"

I sat straight up, surprised my abs were capable of such a feat. "What do you mean?"

"I'm here to pick you up. I can't figure out how to get in. Didn't Ryker just show up at your door? How'd he get in?" He sounded downright giddy, and my heart squeezed.

"Luca, I told you..."

"Listen, I know what you told me. I've decided it was said under duress." There was a beeping noise. "These call buttons don't work."

"No, they don't." I shouldn't have been embarrassed given I paid a normal amount in rent, but the difference between me and the three of them was vast. "You can't just show up here."

"Thank you." The background noise went away, and I knew someone had let him in. "Four-oh-four here I come."

I jumped up, looking around for the robe I usually wore to the bathroom. It was in the high eighties and the wall-mounted air conditioner my place had wasn't the best in the world, so I'd been lying around in just my underwear.

"Paige, you there?"

"Yeah." I finally spotted it on the floor next to the couch and pulled it on.

Just as I was tying it closed, there was a melodic knock on the door. Why was I covering myself up? I didn't *have* to open the door for him.

Neither of us had hung up yet. "I'm not home."

"I just heard you through this paper-thin door. No wonder Ryker practically carried you out of here like a caveman." He knocked again. "I bet your neighbors will love it if I keep knocking."

I shut my eyes and took a deep breath, willing myself to have some self-control. "Luca, please, just leave. I can't talk to you right now."

"Paige, come on. Let me in. We need to talk. I'm not leaving until we do." His voice was insistent and had gotten loud enough that the whole floor could hear.

I hesitated, knowing that if I let him in, things could quickly spiral out of control. But another part of me was curious about what he had to say. I'd never been pursued like this before. Did he really have nothing better to do on a Saturday than try to convince me to hang out with him?

"Look, I know you're scared and confused, but aren't you a little excited too? To see where all of this could go?" It sounded like he was drumming his fingers on the door. "When I want something, I don't give up until it's mine."

I walked to the door, putting my forehead against it. "And what is it you want exactly?"

Luca's response was immediate. "You. I want you, Paige. And I'm not going to stop until I have you."

I closed my eyes, taking a deep breath, and tried to push away the flood of emotions that threatened to overwhelm me. It wasn't that I wasn't attracted to Luca. Hell, every time I thought about him, my body reacted.

"I thought you were okay with being friends." I was starting to sweat in my terry cloth robe and wished I would have taken the time to go up to my loft and grab actual clothes.

"I'll take whatever you can give me."

It would be nice to have a friend in the city, even if it was the most complicated friendship known to man. I knew deep down I'd regret not letting him in.

I unlocked my door and opened it, finding a grinning Luca dressed in navy board shorts with tiny sharks all over them and a light blue tank top.

My mouth opened as I took in his inked skin on full display. One arm was a colorful scene that started with a giant sun wrapping around his shoulder. An ocean scene was on the rest of his arm with sea life and a gorgeous mermaid and merman locked in an embrace. Tentacles were woven through the whole scene, making it look like they were about to squeeze a glass jar. At his wrist was a tap, a few drops of water spilling out.

His other arm was done completely in black ink and started with a moon wrapped around his shoulder. The scene below it was a breathtaking scene of a cityscape morphing into a forest.

"Luca." His name came out entirely too breathy, but I

was taken aback by the display, and I hadn't even checked out his legs yet.

"If I had known my tats would get this reaction out of you, I would have taken my clothes off a lot sooner." He smirked and started to lift the hem of his shirt.

"Don't!" I stepped back, making room for him to come inside.

With a victorious grin, he walked in, bringing the most delicious-smelling cologne known to man. It was so subtle, and he smelled sensual and spicy to match his personality.

"I won't take it personally that you don't want me to take my shirt off." He looked around and then turned to look at me as I shut the door. "Nice place."

I raised an eyebrow. "Bull shit."

Luca chuckled. "Okay, okay, it's not the most glamorous place, but it's got character." He walked over to my couch, flopping down on it and making himself at home. "So, what have you been up to?"

I crossed my arms, a bead of sweat trickling down my back. "Applying for jobs."

"That's no way to spend your weekend." He leaned forward and grabbed the romance novel I was reading. "Ryker has this book."

I quickly crossed the short distance and snatched it from him. It was my first time reading a book that had multiple men with one woman and the last thing I needed was for him to open it up to a sex scene.

"Wait... did you say Ryker has this book?" I hugged it to my chest as if he had laser eyes to see the pages.

"Oh, yeah. My man has quite a few he hides behind

his legal thrillers." He sat back and crossed his ankle over his knee as if he was restless.

"Have you read any?" I couldn't believe Ryker had a secret stash of romance novels. No wonder he didn't want me looking at his books while I was in his office. There was nothing to be embarrassed about.

"No, but I've definitely tried to take a few of his. He shuts that down pretty quickly. He said I couldn't handle them."

I held up the book I was reading. "Do you know what these are about?"

He shrugged. "Sex?"

I brought the book back against me, hugging it. "With multiple men. All together."

"Threesomes? Orgies?" He stood and came toward me, his eyes where I was clutching the book. "Let me read."

I put the book behind my back as he stopped in front of me. "Some, but they are all... in love. She loves them all."

"Oh, really?" He sounded surprised. "So you're telling me that Ryker has been reading romance novels where a woman has multiple boyfriends? Do they have multiple girlfriends?"

"No. That's the whole point of it. She doesn't have to choose, and they are completely devoted to her." I was really starting to sweat now, and my face felt like it was on fire. Of all conversations to have with Luca, why did it have to be about why choose romance?

Luca's eyes were full of mischief. "Interesting concept," he said, his voice low. "I can see the appeal."

I took a step back, running into my counter and dropping the book. "You can?"

He reached toward me and tucked a stray hair behind my ear. "Of course. Why would I not entertain the idea of falling in love with a woman who isn't afraid to go after what she wants? And if it's with my two best friends? Even better."

"But-" He put his finger across my lips.

"Come out with me. Just as friends." He trailed his finger down to my chin, down my neck, and stopped right in the center of my chest. "Being out on the water can give you some clarity."

"The water?" My heart was beating so wildly that I was surprised he didn't say something about it as he circled his finger on my skin. I didn't try to stop him; I craved the touch.

"We'll cruise around on my boat and then have dinner while watching the sun set."

"That sounds, um... romantic not friendly." My lids were growing heavy as he drew random shapes on my exposed skin.

"You're in control of the situation, Paige." He leaned in, his free hand resting on the counter behind me as he gently kissed my cheek and let his lips linger. "If you tell me right now to back off, I will."

Heat pooled in my stomach, and I had to bite my lip to stop myself from turning my head and kissing him. "Just friends, Luca."

He pushed off the counter, the loss of his touch making

me ache and feel like a complete liar. "Go get dressed. Bring a sweater since it's cooler at night."

He picked up the book off the floor and went to the couch, opening it as soon as he sat down.

There was no stopping him from something he wanted; he'd made that abundantly clear.

Chapter 16

That's Not a Boat

Luca

Persistent was my middle name and, once again, I'd proven that even the impossible was possible.

I hadn't known how Paige would handle me showing up to her apartment—if it could even be called that—unannounced after upsetting her a few days ago.

I didn't regret what I'd said because it had given me a glimpse into what was going on in Paige's head. And now? Now I had the confirmation I needed that she was open to being with all three of us.

To say I was happy would have been an understatement.

It made perfect sense that Ryker, Garrett, and I would be in a relationship with the same woman. To be honest, I was a little surprised Ryker never brought it up considering the books he read.

Was that why he read them? To see if that would be something he could handle?

I knew without a shadow of a doubt that Garrett would be able to handle it, but Ryker was more possessive than both of us combined. He had to be in control and a polyamorous relationship took some of that control away.

I skimmed through the romance novel as I waited on Paige to change. It had taken everything in me not to yank the ties on her robe and find out what she had on underneath, but I'd kept my composure. I felt like such a horn dog around her, but I also just craved her touch.

I had been with a lot of women before, but when I looked into Paige's eyes and felt her gentle touch, something clicked. It was like I knew her even though I'd never met her before. I felt a strange familiarity and yet an intense attraction.

Paige's legs came into view on the ladder, and I was more than happy to see a whole lot of leg. She had changed into a pair of jean shorts that hit mid-thigh, and a loose, floral tank top that revealed just a hint of cleavage. My eyes roamed over her body, taking in every inch of her as she climbed down.

"Can I take back the friend thing?" I wanted to run my hands up her legs before wrapping them around me.

"What?" Distress filled her voice, and she bit her bottom lip.

"No! I just meant you look so good that I want to do unfriendly things to your body." I stood, snapping the book I'd been skimming shut and tossing it on the table.

She visibly relaxed. "You've already done enough unfriendly things to my body."

I watched curiously as she went to a cart by the door and pulled off a cover. Looking in a hand mirror she had hanging on a pushpin, she took down her hair, brushed it, and put it in a neat ponytail.

Fuck, ponytails were sexy. Something nice and solid to maneuver her head with as she sucked my cock.

No, down boy.

I cleared my throat and adjusted my stance, giving my inflating dick a little room to breathe. "By the way, your book overuses the word cock. It took me exactly five seconds to locate the first sex scene."

She squirted some kind of cream in her hand and rubbed it all over her face. "Well, there's four of them in that book. What else should the author call them? Meat rods? Pogo sticks?"

"He whipped out his willy, the head glistening. It has a nice ring to it."

"It's not sexy." She used a brush to dab something on her face. "I'd rather read the word cock fifty times than see willy even once."

"And what about the balls? Do authors just use balls or do they throw a testis and scrotum in there?" I was surprised she was even humoring me with this conversation, but maybe these were the kinds of things she talked about with her friends.

"I've only seen balls and nuts. There are really no good options for it. What else could they be called?" She leaned in close to the mirror, doing something to her eyes. Women putting on makeup was so fascinating to watch.

"I don't know about nuts. Someone might be allergic to them, and it might ruin the mood using the word. I guess they're sort of like the ornaments of the penis, and they can't be ignored despite their unsexy names." What the hell was I even saying? Thank fuck the guys weren't here because they would never let me forget this conversation. "Some people like them nipped, swirled, and a little teacup action. A romance author can't just ignore them because of an aversion to the word balls."

She giggled, and it filled me with intense satisfaction. "Hey, baby. How about we go back to my room, and I'll give your penis ornaments some tea bag action."

"Teacup sounds much more sophisticated, and I'm down for that if you are." I winked as she looked at me through the mirror.

"How old are you?" She put the cover back over her cart and turned to face me.

Her makeup was subtle, but the way she'd done her eyes made the flecks of green and gold in her eyes pop.

"Thirty-one and, believe it or not, I'm the oldest out of the three of us. Granted it's only by a month, but I'll take the wins where I can." I shoved my hands in my pockets, suddenly a little nervous that this was an issue. She looked legal for sure—plus she'd been drinking at a bar—but she *did* look young. "How old are you?"

"Twenty-seven." She grabbed her purse and phone and slipped on her sandals before giving me a shy smile. "I think I'm ready."

I looked at her lips. Damn. This friend thing was going to be harder than I thought. "Ready for...?"

"Some tea since you're such an old man?" She rolled her eyes and laughed. She was definitely teasing me. "To go... on the boat."

"I can assure you there is nothing old about me." I took her hand and led her to the door. Friends could hold hands and since she didn't pull hers from mine, I entwined our fingers. "Is this okay? I'm not sure how friends hold hands."

She locked her door, and we walked side by side to the stairs. "Nora and I only ever hold hands if we're super excited or scared."

"Well, I don't know about you, but I'm pretty excited." I squeezed her hand reassuringly. "It's going to be fun."

"We'll see." She reached into her purse as we stepped outside and pulled out her sunglasses. "How far is your boat?"

"It's parked on the Hudson right now. Should take about twenty minutes to get there."

I led her a short walk down the street to where my driver had parked. It had been fairly easy to find a space since it was the weekend. During the week, people liked to park in surrounding areas and then take a quick ten-minute train ride into Manhattan.

"Do any of you drive?" Paige asked as I opened the back door, cold air pouring out.

"Yes, but I didn't want to today." I squeezed the side of the door as she climbed into the back of the SUV, giving me a view of her round ass.

"Luca!" I turned my head on instinct and instantly

regretted it. "Are the rumors true? Are you engaged to be married to Clara Accardo? Who are you with?"

Did they really think I was going to answer that asinine question? "Have the day you deserve, boys." I jumped in the SUV and slammed the door shut.

The driver had the privacy screen up already but didn't need my go-ahead to take off. He knew exactly where we were going.

"Were those paparazzi?" Paige looked past me to the three assholes trying to get pictures through heavily tinted glass.

Idiots.

"Yup. Usually, they don't follow me too often. They mostly bug me when I'm going to events." I pulled out my phone and texted my security team about the incident.

"Who's Clara Accardo?"

I really didn't want to talk about Clara, but I couldn't exactly keep it a secret now that Paige knew her name. "Clara is the only heir of Carlo Accardo, who runs a very lucrative custom jewelry empire in Italy. My family has been trying to get me to marry her."

"That's... wow. That happens in real life?" She buckled her seatbelt.

"Unfortunately." I looked out my window as we pulled away from the sidewalk. "She's nice and all, but we aren't compatible."

"What do you mean?"

I wish she'd just drop it because I promised Clara I wouldn't say anything about her sexuality. It wasn't my place to out her, no matter how frustrating both of our families were.

"Just that we would never work. We both agree on that, our families just keep trying; arranging dinners, putting us next to each other at events, leaking rumors." I loved my family and all, but they needed to calm down. Our empire was big enough as it was.

"I see." She looked out her window as we crossed the bridge into Manhattan.

"Hey, don't do that." I reached over and took her hand from where it was resting against the side of her leg. "It's nothing. They can't force us to do anything, and I've made it very clear they aren't arranging any marriage for me."

"I'm sorry. That's a lot to deal with." She squeezed my hand and looked over at me.

"Don't be. I just wish they would leave me the fuck alone about it." I hated that it was even a thing to people, but I *was* one of New York City's most eligible bachelors.

All three of us were.

"Do I need to worry about being in pictures?" The worry in her voice made me feel like I'd been kicked in the nuts.

"No. My team will get them deleted if they get any. They'll probably hang around your place for a few days to make sure no one saw what building we came from." I hadn't seen them when we'd come out of Paige's building, but then again, I'd been a little distracted by her.

"They've never found out about what you get up to in the bedroom?" Her thumb started to rub back and forth across the side of my hand, making a tingle shoot down my spine.

"No. It's not like I'm a celebrity, but there are some social media accounts and blogs that put out content on New York's rich." I laid my head against my headrest, watching her as she stared out the window at the scenery passing by. "Garrett and Ryker aren't really part of that. At least not yet. Mostly, women know who they are."

She made a hm noise in her throat but didn't respond. It was better for her to know all of the bad that came with the good upfront. I just hoped the good outweighed the bad.

Paige stared up at my yacht thirty minutes later, her lips parted. It was giving me ideas, which I quickly kicked out of my brain.

"Meet *Holy Cannoli*, an eighty-five-foot beauty." I took her hand and walked toward the gangway where one of the staff was waiting to welcome us onboard.

"You said boat, not yacht. Garrett said you had a yacht but then Ryker was joking about feeding the fish and sharks. I thought they were joking."

"I hate to break it to you, Paige, but a yacht is a boat. Plus, it has a regular boat on it too named *Bubba*."

I could feel her eyes on my back as I made my way up the gangway with her following close at my heels. She held my hand tightly.

"Welcome aboard, sir. We have everything prepared as

you requested. Please enjoy your evening and let me know if you need anything else." Tom moved out of the way and did a sweeping motion with his arm.

"So fancy," Paige muttered as she walked next to me onto the yacht and toward the main deck. "This is surreal. I can't believe... never mind."

"No, what were you going to say?" I stopped her at the bottom of the stairway, turning her to face me because her tone had changed.

"It's not important." She had her sunglasses on so I took them off and put them on top of her head so I could see her eyes. There were tears in them.

"What's wrong?" I asked softly, bringing her hand to my lips and kissing her knuckles. "Is it too much? Did I say something to upset you?"

"We just live in two completely different realities is all. It's like... when someone says they've bought their fifth Bentley while you watch a rat steal an Oreo that you shouldn't have bought with what little money is left in your bank account." She blew out a breath and looked over at the lower deck seating area. "Sorry, I sound bitter."

"No, it's understandable. I try to give back, but you're right. It's excessive." I'd had this conversation quite often with Ryker, especially when he had days of guilt over spending his money. "I wish I had something philosophical to say. We do pay our employees on board well and they work full time since we also rent it out."

"I guess I never thought about it that way." She still had a sparkle in her eyes but gave me a soft smile. "Maybe I should apply for a job on your yacht."

"And deal with rich assholes all the time? Hell no." I pulled her into a hug, and she didn't hesitate to wrap her arms around me too. "I just thought you'd like the experience. We can go do something else if it makes you uncomfortable."

"No, this is fine. Besides, don't you have friends coming?" She started up the stairs, leaving me to look at her ass.

I didn't know whether to tell her now or just wait for my friends to show up to deal with her ire. "Yeah, my friends will be here in a bit."

"Looking forward to meeting them," she said over her shoulder before coming to a stop at the top of the stairs. "Oh, wow."

The main deck wasn't even the best deck in my opinion, but it had a smaller outdoor area with seating and opened up into the main living area. "There are five bedrooms on this level and the VIP suite."

She walked into the living room and ran her hand across the back of the leather sofa as she walked past it.

In the middle of the room was a large entertainment space with three couches surrounding a large coffee table. At the end was a console with a hidden television that separated the space from the ten-seat dining table.

She went to the next set of stairs—which curved up to the upper deck—which had another indoor living space and an informal outdoor dining area under the cover of the deck above it.

"There are four rooms on this one, with one of them

being the owner's suite. Plus, the helipad." I cringed at that because it was crazy even to me.

"A helipad?" She wheeled around, her eyes wide. "Do you have a helicopter?"

"No." I chuckled. "Some guests have really busy schedules and it's convenient. It's good for safety too."

"Right." She walked right up the next set of stairs. "How big is this thing?"

"There are two more decks. The bridge deck has a small pool, more living space, a gym, captain's quarters, and is where everything is controlled from." I was getting a little nervous because she was quiet, only speaking in one or two words when she did say something. "Then the next level is the flybridge and there's more lounge space and dining."

She sat down on one of the lounge seats by the raised infinity pool, which had a glass wall on one side of it to see what was going on below the water.

I couldn't help but wonder what it might be like to watch her get fucked in the pool and see everything.

"Say something." I sat down at the end of her seat, putting my hand on her ankle. "We can leave."

"We should." My heart sank as she leaned back against the pillows, slipping her sunglasses back on. "Your boat isn't quite big enough."

And just like that, all my worries dissipated. "It's not about the size of the boat."

She smiled and I could feel her looking at me. I couldn't stop myself from running the tips of my fingers up her calf, causing goosebumps to spread across her skin.

"Luca." Her voice lacked any conviction. "You can't touch me like that."

"Like what?" I leaned down, kissing her knee. "I'm just being friendly." I didn't kiss her skin again but kept my hand on her ankle.

"Like you're up to no good." She bit her lip like she was holding something back.

"Friends can get up to-"

"Sir, your other guests have arrived. Would you like them to come up and I'll serve drinks here?" Cynthia, the lead stewardess seemed to appear out of nowhere.

Paige sat up quickly, swinging her legs over the edge of the lounger.

"That would be perfect. Thank you, Cynthia." I turned back to Paige. "You have to promise me you won't get upset."

"About what?"

I cringed. "Well, my friends. You see... you know them already."

"You didn't mention any names." She lifted her sunglasses so she could shoot laser beams at me.

If it was possible for a look to castrate a man, that would have been it.

Chapter 17

Emotional Support Bottle

Paige

When Luca said he was hanging out with friends, I didn't think he meant Garrett and Ryker. I mean, I should have, but he would have said their names, not just lumped them with a generic term. At least that would have been what I would have said had I invited someone the other person already knew.

But was I really that surprised?

Luca put his hand just above my knee and squeezed. "It's going to be fun. We haven't all hung out and I think it would be good."

"It's going to be awkward." I put my sunglasses back down and stood, putting my hands on my hips. "Withholding information you should have given me is lying."

He squinted up at me, putting a hand over his eyes to shield them from the sun. "Would you have come still?"

"That's not the point, Luca." I sighed. "What are you trying to do?"

The smallest of smiles appeared on his lips but disappeared quickly. "Nothing."

How was I going to stand being around all three of them alone? My body, and quite frankly my mind, kept betraying me when they were near. Even then, I was letting Luca touch me in more than a 'just friends' way.

Female laughter came from the next deck. "Stop it, Gare."

"You have got to be kidding me." Jealousy like nothing I'd ever experienced before took hold and made my blood run hot.

"What's wrong?" Luca looked confused as I backed away, the sound of footsteps on the stairs only making me panic.

It was like Daniel all over again but worse, which was ridiculous because none of them were mine. It felt like someone was stabbing me in the chest.

"I have to go to the bathroom." I didn't want him to follow me, that was for sure.

Before I had to see the women that were with Garrett and Ryker, I practically ran to the other set of stairs and went down them. I had no clue where they led, but I needed a minute to get myself together.

"Paige! Where are you going? There's a bathroom up here!" Luca's voice was still up on the deck.

I ran into the indoor part of the yacht. I went through a living room, down a short hall, through a sitting room, and finally down a hall with bedrooms. Why was this damn yacht so big?

There were four doors and all of them were closed so I picked one, hoping for the best. Once inside, I shut the door and leaned against it, closing my eyes.

"It's going to be fine. Everything was fine." I tried to reassure myself, but the lasso around my chest was pulling tighter and tighter. "You aren't with them. It doesn't matter."

I slid down to the floor, even though there was a perfectly made queen bed and a chair in the corner. I just needed to put my head between my knees or something to calm down, that was all.

Why had Luca done such a thing? Was it to make me jealous? To stake his claim on me? He could have at least told me beforehand and then maybe I wouldn't have felt so... deceived.

I pulled my phone from my crossbody purse and called Nora. She'd talk me down; she always knew just what to say.

But of course, she also was the one who got me into this predicament.

"Paige! What's up?" There was noise in the background and when I heard a whistle, I knew she was at hockey practice.

"Are you busy?" My voice trembled and I bit my lip.
Do not cry.

Who was I kidding? That never worked.

"I'm never too busy for you. Just assessing skating skills during drills. Phew. They need a lot of work; they don't even know what's about to hit them." She sounded like she was going to get great satisfaction out of coaching a bunch of NHL players to skate gracefully. "What's wrong?"

I told her everything I hadn't already, which only covered that day, but was still a lot. By the time I was done, I was choking back sobs and wiping my eyes.

"Babe..." She sighed. "Are you listening to yourself?"

"Yes." I got to my feet and went into the attached bathroom to grab a tissue before going to sit on the bed.

"I don't think you are. They want you, Paige. All three of them. You want them. I really don't see what the hold-up is besides your own fear."

"Did you not hear me say that there were women with them?" I wiped furiously at my tears, but they just kept on falling. "I'm such a mess and it's all your fault."

She laughed, and not just a haha funny laugh, but one that I was sure drew attention to her. "My fault? Fine, I'll take the blame for you about to have the most epic sexual experience of your life."

"I already have." I took my purse off and lay back on the bed. "I can't go back out there."

"Yes, you can and you will. March your cute little self out there, introduce yourself as their girlfriend, and there you go. You can throw those hussies overboard and let the sharks feast on them."

"You've been around hockey players too much. And I'm not their girlfriend. It's a little presumptuous to assume they want that." It was so unconventional of a concept that I didn't even know how to bring it up without feeling like a fool.

"They haven't killed each other yet, have they? And they know about all the sex and whatever else you've been up to with each of them?"

"Yes. They share everything with each other it seems." I picked at a loose thread on the comforter. "Is it weird that I feel like this and barely know them?"

She was quiet for a few moments and when she spoke, her voice was soft. "I asked my dad once when he knew Mom was the one and he said he knew the moment she smiled at him. I know it's corny, but sometimes there's just an undeniable connection."

"I don't know if it's that simple considering there are three of them." I sighed, overwhelmed by the situation and my own emotions.

"It's not always simple, but it's worth taking a chance on. You don't want to look back one day and wonder what if."

I sat up, wiping away my tears once again. "You're right. I should take a chance on them."

"That's the spirit! Now go out there and claim your men."

My men.

Oh, God, what was I even thinking?

It was terrifying, and my heart was still in pieces from the last time I'd let someone have it. But Nora was right. I couldn't let fear hold me back from something that could be amazing.

Nora and I said our goodbyes, and I went back into the bathroom to make sure I didn't look like I'd had a breakdown.

My eyes were a little red, but that's what sunglasses were for.

As I walked out of the room and headed back toward the stairs leading up to the next deck, I psyched myself up. I wasn't a confrontational person, but the closer I got to the voices, the more I gritted my teeth.

I stopped just before I got to the top of the stairs, staying out of view. There were definitely two women, but then a man who wasn't Ryker, Luca, or Garrett said something.

That voice sounded very familiar.

After reminding myself that there were copious places on the yacht I could hide if things didn't go well, I ascended the last few steps.

Ethan was sitting with the two women, their heads together as if they were gossiping. He saw me first, and his face lit up.

"Paige!" He jumped up and rushed over to me, looping his arm through mine and leading me to the two women. "There you are! We were just talking about you."

"Uh... okay?" If Ethan was already friends with these women, that must have meant they'd been around for a while.

I felt like I was going to puke as we stopped in front of them. They were both gorgeous.

"I was telling them all about how you wrote 'fuck you' and 'I quit' on sticky notes and left them on your desk. It was really epic."

"Ry must have had steam coming out of his ears," the

blonde woman said quietly before she stood and *hugged* me. "I'm Libby."

The other woman with brunette hair stood and hugged me too. "And I'm Harper. Ethan was just catching us up on the woman who made our brothers act like idiots just a minute ago when Luca said you were here."

Sisters.

My shoulders sagged in relief, and I felt like crying *again*. I used to think something was wrong with me until my mom told me people who cried a lot were highly in-tune with their emotions and to stop getting upset over getting upset.

"It's nice to meet you both." I tried to keep the tremble out of my voice, but it was a struggle. "They um... acted like idiots?"

"Oh, girl. You have no idea." Ethan pulled me down next to him and then nodded his chin toward the inside part of the deck we were on.

Luca, Ryker, and Garrett were right inside the gym, the door cracked just enough to see them having a very heated conversation. I assumed it was about me, but was it a good conversation or one that would leave me feeling uncomfortable for the rest of the afternoon and evening?

Before I could dwell on it any further, Libby spoke. "Don't worry about them. Luca vaguely told us what was going on when he invited us." She was the opposite of Ryker personality-wise. While he was assertive and confi-dent, she was soft-spoken and almost seemed shy.

"Did he want me to think you were their girlfriends?" I didn't want to look away from the three men, but they moved farther into the gym, and I couldn't see them anymore with the gym windows being tinted.

"I think Luca's intention was to have us smack some sense into our brothers if needed." Libby put her hand on my arm, and I looked at her. "I don't think we need to do that, though."

Cynthia, the stewardess, appeared carrying a bucket with champagne and flutes. "Would you four like me to pour your drinks?"

"Yes, please." I was in desperate need of some liquid courage and was grateful for the distraction.

Cynthia expertly poured each of us a flute of champagne, and we all raised our glasses.

"To an evening that I'm sure will be full of surprises." Ethan winked at me and my face heated.

We all clinked glasses, and I drained mine in one go. It was probably a bad idea since champagne seemed to make me tipsy quicker than anything else.

"Dang, girl." Harper smiled and took another sip of her drink. "Oh! The yacht is starting to move! Let's go upstairs."

"I'll grab the champagne." I stood, putting my glass down on the small table and grabbing the champagne bottle by the neck.

We walked to the stairs leading to the flybridge and I stopped, causing Libby to bump right into me.

"Just go." She pushed me toward the door into the gym.

"What if they're having a business meeting?" I took a drink from the bottle I was holding.

"Doubtful Luca would let that happen when he's wearing shorts." She looked away from me, her cheeks turning pink. "I know it's weird, but it's not like Ryker isn't open to the idea... he's stolen a lot of my books thinking I didn't notice."

I stared at her with wide eyes. "That's..."

"Gross, yeah I know. Knowing that my brother has read the same books I have, gives me nightmares. He's also the worst at returning them and I'm not sure if I even want them back." She made a gagging noise.

"Are you two coming?" Ethan yelled from upstairs.

The faint voices inside the gym stopped, and I knew they saw me through the windows despite them being heavily tinted on my side.

"Go on. We'll see you at dinner, or maybe not at all." She wiggled her eyebrows and then went up the stairs.

Both sisters seemed nice and welcoming, but I was a little surprised at how open they were about what was happening. I was sure there were a lot of people who would not be okay with what I was about to suggest, but the only person's opinion that mattered was my own.

Although, saying it in my head and putting it into practice were two entirely different things.

"Time to claim my men," I muttered to myself before striding toward the door and sliding one side open. "Hi."

Three sets of eyes stared at me as I walked into the small gym and closed the door. The air in the gym felt thick as I walked a few steps closer to where they were gathered around a bench. It was a bit of a strange place to huddle together, but maybe they liked the smell of the workout equipment.

Nothing like the smell of rubber while you poured your heart out.

I did a slow perusal of Ryker and Garrett. They both had shorts on, showing off their sexy man calves just like Luca. Garrett had on a tank like Luca did, but Ryker wore a t-shirt that didn't disappoint in the arm muscle department. He looked like he was back to his normal self, not a hair on his head out of place.

Why was it so hot in there?

I took a swig of the champagne and then hugged it to me. It could be my emotional support bottle.

Luca cleared his throat. "Are you okay? You ran off."

"Had to pee," I lied.

Garrett pointed toward a door. "There's a bathroom down that hall."

"I don't have to pee now." This was totally turning awkward. "We need to talk."

Ryker cleared his throat. "Can you take your sunglasses off?"

I took a deep breath and pushed my sunglasses up onto my head, revealing what I knew were red-rimmed eyes. "I'm sorry for running off like that. I just needed a moment to collect my thoughts."

Luca's concerned stare made me want to run. "I'm sorry, Paige. I didn't think it would be a big deal. I thought maybe a fun day together would help things along."

Ryker pinched the bridge of his nose and Garrett made a noise in his throat.

I took another drink of champagne before lowering it to my side. I kept my eyes down because I really couldn't bear to see their reactions to what I was about to say.

It was time to rip off the Band-Aid and get this over with. It was now or never because I couldn't keep doing this to myself. The uncertainty and wondering were destroying me, and I didn't have much left to destroy.

"I want you all and I don't know if it's even possible or reasonable to ask that of you, but it's how I feel. I can't just choose one of you even though that would be a hell of a lot easier." My feet were tingling with the urge to flee but I didn't move. "I'm sorry."

It was quiet and I peeked up at them through my eyelashes. Luca was grinning like he'd just been given everything on his Christmas list, Ryker looked like he was about to say something, and Garrett's jaw was clenched so tightly I thought it might break.

"I'll um..." I turned my torso and pointed to the door with the bottle. "Let you three discuss."

"Stop running." Ryker's command made me stop mid-pivot. "Stop running and maybe we'd catch you."

"I'm sorry if you run too slow." It was out of my mouth before I could stop it, and my eyes widened as Garrett stalked toward me.

I was frozen in place as he stepped right in front of me, reaching around to grab the base of my ponytail. It wasn't rough but it also wasn't gentle. He surprised me so much I almost let the champagne bottle slip from my hold.

Garrett finally spoke, his voice low and controlled. "Are you sure this is what you want?"

"Yes, I'm one hundred percent sure. If you'll-" I was going to say, 'if you'll have me' but Garrett silenced me with his mouth.

I groaned, clutching at his shirt with my free hand. It was overwhelming to have him finally kiss me again, and to do it in front of Ryker and Luca just made it that much more real.

I wanted this and now there was no turning back.

Chapter 18

Rock The Boat

Garrett

It was about fucking time I could kiss and touch Paige without worry twisting my stomach in knots.

When I'd heard Luca call Paige's name as we'd come up the stairs, I'd felt a sense of dread wash over me. Not because of her being there, but because of Luca and Ryker. They both wanted more with her, and so did I.

Things had already been strained between us, and the last thing we needed was to be fighting or disagreeing over a woman.

But then Luca had broached the subject of us *all* having more with her. I'd briefly thought about it before, but realistically, it was a tough arrangement. But what if it could work?

While Paige had seemed to want the same thing, it was a completely different ballgame when it came to putting it into action.

'I want you all' played on repeat in my head as I used Paige's ponytail to move her head and deepen our kiss. She didn't just want Luca or Ryker. She wanted me too.

Paige moaned, her hand gripping my shirt as she tried to press closer to me. The feel of her body against mine was something I dreamed about nightly ever since I'd kissed her on the street. It sent a jolt of desire through me that I couldn't ignore, but probably should have considering we were in the middle of the gym.

We needed to talk about this to set some boundaries and figure out what exactly we all wanted out of this. We'd been starting to hash things out when she'd walked in, champagne bottle clutched tightly in her hand like it was her life preserver.

I pulled back from the kiss, my lips tingling, and my breath coming out in ragged gasps. Her eyes were full of desire, but I didn't know if I wanted an audience the first time I was with her. If I didn't stop kissing her, that was exactly what we'd have.

A shuffling noise came from behind me, and Luca came to the side of us, cupping Paige's cheek and turning her head toward him. He kissed her right there in front of me, and fuck, it made my dick stir even more. It wasn't going to be easy to hide my hard-on in the shorts I was wearing.

She still had that damn bottle in her hand, and I grabbed it from her, stepping back to give them space and to put the champagne on the bench.

Ryker stood watching, which was new for him. He'd never liked to watch before, which was why we'd had the arrangement we did. But Paige was different. I think we knew that from the moment we saw her on her knees.

Luca had his arm around Paige's waist as they continued to kiss, and my jealousy flared up. I couldn't help but feel like an outsider even though I'd just kissed her myself.

I needed to get past this feeling if we were going to give this a chance. I stepped closer to them and ran my fingers up her arm.

She broke her kiss with Luca and turned her face toward me again. I leaned in and kissed her, my tongue pushing at the seam of her lips. She opened for me, and I groaned as our tongues brushed against each other.

"I think I hear someone coming," Ryker interrupted. "Down the hall."

While I liked the thrill of almost getting caught, there was a time and place for that and now wasn't it. I wanted this moment all to us.

Paige pulled away first, her lips swollen and her eyes heavy-lidded. "Wow."

"You got that right." Luca stepped back just as the door on the other side of the gym opened and the captain walked in.

He stood there for a second and looked between us, one of his eyebrows lifting. Seeing as we'd had some wild parties on the yacht, he didn't seem too shocked. "Sorry if I'm interrupting, sir. Cynthia said you were in the gym. I need to know if you've decided if we're staying on the Hudson or going out to sea."

Paige's head whipped in Luca's direction so fast her ponytail whacked me in the face. "Out to sea?"

Why did she seem so surprised? Had Luca also left out that he'd planned to make this an overnight trip?

"Well, that's up to you." Luca took one of her hands and brought it to his lips. "We can just cruise the Hudson and stay through dinner, or we can go out in the Atlantic and sleep on board."

"I didn't bring anything." She looked down at herself.

The captain cleared his throat. "Ma'am, we have laundry on board and personal care items in most bathrooms. Anything you need, we can order to be brought to us."

Paige's mouth opened. "Like someone gets in a boat and delivers it to the yacht?"

I put my hand on the small of her back, sensing her uncertainty. "We can go out to sea and then if she decides she doesn't want to spend the night, we can use the boat to come back. Unless you're scared of the ocean."

She snorted. "I'm not scared of the ocean, just surprised is all." She looked at Luca again, and I caught her glare in the mirror.

"Then we'll be on our way. Perfect weather for a quick overnight trip out." The captain extended his hand to Luca for a handshake and then went back through the inner hallway to the bridge of the yacht.

"This could be considered kidnapping, Luca." Paige turned toward him, her hands going to her hips. "You have some explaining to do."

"I didn't see any cement bricks when we got on board.

I think we're all safe." Ryker finally moved from the spot he'd been glued to, leaning in and kissing Paige's cheek. Was he all modest now? Maybe being around his sister had rubbed off on him.

Luca rolled his eyes and snatched the champagne bottle from the bench. "It's a big boat, Ryker. I could have them stashed anywhere to use when you least expect it."

Ryker leaned in again and kissed Paige's neck before whispering in her ear loud enough for both me and Luca to hear. "I plan on punishing you for leaving without saying goodbye yesterday." He bit her earlobe, and she shuddered, her breath hitching.

I crossed my arms, wanting to steal her away from them and be alone together. They'd both been inside her and yet I'd only kissed her.

Did I feel like a petulant child? Yes, but I couldn't help but feel like I was the odd man out. What if when we did finally sleep together, it wasn't up to par with what she wanted? Would she go back on what she said about wanting us all?

"Perk up, Gary." Luca nudged me with his elbow. "We might see your friends while we're out at sea."

"Gary?" Paige turned to us, putting her back against Ryker's chest.

I sighed, shutting my eyes in frustration. "Can we not."

Luca slung his arm around my shoulder and took a sip of champagne from Paige's bottle. "Gary Wilson Jr."

"What about it? I thought Garrett's nickname was Gare." Paige looked confused and leaned back into Ryker, who'd wrapped a possessive arm around her chest.

"Do you not know who I speak of?" Luca feigned shock, and I rolled my eyes. He hadn't brought this up in years besides occasionally saying Gary to annoy me.

Paige shook her head and Ryker hid his smile against the side of her head.

Luca bent his elbow so Paige could see the back of his forearm. "This right here is Gary Wilson Jr." He pointed right to the very out-of-place sea snail amongst the beauty of his tattoo.

Paige leaned forward, her eyes narrowing in assessment. "Isn't that SpongeBob's pet?"

I groaned, snatching the champagne from Luca and taking a long drink. The bottle was almost empty to my dismay.

"It is. And look! He's going to drink himself into a stupor and probably will start meowing for you if you ask nicely. At least he did in college for pretty women." Luca wiggled his eyebrows.

"How did this even come about?" Paige wiggled free of Ryker's hold and wrapped her arms around me and, damn, if all my insecurities and annoyance didn't just melt away.

"I answered my phone once on speaker and my mom called me Gary. It's all her fault for naming me after my dad and needing a nickname he hadn't already claimed." I put my cheek against the side of Paige's hair and let out a contented sigh. "So, we're actually doing this? Even if my nickname is a sea snail that meows?"

She laughed and nuzzled into my neck, her lips brushing against my skin. "I want to try. We should take things slow... maybe. I don't know. It just all clicked together over the last few days and I haven't given much thought to the logistics of it."

"We have a lot we need to figure out." Ryker shoved his hands in his pockets, looking a little out of his element. "Not fighting should be at the top of our priority list."

I clenched my teeth, stopping myself from lashing out at him. Why did everything have to be like a business transaction? Hell, even watching him with a woman had rules we had to follow.

"We don't have to figure out everything right now. Let's just go with the flow and let things unfold how they unfold." Luca looked out the glass doors. "I should probably go find our guests and be a proper host. Would hate to start something here and have one of your sisters stumble in on it."

"I don't even know why you invited them and Ethan." I hadn't thought anything of it when Luca invited me and her.

Luca's face softened. "A safety net for Paige. I didn't know how things would go down and wanted there to be some other people here besides just us."

"That's really sweet... for a kidnapper." I could hear the teasing in Paige's voice. "Does this mean I already have Stockholm Syndrome?"

"I'll make it up to you." Luca moved behind her, grabbing her hips.

"Luca, let's give Paige and Garrett a few minutes." Ryker grabbed the mostly empty bottle from me and walked to the door, sliding it open. "Remember you wanted to check on your guests?"

Luca backed away reluctantly. "I should have planned this whole situation out a little better."

Ryker gave me a tight smile and was out the door, Luca right behind him. The door clicked shut and, finally, I was alone with her.

She pulled back just enough to look me in the eyes. "Are *you* okay with this?"

I took a moment to gather my thoughts before answering. "Things have been strained for a while between the three of us. Not just because of what happened last time with me going rogue, but at work."

She lifted her hand to my jaw, rubbing her thumb along the line where my light stubble met my smooth cheek. "And you're worried this is going to make it worse?"

"I'm worried that if I end up leaving the company, it's going to make things worse and ruin this before it's even really begun."

"They'll understand if you do, Garrett. They're your best friends." She moved her thumb over my lips, and I forgot for a second where we were and what we'd been talking about. "You need to tell them how you feel. Tell them what you need from them."

I opened my eyes to find hers burning right into my soul. "Right now, I need you."

Her eyes darted to either side of the room before coming back to me. "Then have me."

I pressed my lips to hers in a deep and urgent kiss. I wanted all of her focus on me; not on the slight possibility of someone walking in on us or on the others.

I grabbed her ponytail again, a little rougher this time

and tilted her head to the side like I was a vampire, and she was my meal. She gasped as I ripped my lips from hers and bit her neck just hard enough to sting.

She slid her hands down my chest to the waistband of my shorts, her fingers dancing along my skin. "Let me taste you, Garrett."

I let go of her hair and moved back just far enough to shove the waistband of my shorts down. Who was I to deny her?

She wrapped her fingers around me, and I groaned, my hips moving forward of their own accord. Her touch felt so good, and she'd barely touched me. Her mouth was going to destroy me.

I grabbed her hair again and she started to get to her knees, but my attention caught on the rower right behind us.

I tugged at her hair since she seemed to like it and stopped her. "I don't want you on your knees."

"No?" She was confused until I directed her to look over her shoulder. "Sit on the rower?"

"Yes." My voice was low in my throat as images floated through my head of just how much I wanted her to be able to slide back and forth.

I let go of her as she sat down, her feet flat on the ground, and slid back and forth a few times. "Do you think you can handle that, Paige?"

"Yes." She slid in little pulses, her eyes on my cock.

That was all I needed to step out of my shorts and boxer briefs and straddle the rail in front of her. She was at the perfect fucking height, and I knew I'd be buying a rower for my gym after this.

"Take off your shirt and bra." I knew it was a big ask given where we were.

She bit her lip but then slid farther away from me to give herself space to pull off her tank top and unclasp her bra.

Her tits were even more exquisite than I remembered, the dusty pink of her nipples hardening into hard points that I wanted to spend hours torturing.

She slid back and forth at the other end of the rower, her breasts moving with her motions. Her smile was playful, and she pushed them together, her thumbs rubbing over her nipples. "Do I get rewarded for heeding your command?"

Pre-cum beaded at the head, ready for whatever she was willing to give me. I grabbed the base of my cock, stroking myself a few times. "Your reward is my cock in your mouth. Come here."

"Bossy, bossy." She slid forward, stopping herself by grabbing onto my hips. She looked up at me as her tongue darted out to lick the tip.

"Fuck." I groaned as she traced the veins down the length. "In your mouth. Take me in your mouth."

"Yes, sir," she said in a singsong voice.

Well, now she'd gone and done it.

I grabbed either side of her head as she wrapped her lips around me and thrust into her mouth. Her eyes widened in surprise, and she dug her nails into my thighs as I hit the back of her throat.

"Fuck my cock with your mouth, baby." I kept hold of her head as she used her legs to slowly push back on the rower until she just had the tip in. "That's my girl."

She pushed forward, taking my cock to the back of her throat again. This was the single greatest idea I'd had for a blow job. As she slid back again, she sucked, hollowing her cheeks.

"You suck my cock so good." I couldn't take my eyes off her as her pace increased and she found just the right position for her mouth. "Yes, Paige. Fuck it harder."

She moaned and the vibration sent heat down my spine. I was going to come so hard and fast if I let her continue to work my cock like she was.

After a few more strokes on the rower, I pulled away from her lips and a small, sad noise escaped her.

I grabbed her chin gently and leaned down to kiss her. Kissing her would never grow old and I'd die a happy man if that was all she let me do for the rest of my life.

She pulled away, her eyes glossy with emotion. "Fuck me, Garrett."

"Stand up." My voice was a harsh rasp, the need to be inside her affecting my whole body.

She stood and I unbuttoned her shorts, pushing them along with her panties down her hips. She put her hands on my shoulders as she stepped out of them, kicking them to the side.

"Shit. I don't have a condom." I ran my hand down my face. "My wallet is in my bag which they took to my room."

"It's okay. I'm on birth control, and after that night at the hotel, I went for tests." She bit her lip.

"I'm clean." I'd never not used a condom, but I trusted her.

"I mean, yeah, Ryker used a condom, but I didn't always use one with-"

I kissed her because the last thing I wanted her to think about was her ex. It took her a few seconds, but she relaxed.

I wasn't sure how to explain what I wanted her to do, so I walked to the side of her and pushed the rower seat all the way to the back of the rower. "Get on your knees and straddle the rail. You're going to lean forward over the seat."

In my head, it was going to work perfectly. The rail wasn't that high off the ground and my nuts hadn't even come close to touching it when I'd straddled it.

She did as I asked and used the seat to rock her hips. "Oh, God, Gare. This is going to feel so good when you're inside me." She looked up at me, her cheeks a beautiful shade of pink. "What are you waiting for?"

Chapter 19

Sea Legs

Paige

My body was on fire as I slowly rocked using the seat of the rower. I'd only ever used the machine once before, and after five minutes, I had collapsed into a heap on the floor next to it.

This time I'd be collapsing into a heap from the sheer pleasure this was about to bring. I never knew sex could be so good until these men came into my life.

And Garrett? What a surprise he was. I never thought I'd like to be bossed around and have my body used like he was using mine. It made me feel like the most powerful woman in the world.

Garrett got on his knees behind me, straddling the railing without saying a word, which just heightened my awareness of everything he did.

His hand ran down my spine, across my ass, and

between my legs. He hummed in satisfaction as he slid a finger between my folds.

"Garrett, please." I rocked a little, making his fingers slide back and forth. "I want your cock."

He didn't give me what I wanted, though, keeping his hand still as I rubbed on it. His silence was killing me. I wanted to hear his praise and the dirty things that came out of his mouth.

With how the seat slid, I couldn't exactly reach back and grab him without face planting into the rail. I had to keep my torso centered on the seat.

Finally, he moved his hand, his finger pushing at my entrance. The tip slipped in, and I pushed back until it was buried inside me.

"Mm. You want to fuck my fingers, baby?" His other hand gripped my hip as I started pulsing on the one inside me. "How many can you take?"

"Two." I panted, adjusting my body so his one was tilted just right inside me.

He moved a second one to join the first, his hand steady as I groaned. It wasn't enough.

I was practically bouncing off his hand now, chasing the orgasm that felt so close yet so far. "Three."

He slid a third in and twisted his hand to position them to rub against my G-spot. "You're so fucking wet from fucking yourself on my hand, aren't you?"

"Yes, yes, yes!" My voice was louder, and I didn't give a shit if the captain or everyone upstairs heard.

He pulled his hand away, leaving me rocking into

nothing but air. I cried out in frustration and reached for my clit.

He grabbed my wrist and pinned it behind my back. "Tell me what you want."

"I want to come." I felt his cock between my legs, and I pushed back, making it slide between my folds and bump against my clit.

He chuckled and moved the tip to my opening. "Fuck me, Paige. Make yourself come all over my cock."

I now knew why men loved to hear women tell them to fuck them. Garrett saying it was like jet fuel to the fire burning in my core.

He let my wrist go and I held onto the rail as I used it to help me push back, impaling myself on him with a cry. His fingers dug into my hips as I began sliding in short little pulses, adjusting to his size.

"That's it, baby. Show me just how you like to be fucked."

Who was I to deny him? I moved faster, sliding myself just enough away before pushing back hard. My core was aching with my building release, and I walked my knees a little wider to get him in deeper.

"Fuck, Paige. I wish you could see how my cock looks as it slides in and out of you." He started to help me, pushing me out and pulling me back in, his hips meeting my ass in a steady rhythm.

Keeping a firm grip on me, he reached under me, finding my clit and pinching it.

"Garrett!" My orgasm was right there, peaking its glorious little head of pleasure over the edge.

"Are you going to come for me, baby?" He began to move faster, his fingers stroking me in firm, quick movements. "Are you going to let me feel you come around my cock?"

"Yes! Oh, God." I closed my eyes as my orgasm slammed into me. "Garrett!"

He took over, his hips slamming into me over and over. "That's it, baby. Take it all. Fuuuuuuccck!"

Warmth filled me and he buried himself deep, his hips grinding into me as he filled me with his cum.

My body tingled everywhere, and my pussy burned with a satisfaction I would be feeling for hours.

Garrett stroked my lower back as he caught his breath, his hips still moving in small circles. "Paige... you're... amazing."

I let go of the rail I'd still been clutching onto, letting my arms hang limply. "I can hardly feel my legs."

He finally stilled inside me but didn't pull out. "That's the greatest compliment you could give me."

I giggled and squirmed a little. "I need to get up."

"Just stay here while I get a towel." He slowly slid out, leaving me feeling an emptiness I already wanted to fill again.

He groaned as he stood up and shuffled across the gym to a cabinet, where he pulled two towels out. His cock glistened with our releases as he walked back and knelt beside me.

"Garrett?" I rested my chin on the rail as he moved the towel between my legs and made a sound of acknowledgment. "You're a bit wild."

He laughed as he worked to clean me up the best he could. "I can be. I'm comfortable with you so I'm more... free. Here. Let me help you up."

He got to his feet and held out his hand so I could sit up. My legs were not functioning properly as I stood; I could hardly lift my leg to get it over the rower. He moved me to the arm of the treadmill where I could steady myself as he gathered our clothes.

"So..." I bit my lip as Garrett held open my underwear like I was a toddler who needed help getting dressed.

"So..." A smile spread across his face as he pulled my underwear up. "You're going to have my cum dripping out of you the rest of the afternoon."

He held open my shorts for me the same way and I used his shoulders to steady myself. I could have probably dressed myself, but I liked him doing it for me. It made me feel cherished and I don't think anyone had ever made me feel like that before.

"That's a little gross, but also oddly sexy if I'm being honest." I put my arms through my bra and turned so he could clasp it. "Thank you."

"You don't need to thank me for sex, Paige. If anything, I should be thanking you." He kissed my shoulder. "Thank you."

I laughed and turned around, wrapping my arms around his neck. "I meant for taking care of me after you fucked my brains out."

"Oh, yeah? But I wasn't the one who fucked your brains out. You fucked your own brains out." He kissed me tenderly and my heart fluttered. "You'll know when *I* fuck you."

I arched an eyebrow. "Is that so?"

"You think it's hard to walk now..." He backed away and pulled on his light blue boxer briefs and dark blue shorts. Instead of putting his tank top on, he put it over my head, and I put my arms through the holes.

"What about a shirt for you?" I took in his torso, which was muscular but not bulky. I wouldn't have minded staring at him for the rest of the day.

"I'd rather you wear my shirt." He gathered the extra fabric and tied it in a small knot on my hip. "Is this okay?"

He'd tied it so the shirt barely touched the top of my shorts and if I moved a certain way revealed a sliver of skin. Normally, I wouldn't dare show even a hint of skin there, but if he wanted me to, I would.

"It's perfect." I ran my hand down the front of it, smoothing the wrinkles. "Everyone is going to know what we were up to."

"I don't care what anyone thinks." He gathered the towels and put them in a hamper in the corner. "Ready? There's probably more champagne and snacks by now."

"I probably should stay away from the alcohol, but I could definitely go for a snack after that workout." I took his hand as he held it out to me, and we exited the gym.

The air was cooler than it had been when I'd gone into the gym and the breeze from the yacht moving whipped a loose strand of hair into my face.

"Here." Garrett let go of my hand and moved behind me, pulling my hair tie free. "Do you want me to braid it really quickly? My sister always used to need hers done so I learned how."

"Yes, please." I felt a bit emotional as he ran his fingers through my hair and positioned me so the breeze wouldn't hit it as he worked.

"I'd prefer it down, but I wouldn't want you to get it all tangled." He worked quickly, and I closed my eyes, savoring the touch. "Well, actually, a ponytail is nice to grab on to."

I snorted. "I didn't think I'd be into it, but I wish you'd pulled harder."

His hands stopped moving and he put his mouth against my ear, making my skin prickle with goosebumps. "That can be arranged."

Laughter came from the deck above us, and Garrett kissed my neck before returning to his task.

How was it that in such a short time, I already felt myself falling for all three of them?

"Are you okay? You got all quiet." He tied off the end of the braid and took my hand.

"Just thinking." I turned and smiled. "Let's go before they send a search party."

He took my hand and led me up to the flybridge. It was the very top of the yacht and had a large sectional at one end, a table with chairs under the hard top.

Ryker and Luca noticed me immediately and their gazes burned into me as they watched us walk toward them to the sectional where everyone was gathered.

There was just enough space between Ryker and Luca for me to squeeze in, so I let go of Garrett's hand and sat there. I really wished we were alone to figure out this group thing without an audience. I didn't know how to act and I was sure they didn't either.

Ryker leaned in so only I could hear. "You look freshly fucked. It's a good look, although I'm not too keen on you wearing his shirt." He pinched the material before dropping his hand to my thigh and squeezing possessively.

"We were just talking about you," Harper said from across the table that had an array of drinks and an impressive charcuterie board.

"A bunch of gossips." Garrett sat down next to his sister and reached for an unopened can of hard seltzer.

"If you want us to gossip, we can talk about why she's wearing your shirt but is now cozied up between Ryker and Luca." Ethan offered me a seltzer and I shook my head, leaning forward and grabbing a bottle of water instead.

"We were telling Ryker all of the benefits of hiring Paige to come back as your assistant." Libby smiled across the table at me. "We just about had him convinced."

"Oh?" I took a drink and looked at Ryker and then Luca. "What about you?"

"I don't need any convincing." Luca slipped his hand behind me and rested it on my hip. His fingers immediately began stroking the skin above the waistband of my shorts. "You're the best assistant we've ever had."

I laughed and put my hand on his knee, which was somewhat in my space since he had his ankle on the other one. "I literally worked for you for an hour."

"Best hour of our lives." He raised his glass to his

mouth but didn't drink it until he said, "Imagine if you'd worked for us for six... or nine."

Ryker's hand tightened on my thigh. "I'll talk to Sue and get you a position in another department."

"Oh, come on, man. We haven't found anyone yet, and it would be perfect." Luca leaned forward so he could see Ryker. "Or is your willpower to remain professional that weak?"

Ryker tensed, and I put my hand over his. He was so on edge all the time when it came to work, it was concerning.

"In my experience working with someone you're romantically involved with is tough. And with three?" I realized what I'd just said a little too late and inwardly cringed.

I didn't want them to know just how complicated the whole situation with my ex had been. It's one thing for a relationship to fall apart, but another thing entirely when work is involved.

Libby looked between the four of us. "Well, I think it would be good, that way you have more time with each other. It's romantic, really."

Ethan was staring at Ryker. "It would be good to have someone there to remind you it's five o'clock and time to go the fuck home."

"Or to convince you to take time off because you're hacking up a hairball," Luca muttered.

Ryker flipped his hand over, lacing our fingers together. It was unexpected and heat crept up my neck to my face. Everyone seemed to be watching his every move.

"Does anyone care what I think?" Garrett had been quiet and now had his arms crossed over his chest.

An awkward tension passed between my three men, and I remembered what Garrett told me about their professional and personal relationships being strained. I'd never noticed it before, but now that I thought about it, I could see what he meant.

I squeezed Ryker's hand because he was just staring at Garrett.

"Of course we care what you think." Luca reached forward and grabbed a cracker, a piece of cheese, and a slice of salami.

"Go ahead," Ryker said, his tone indifferent but also having a bit of a quiver to it.

"If that night had never happened, we'd hire her in a heartbeat. I looked at her resume and the notes Sue took during the interview. She's more than capable of handling the workload... and us." He finally broke his stare down with Ryker to look at me. "You can work for me and Luca."

Harper stood, drink in hand. "Well, I think that's our cue to go get our rooms all situated. I want to go in the pool too."

"That's a great idea." Libby stood and looked down at Ethan, tilting her head as she stared at him.

"Fine. I guess I'll go too to keep you girls out of trouble." Ethan winked at me as he followed the girls downstairs.

Luca sighed. "This is why there's a no-work policy on this yacht."

Ryker was the quiet one now and I looked over at him to find red creeping up his neck to his jaw.

"For fuck's sake." I stood, ignoring Luca's protest, and went to the part of the sectional where they weren't. "Why would I want to work in an environment where the three of you are one wrong comment away from biting each other's heads off?"

"What did you mean 'from your experience' regarding workplace relationships?" Ryker leaned forward, his hands clasped between his knees.

Ah, shit. I should have known he'd want to circle back to that. "I've seen a friend struggle with the aftermath of a breakup." I could consider myself my own friend, couldn't I?

Ryker didn't seem convinced but let it go, turning his attention back to Garrett. "You can't just make position description decision changes and not include me."

"You can't decide to fire someone because you're scared," Garrett scoffed.

"You wanted her gone too!" Ryker raised his voice and I grimaced.

Luca looked between his two best friends, a helpless expression on his face.

Was this how it always was between the three of them? Surely if it was, they wouldn't still be friends or work together.

Luca leaned toward me like he was going to tell me a secret. "For the record, I didn't want to fire you."

Garrett finished taking a long gulp of his drink. "Why

would I care if she worked for us when I don't even want to work for us?"

"What are you talking about?" Luca's moment of playfulness was gone.

"I'm not happy." Garrett slouched in the sectional, resting his head on the back of it. "I haven't been for a while."

"I don't think any of you have," I said quietly, but loud enough for all three to hear. "Is the money even worth it if none of you are happy?"

Luca looked like he wanted to say something but didn't. I was grateful because anything he said regarding money would piss Ryker off.

"Aren't you exhausted? Of always adding more to your plate? To ours?" Garrett didn't have to look at Ryker for us to know that's who he was speaking to.

Ryker ran his hands over his hair before covering his face with them. "I'm sorry."

"He asked if you were exhausted, not to apologize." Luca surprised me by scooting closer to Ryker and putting his hand on his shoulder. "You never stop, Ry."

Ryker shrugged off Luca's hand and stood, avoiding looking at any of us. "I can't."

He turned his back on us and walked away, leaving me wondering how I was going to fix this and if I even could.

Chapter 20

Monday Morning Blues

Ryker

Monday mornings usually were my favorite time of the week. Nothing felt as good as getting back to the grind and feeling the satisfaction of securing another client.

But as I stood in the empty elevator whizzing me to the seventieth floor, there was a sense of dread in the pit of my stomach. It was the same feeling I had so many times before when too much changed all at once.

With change came too much uncertainty. Too many variables. Too many what-ifs.

The future was filled with endless possibilities, but the fear of not knowing what those possibilities might be left me feeling unsteady. Every day held new surprises and decisions that could be life-altering. I had to be prepared for the worst outcome because there was always a chance for the worst.

"Aren't you exhausted?" Exhausted was too weak of a word for what I felt. It wasn't a physical exhaustion; on that front, I was fine. It was mental depletion that had my emotions feeling frazzled.

The doors slid open, and I stepped into the dimly lit reception area. More often than not, I was the first one to arrive and the last to leave. Even in college, there was an urgent need to be the best, and to be the best, I had to work the hardest. That was how it had always been and how it would always be.

I walked toward my office, trying to shake off all the feelings from the weekend. Garrett might as well have punched me in the gut on Saturday. *"I'm not happy. I haven't been for a while."*

How had I let it get this bad? Everything we'd built together was uncertain now; our business, our friendship, Paige.

Paige wasn't going to stick around if I couldn't get my shit together. She had two other men who wouldn't put her on an emotional rollercoaster.

I sat down and pulled my laptop out of my bag, my mind racing trying to come up with a plan to fix things. But I didn't know where to start. For the first time in a long time, I didn't know how to keep pushing forward.

I took a deep breath and leaned back in my chair, closing my eyes. There was no use stressing out now. I needed to focus on work. That was what I did best, after all. If Garrett wanted to leave, he was going to leave. All I could control was myself and what I did. That just meant to protect what we'd built I needed to work harder than I ever had before to pick up the slack.

I opened my eyes and stared at the ceiling for a moment, making a list of everything I needed to do. There was a lot I'd put to the side while I was sick, and Sunday had been a clusterfuck, so I'd gotten nothing done.

My phone buzzed, and I pulled it out of my suit jacket's pocket. I sucked in a sharp breath at Paige's name in my notifications. She'd messaged me a few times over the weekend, concerned about me. I'd told her I wasn't feeling well and not to worry.

It didn't change the fact that I'd ruined their weekend by leaving the yacht. I didn't deserve to have Paige concerned about me.

Paige: *Good morning! I'm stopping for drinks on my way in. Do you want your usual green tea? Did you eat breakfast?*

Me: *Good morning. I got it. Thanks.*

Paige: *Okie dokie artichokie! See you soon.*

I threw my phone on my desk and pinched the bridge of my nose. She was the only bright spot in my life, and I'd just lied to her. It didn't matter that it was a stupidly small lie. But it wasn't just a small lie, was it? Pretending everything was fine was a big lie.

I stood from my desk and walked to the wall of windows, staring out into the gray, overcast sky. My mood was just like the weather. Ignoring things wasn't an option anymore, not if I wanted something to grow between me and Paige, and especially not if I wanted to mend the rift between me and my best friends.

But I didn't even know where to start.

I turned back to my desk, needing to distract myself with something else. If I let them, my insecurities and issues would plague me the entire day.

Putting on my glasses, I opened my laptop and got to work.

No one bothered me as the office slowly came to life outside my closed door. That was probably for the best since I wasn't the best company when I was in a bad headspace.

Eventually, my cone of solitude was broken, and Sue knocked on my door before poking her head in. "Do you have a minute?"

"I always have a minute for you." After our last interaction, I'd make time for her. I'd been a complete asshole and she'd been right; Paige had been good for me, just not in the way she meant.

"How are you feeling?" She shut the door behind her and sat down across from me.

"Good. I was lucky it just seemed to be a mild bug. I was feeling much better on Saturday." Better enough to go on the yacht.

"I'm glad..." She gave me a knowing look and I didn't have to ask to know that she knew Paige had taken care of me. "Javier let me know that Paige would be starting work again today as Garrett's and Luca's assistant."

Hearing it from her made it that much more real. I nodded, not trusting myself to keep the emotion out of my voice. It wasn't that I didn't think Paige was a good fit. Things would just get complicated fast with her working for us. It was already going to be hard enough with all three of us in a relationship with her—if that was even still on the table for me.

Sue leaned forward, placing a hand on the edge of my desk like it was my arm. "I've been worried about you for a while, and now only Luca and Garrett are going to have an assistant?"

I sighed, taking off my glasses and rubbing my temples. It still felt odd to talk about this with Sue. I'd been so closed off about personal matters, especially when it came to my love life.

"Seems so."

Sue's brows furrowed. "Do you want me to find you your own assistant?" With her doing the hiring, she could easily find me my own assistant.

On one hand, it would be nice to have someone who just worked for me, but on the other, there would always be a certain level of coordination and communication that had to happen with the other assistant.

We'd tried having three separate assistants before and it had been more of a headache than it was worth.

"You don't need to do that."

"You're going to do everything yourself? Set your own

schedule? Keep notes? Respond to all your emails?" She shook her head in disbelief. "You already work enough as it is."

"I'm sure it will be fine. I like to stay busy." I looked back at my computer screen not believing my own words.

When I was busy, I didn't have the time to worry.

With a heavy sigh, she stood and walked to the door, stopping with her hand on the doorknob. "You only get one life, Ryker, and you've been blessed with what you have. It's time to enjoy it a little."

She left without another word. I knew deep down that she was right—that Garrett and Luca were right—but every time I thought about slowing down, worry crept in.

Working all the time wasn't living. Knowing it was one thing, but being able to move forward in my life wasn't so simple.

My computer dinged, a meeting reminder popping up. I shut my laptop and grabbed the file for the client I was meeting with before venturing out of my office for the first time since I arrived.

I glanced down the hall where Paige's office was, but it was empty. Having a few minutes before I needed to be in the conference room, I went to her door and poked my head in.

She hadn't made it her own yet, but there was a vase on her desk with an assorted array of pink flowers. I looked behind me before I walked to her desk, picking up the small card lying next to them. *Have a great first day. Luca and Garret.*

"Ryker?" Paige's voice made me jump and drop the note and the file I was holding. "What are you doing?"

I spun around to find Paige standing in the doorway, a puzzled look on her face.

Wearing. *The*. Dress.

Why the hell would she pick the dress she wore the night we'd met?

My cheeks flushed as I bent down to pick up the card and file I had dropped. "I was just ... um... looking for something."

Her eyes narrowed as if she didn't believe me, and took the card from me, her lips tipping up into a smile. A twinge of jealousy crept in; I wanted to be the one to make her smile like that.

She set the card back down on the desk almost reverently and looked around the office. "It's still kind of bare in here."

I nodded in agreement. "It will be nice once you get settled in."

The smile she gave me didn't make her face light up like a genuine one did. She turned away from me, running a finger along a bookcase. "It's hard starting over again, you know? It makes me feel off balance."

It was easy to forget that she'd very recently left her life behind to start a fresh one here. There was still so much I had to learn about her.

I felt a sudden urge to protect her, but from what I wasn't sure. Me?

Before speaking again, I cleared my throat. "I want to apologize for my behavior this weekend."

She turned toward me, stepping closer and putting a hand on my chest. "There's no need to apologize to me."

I put my hand over hers. "But it affected you. You got put in the middle of it."

"I understand where you're coming from, though. I think maybe Garrett and Luca need you to spell things out for them because they didn't grow up in your shoes and just don't understand how those things change a person."

She was right. Luca and Garrett knew I grew up poor, but I hadn't painted a picture for them because it was hard to. The only two people who knew the extent of things were me and Libby.

Removing her hand from my chest, she stepped back, tucking her hair behind her ear. "Why don't you explain it to them? I think that's what's upsetting both of them. Luca might not show it like Garrett does, but he was just as invested in that conversation."

Being open and honest despite the pain it would cause me was the best thing to do if I wanted to make things right again.

I reached out and gently touched her arm. Her eyes met mine and there was so much understanding and compassion in them she might as well take my heart now.

She closed the distance between us, wrapping her arms around my waist. I swallowed the lump of emotion in my throat and hugged her back, desperately needing the comfort she was offering.

"I know it's not easy to open up, Ry, but you have to let people see you," she said softly.

Burying my face in her hair, I nodded and breathed in

her sweet scent. She squeezed me tighter before pulling away just enough so that we could look at each other again.

"I'm so scared of ending up back in that place, even though logically I know I won't. It's embarrassing how much I've let this consume me and impact my relationships. And the pressure..." My words started to shake the tiniest amount.

She took my hand in hers, and I had to rapidly blink to keep the moisture away.

"You have nothing to be embarrassed or ashamed of." She squeezed my hand reassuringly. "Your past doesn't define who you are, your heart does."

Fuck.

A traitorous hot tear slipped free, but she didn't reach up to wipe it away. Instead, she leaned in and pressed her lips against mine.

Someone cleared their throat, and we broke apart. Garrett stood frowning in the doorway, his arms folded across his chest. "Your ten o'clock is waiting on you."

I wiped the few stray tears from my face and gave Paige another quick kiss. "Thank you."

Garrett's arms fell to his side as he stepped out of my way. "Do you want me to do the meeting?" He reached for my folder, and I tucked it under my arm.

"I'm fine." I smiled, but my cheeks quivered from the strain of fighting a frown. Now wasn't the time to get into it anyway.

"If you say so." He shook his head and walked into Paige's office.

Now wasn't the time to fix my problems, so I squared my shoulders and walked to the conference room. Right then, our client was more important. But for some reason, for maybe the first time ever, I knew that wasn't true.

Chapter 21

Field Trip

Garrett

"You won't believe what Ryker just did." Ethan was out of breath despite the reception area only being twenty feet from my office. He stood there for a moment like a runner at the end of a race, chest heaving.

"What the fuck did you do, sprint?" Luca paused the marketing video we were reviewing before we had to send it to a client. "He didn't try to fire Paige again, did he?"

"Why would he do that? The man had the goofiest grin on his face after lunch when he found that cookie she left on his desk." Ethan looked like he was about to swoon. "If only Paige were my type."

"I'm glad because you'd be giving us a run for our money." I sat back in my chair, trying to recall if Ethan had ever gone on an actual date in the time we'd known him, which was quite a few years. "When was the last time you went on a date?"

"The inventory lately is not up to my standards." Ethan examined his nails. "Plus, men are assholes."

Luca snorted. "You're a man."

"Exactly." He stood up straight again, suddenly energized. "Back to why I came in here; Ryker left work early."

I looked at the clock on my computer. "But it's barely four."

"I know! I asked him where he was headed since nothing was on his calendar, and he said he was done for the day." Ethan smoothed out his tie. "Does him leaving mean I can head out?"

Luca laughed. "Nice try. Can you make sure Paige isn't pulling her hair out over our to-do lists?"

He smirked. "I've checked on her a few times this afternoon. She is rocking it. I'm not sure about the last item on yours, though, Luca."

I groaned. "Luca. What did you put?"

"That's between me and Paige... and I guess Ethan now too." Luca smirked.

Ethan cringed and shook his head with a laugh, heading for the door. "Some things I do not need to see and hear," he said before shutting the door behind him.

"Maybe if he wasn't so nosy he wouldn't see and hear things he doesn't want to." Luca looked up from his computer screen. "What's that look for?"

I steepled my fingers in front of my lips, tapping them there for a moment. "What did you put on your list for her?"

"Answer emails, lunch reservations with a client next week-"

"The last thing."

Luca grinned and leaned back in his chair, kicking his feet up on the table. "We both know it wasn't a business task." He paused for a moment, letting the suspense build to my annoyance. "Take her panties off, sit on my desk, and wait for me."

I fought the urge to throw something at Luca's smug face. "This is a business, Luca. You're her boss."

He shrugged, unbothered by my reprimand. "You're telling me that when she walked in this morning in that fucking dress you didn't get hard and want to bend her over something right then and-"

"Don't." I picked up a stray paperclip and started flipping it between my fingers.

"Why? Is it making you hard thinking about her spread out on my desk, me feasting on that delicious pussy? I'd let you join, you know." There was an unmistakable glint of desire in his eyes.

I shook my head, trying to clear it of the mental images that were flashing through my head. The truth was, it was all I could think about since she'd agreed to work for us. "I don't think she would do it."

"Do what? Have some fun at work or let us at the same time? Is that even something you're open to?" Luca seemed to forget all about getting our work done so we could leave for the day.

Although we'd watched each other a few times before, we ultimately decided we liked watching Ryker better.

We'd never broached the subject of threesomes or more. We all had a bit of possessiveness to us and the thought of a woman dividing her attentions wasn't appealing.

But with Paige? Part of my pleasure was her pleasure.

I flicked the paper clip I'd been twirling at him, hitting him in the chest. "I'm open to it."

Luca opened his mouth to say something, but both of our phones pinged at the same time.

I opened the message from Ryker, reading it out loud since he'd sent it in a new group text, which included Paige. "Sending you directions. Meet me there in an hour. There's something I want you to see."

"That doesn't sound sketchy at all." Luca opened the message. "Not the best part of Queens."

"Why would he want us to go there?" I clicked the link to the map, but I didn't go to Queens very often, so I had no idea where the location was.

There was a soft knock at the door before Paige came in with a slightly worried expression on her face, her phone clutched in her hand. "Did you see Ryker's message?"

Luca closed out of the video and shut his laptop. "We did. Not sure if you should go, though. It's not the best area."

She rolled her eyes. "So? It won't be dark, and I'll be with you guys. We should get going. The map says it's forty minutes away."

~

We joined Ryker, where he was standing on the sidewalk, looking at a vacant lot filled with trash and weeds. Paige put her arms around his waist, and he lifted his arm to tuck her into his side. None of us spoke while we waited for Ryker to tell us what the hell we were doing out there.

He looked first at me, then at Luca, before returning his eyes to the field. "I told you guys that I didn't have much growing up, and that things were... rough. But I didn't tell you exactly how rough. I only lived in Connecticut from the time I was thirteen... we were in foster care until they adopted me and Libby a few years later and moved out of the city. Before they took us in, we lived here." He gestured to the empty plot of land between two abandoned buildings. "There used to be a building here. This was the last place of many that we lived before my mom died."

Luca spoke first, his voice gravelly with emotion. "That must have been tough for you and Libby."

"It was and it wasn't." A muscle ticked in Ryker's jaw before he put his cheek against Paige's hair. "When my dad left after Libby was born, she stopped being our mom. Diane and Hugh are our parents; have been since the moment we were placed with them."

I shoved my hands in my pockets, not knowing what to say or do. Luca and I had no clue it had been like this, and since we only knew Diane and Hugh, we never dove deeper.

"This is why I'm the way I am. It's not just wanting to never come back to this kind of life, but it's wanting to take care of the people who took care of me and Libby." His voice cracked and he cleared his throat. "I want to be better... a better friend. A better boyfriend. A better business owner."

"You have to start with being better to yourself." I put my hand on his shoulder and squeezed. "Thank you for sharing this with us. It means a lot."

He gave a single nod, his Adam's apple bobbing as he swallowed hard.

Paige looked around, her eyes glossy. "What do you think they're going to do with this lot? It looks like they're building new apartment buildings on the street we drove down before this one."

"A lot of the buildings around here have been condemned, so they're tearing them down and building low-income and transitional housing. Something they should have done a long time ago." Ryker kicked at a rock on the ground, getting his shiny shoes dusty. "As for this lot and the two buildings on either side... I haven't decided what I'm doing with them yet."

"Wait. What?" Luca moved in front of us and then looked behind him.

"A while back, when we first really started earning money, I found the owner, made him an offer, and he accepted. First thing I did to it was tear down the building I lived in." Ryker's frown suddenly turned into a grin. "The crew even let Libby do a bit of it."

It was good to see him smiling when he'd just ripped open his chest and showed us what was inside. "Why not knock down the other buildings too?"

"I didn't want to go overboard since I didn't know what

I was going to do." Ryker let go of Paige and walked out into the middle of the field, between the two buildings.

On the outside, the three-story brick buildings looked solid despite the boarded-up windows and the graffiti everywhere. The ground floors both had almost the entire fronts covered with plywood, indicating that they used to be businesses.

"Let's give him a minute." As much as I wanted to go out there and hug him, he seemed to be having a moment.

I took Paige's hand while Luca took the other, and we walked to the SUV idling across the street. Ryker's ride was nowhere in sight.

We sat in silence, watching a man who'd been through so much turn in a few circles before putting his hands on his hips. I'd seen him take that stance several times before when he'd had an idea buzzing around in his head.

Paige turned around to look at me and Luca in the back row. "You're too quiet."

"It's a lot to take in," Luca said, ignoring his phone that had been buzzing off and on since we'd gotten in the car. "So many things make sense now."

"I just wish he would have felt comfortable enough sharing this with us, you know? We could have helped him work through it. It's a big secret to keep." I couldn't help but think of all the conversations we'd ever had about money and how ridiculous I'd thought his fears were. Now they didn't seem so ridiculous.

"I know I haven't known you all that long, but Ryker doesn't strike me as the type that likes to depend on other people." She rested her chin on her stacked fists. "But maybe that will change."

"Makes me grateful for everything I have." Luca pulled out his phone. "On second thought, I take that back."

"What is it?" I glanced over as he furiously texted something back to his mom.

"Some charity gala at the end of October. My mom wants to make sure I have enough notice so I clear my schedule. The Accardos will be there." Luca tossed his phone on his seat and scrubbed his hands over his face. "You guys want to go?"

"It's been on my calendar for months. You don't remember we got tickets ages ago? I'm always down for some family drama." I tried to hide my smile, but I loved to see Luca squirm.

Paige's lips twisted like she was thinking about it. "What day?"

"Saturday the twenty-eighth. It's formal, so we'll have to find you a gown." Luca rubbed his hands together, excitement in his eyes. "Time for a shopping trip."

Paige had zoned out, her eyes focusing on the empty seat between me and Luca.

"Paige?" I waved my hand in front of her face, and she jumped back. "You okay?"

"Yeah, sorry. It's been a long day. Everything is moving really fast." She smiled at Luca, but it was forced. "I'd love to go to the gala, but I can't afford a fancy dress and all that."

"Don't worry about that." Luca picked up his phone,

his mood much better than when he'd checked it. "I'm inviting you, so all the expenses are on me."

Paige opened her mouth to protest, but the back door opened, and Ryker slid in next to her, a determined look on his face.

"I know what I'm going to do." He turned in his seat so he could talk to the three of us. "I'm going to tear it down and build a place where kids can come to feel safe. There can be an after-school program with tutoring and a sports program. Dance. Art. Whatever. We could partner with professional sports teams even." He looked at me, his eyes lit up in excitement.

"I'm sure Dom would help us connect to the right people to make that happen." My brother might have his head stuck up his ass half the time, but he'd at least give me some contacts.

"And Libby can run the whole thing... well, maybe with a lot of help at first until she grows into that kind of role." His smile faltered but then was right back in place again. "Or she doesn't have to run it. She can do whatever she wants."

"And what about you?" Paige touched his cheek tenderly. "You already work so much."

Well, that took the wind right out from his sail. I was glad she was the one who brought it up and not me or Luca.

"We can hire a team with a project manager to do all the heavy lifting and be more selective about the clients we take on," Luca suggested.

Ryker suddenly seemed unsure. "I'm getting ahead of

myself. It just came to me and it's like all the negative feelings associated with this place disappeared."

"I think there's a lot we'll need to discuss and figure out. Fundraising is going to be a major component." I buckled my seatbelt. "But I'm in if you want help."

"Me too." Paige leaned forward and kissed his cheek before turning forward.

"So am I, whether you want my help or not." He smirked and rolled down the privacy screen between us and the driver just enough to tell him where to go. "We're going to head to Garrett's place."

"Why my place?"

Luca shrugged. "Just feels like the place to go. You also have a grill and will hopefully feed us."

As the SUV pulled away from the curb, my shoulders relaxed and I sat back in my seat, watching Ryker and Paige talk quietly in front of us.

I wasn't sure if he would have ever shared this with us if it hadn't been for her. We still had a long way to go to fix what we'd slowly let crumble, but for the first time in a long time, I felt a flicker of hope that things would get better.

Chapter 22

Bon Appétit

Paige

"That is just... so wrong, but so sexy. Why is that turning me on? Is there something wrong with me?" I pressed my thighs together as I sat at Garrett's island and watched him touch a chicken breast very inappropriately.

"Food can be very sensual." He smirked and gave the chicken a smack. It reminded me of the way Luca had smacked my pussy, and my core clenched.

I'd never be able to look at chicken the same way again.

Luca wrapped his arms around me from behind, making me jump. He'd disappeared into a corner of Garrett's house somewhere with Ryker, and I hadn't even heard him come back into the room.

"Jesus. Give a girl a heart attack." I shivered as he trailed his nose along my neck.

"Maybe Gare can smack your pretty little cunt just like

that later." His breath against my ear made my nipples tingle, and a shiver worked its way down my spine. "While I'm taking you from behind."

I needed to put a stop to this before I ended up on the counter again. "So... what were you and Ryker talking about?"

Luca buried his face against my neck, and I could feel his smile against my skin. "Stress relief."

"Why don't you come over here and cut all these potatoes in half." Garrett set the chicken to the side and went to the sink to wash his hands.

"Oh! I can do that!" I tried to get up, but Luca moved his hands to my shoulders. "Come on, I burned soup once."

"And there's still the faint smell of burned tomato in my apartment." Ryker sat down next to me, his leg pressing against mine. "When's dinner?"

Garrett gave him a fleeting glance before very aggressively slamming a head of lettuce on the counter. "Nothing is stopping you from helping." He took the core out of the lettuce and tossed it at Ryker, who nearly knocked me off my stool avoiding it.

"Children, not in front of our guest." Luca had the colander of baby gold potatoes Garrett had washed next to him and started cutting them in half.

It was fun to see the three of them interact when they were in such a relaxed atmosphere. As soon as we'd entered Garrett's house, it was like there was a shift in their demeanors.

Shoes and socks were removed, jackets and ties thrown over a chair in the living room, and shirt sleeves rolled up.

It was like all of the tension from the day was gone and what was left was *them*.

Garrett's movements in the kitchen were unlike anything I'd seen before. He looked at complete ease but also had a sensuality to his movements. I didn't know if he was just doing it for my benefit or what, but it was turning me to goo inside.

"Paige?" Ryker touched my arm, and I looked over at him. His face looked more relaxed than I'd ever seen it, the wrinkles that usually lined his forehead nowhere to be seen. I'd never really noticed them before until they were gone.

"Hm?" I looked at his lips, wanting to kiss him and feel the prickle of his stubble against my skin. But who was I kidding? I also wanted to feel it between my legs.

They'd woken up a sexual beast inside me, and it felt like my mind was constantly being inundated with images and thoughts of them.

"I asked if you wanted more wine." His tongue darted out and his lips stayed parted the tiniest bit as if he was opening the door for my tongue.

"I think she wants something." Luca chuckled, putting his knife down.

"Yes, please." My voice came out barely above a whisper and it took all my strength not to lean forward and kiss him.

"I'll get her another glass." Garrett leaned over the counter and grabbed my empty glass. He had a wine cellar that was bigger than my apartment in his basement with everything a wine connoisseur could ever want.

Ryker rested a hand on my exposed knee, sending sparks through me. "So how is this going to work between the four of us?"

The question hung in the air for a moment before any of us spoke. I had thought about it a lot, and it was something that scared me but also excited me. I'd only ever read poly relationships in books, and most of the time they were paranormal romances with magic or a prophecy involved.

"We take our time and go with the flow." Garrett drizzled olive oil on the potatoes Luca had put in a grill pan. "It's been working so far. Not that it's been that long."

Luca jumped up on the counter, grabbing his wine glass and swirling it. "I think we should make sure we're all comfortable and take it one step at a time."

Ryker squeezed my knee reassuringly as he looked at each of us, his eyes lingering on mine for a moment longer than necessary. "And the sex?"

Garrett paused, a pair of tongs in hand, and looked at me, his stare heated. "Whatever Paige is comfortable with... whether it be one of us at a time, two of us, or if she's brave, all three."

Was it getting hot in here? And why did I suddenly want to take my clothes off?

Luca sipped his wine, a thoughtful expression on his face. "We all need to feel comfortable and respected and make sure that everyone's needs are being met. If someone isn't feeling safe, they need to speak up. But more importantly, we need to be okay if our dicks touch or a hand slips where it doesn't belong."

The four of us looked at each other for a moment

before breaking out into laughter. I'd let them worry about that aspect of all being together.

This was both exhilarating and terrifying, but it was definitely something I wanted.

The daylight was quickly fading as Garrett switched on strand lights on his patio as he and Luca took the food to put on the pellet grill. The weather had shifted since the warmth over the past week, and the air had a bit of a bite to it on my exposed arms and legs.

"Let's go sit in the living room." Ryker stood and put his hand on my lower back as I did the same.

Garrett's house was nothing like Ryker's thirty-eighth-floor condo. While Ryker's place was comfortable enough, it didn't feel lived in like Garrett's house did.

The living room was painted a muted green with dark hardwood floors. A large navy sectional was in the center of the room and there was a reclaimed wooden coffee table in front of it. The entertainment center was white and spanned almost the entire length of the room with shelving and the large television front and center.

My toes sank into the plush rug as I walked to the couch, ready to curl up and enjoy the evening with my boyfriends. My God. I had three boyfriends.

Before I managed to sit down, Ryker took my wine glass from me, setting it on the coffee table along with his. His arm wrapped around me, and then we were falling onto the couch, our lips colliding as soon as the risk of knocking out each other's teeth was gone.

One of Ryker's hands ran through my hair as he deepened the kiss, his tongue exploring my mouth. His other hand ran up my thigh and there was no question about where it was headed.

I untucked his shirt, needing to feel his skin under my fingertips. He groaned at the first brush of my fingers across his stomach.

Ryker pulled away, our eyes meeting in a silent conversation. At least, that was how it felt. We both knew Garrett and Luca were right outside and would be back in to find us.

I rolled my hips against his, digging my nails into his abs, spurring him on. With a sound that sounded an awful lot like a growl, he kissed and nipped down my jaw to my neck, his fingers skimming the apex of my thighs.

"Fucking soaked already, aren't you?" He sucked my skin, no doubt leaving his mark on me. His fingers teased me, barely brushing over where my clit lay waiting for him to find it. "Do you know how many times today I wanted to bend you over something and fuck you?"

"How many?" I whimpered as he pushed my panties to the side and slid his finger up and down my slit in teasing strokes.

"So many times that I've been aching all day." He pushed a finger inside me, and I arched into him, gasping. "And now? Thinking about what's going to happen when Gare and Luca come back in? Fuck, Paige."

Hearing the pure need and desire in his voice made me clench around his finger. I wanted them any way they wanted to have me. The connection I felt with all three of them burned hotter and brighter with each passing second.

I fumbled with his belt, my hands shaking as he pulled

Maya Nicole

his finger out and circled my clit with it. And then he pushed two in.

I cried out as he crooked his fingers, hitting the spot that made everything burn with the need for release. He chuckled against my breast, where he'd pushed down my dress and bra on one side. He sucked my nipple into his mouth, much like how I wanted him to suck on my clit.

My hands finally cooperated enough to get his belt unbuckled and his pants undone. His cock was hard beneath my palm as I stroked him through his boxer briefs.

"I really don't want to clean up jizz from my couch." Garrett's voice shocked us both and we scrambled apart like two teenagers caught in a compromising position.

"Too bad. Buy a new one." Ryker stood, pushing his pants and boxers off before unbuttoning his shirt.

I watched him, squeezing my thighs together. Luca stepped in between me and Ryker, holding out his hand. Not exactly sure what was happening in my lust-filled daze, I took it, and he pulled me to my feet.

He hooked his arm around me and lowered his mouth to my exposed nipple, biting it harder than expected. I yelped, grabbing onto two handfuls of his hair.

As if they were speaking to each other through some kind of telepathic connection, Luca turned us so I was against Ryker. His erection pushed against me as he moved my hair over one shoulder and kissed my neck.

"Take off her dress." Garrett had moved the wine glasses from the coffee table to a shelf on the entertainment center and pushed the coffee table out of the way.

Luca released my nipple with a pop and lifted my

240

dress over my head, throwing it to the side. "God damn, your body." He grabbed hold of my hips and squeezed. Before them, I might have blushed or even thought there was somehow a joke being made, but feeling their heated stares took all my insecurities away. They didn't care my stomach wasn't flat, that my skin was a bit bumpy in places from stretch marks and life.

Ryker unclasped my bra, and it slid down my arms. I trembled, wondering what they would do next. With all three of them involved, anything was possible. They were all dominant lovers, and I just hoped their personalities didn't clash and make things awkward.

Ryker cupped my breasts from behind, his thumbs brushing over the sensitive points of my nipples. "Tell us if you want us to stop."

"Never." I leaned back against him as Luca slid down my panties.

"Get undressed, Luca." Garrett was apparently the director of this little soiree and came to stand at my side, guiding my mouth to his.

This was happening. I was going to have my very first orgy. I giggled against Garrett's lips, causing him to pull away with a confused expression.

"Orgy is such a funny word. Don't you think?" I covered my mouth, trying to stifle my laugh.

Garrett grabbed a handful of my hair, using it to turn my head to look at Luca, who was sitting naked on the couch, his fist wrapped around the base of his cock. "Get on your knees and we'll see how funny you think it is."

My last giggle died on a gasp as Ryker pulled me down

to the floor with him. I was suddenly nervous. Nervous I was going to somehow mess up and bite someone's dick if a thrust hit at the wrong moment. "Our food is going to burn."

Garrett used my hair to make me look up at him. He looked like he didn't care if dinner burned, and he was about to devour me instead. "It won't. And even if it does, you're about to eat your dinner right now. Show Luca how good you are with your mouth."

Ryker walked me forward just enough, nudged my legs apart, and with his hand on the back of my neck, pushed me forward just as Garrett let go of the hold he had on my hair.

I ran my hands up Luca's tattooed thighs, trying not to giggle again because on one was an angel and on the other a demon-looking devil creature.

"You're killing me here, Paige." Luca stroked himself, his thumb running over his piercing.

"What if I chip a tooth?" I swirled my tongue around the tip before flicking his ring.

"Then I'll buy you a new tooth." Luca buried one of his hands in my hair, not to control my movements, but to urge me to take him in my mouth. "Don't be nervous. We've got this."

There was no question about that, but I couldn't help but be a little bit. When I'd come home with the three of them, I hadn't imagined this would be what was in store for me.

I wrapped my lips around him, humming lightly as I sucked.

"Oh, fuck." Luca's thumb rubbed against my brow bone. "Your mouth feels amazing, baby."

I glanced over at Garrett, who was getting undressed like his clothes were made of something precious. It was so slow and methodical that it made me remember what he'd said back on the yacht. *"You'll know when I fuck you."*

My heart raced in my chest, wondering what he meant by that because I *had* thought he'd fucked me.

Ryker, who I'd almost forgotten was behind me, cupped me between my legs possessively. "Do you want my cock too, Paige? Right here?"

I mumbled my answer around Luca's length, which made him groan a string of curse words. I'd never given a blow job to someone with a piercing, but I imagined he was more sensitive, especially with vibrations.

"Take her." Garrett was undressed now and knelt next to me but didn't touch me.

Did they both know he would be like this? I would have guessed Ryker would be the more dominant one when all three were involved, but it seemed he only was when they were watching. Neither seemed that surprised Garrett was bossing them around, but then again, they were best friends.

Ryker pressed the head of his cock against my entrance and slowly eased in. I was ready for him, my pussy giving no protests to his intrusion.

How was I going to suck off Luca and handle being fucked at the same time?

"Every time you stop, Ryker will stop. Do you understand?" Garrett's hand reached under me and pinched a nipple. "You should see how sexy you look taking both of them like this. So perfect."

His praise only spurred me on more, and I took Luca all the way to the back of my throat as Ryker began moving inside me. Luca's piercing tickled my throat, and I slid back a little, hollowing my cheeks as I sucked.

"I'm not going to last long." Luca's eyes were heavy-lidded as he watched the scene playing out before him. He had the best seat in the house.

Garrett kissed my shoulder and then put his mouth next to my ear. "How many fingers can you take?"

My brows furrowed in confusion, and he let go of my nipple and moved his hand down between my legs. I clenched so hard around Ryker that he groaned, grinding against me, trying to get more of his cock in.

Garrett pinched my clit. "How many fingers, Paige?"

"One," I muttered around Luca's cock.

"Good girl." He lay down and then his finger was there, sliding right in alongside Ryker.

"Garrett." Ryker stilled behind me, his fingers digging into my hips. "What are you doing?"

"Getting her ready for us." He worked his finger in and out; each time, it brushed along my G-spot. "She's so wet and ready. I think she can take two."

I cried out around Luca's length, my fingers grasping at the couch cushion. It was too much yet not enough all at the same time.

"This might be too much." I sucked hard, stopping Luca from raining on my orgasm parade.

"It's going to feel good, Ry. For all of us. Now start

fucking her again or I'll kick your ass." Garrett's soft words toward Ryker was in such stark contrast to how he'd been talking to me, I couldn't help but giggle.

At least until Garrett lifted his head and upper body off the floor, his abs straining, and sucked my clit into his mouth.

That, in combination with his fingers moving against my G-spot and Ryker starting to move inside me again, sent me over the edge. I released Luca's cock, opting to wrap my hand around it, while I buried my face against his balls and let out a guttural scream.

Luca's hand covered mine, guiding me up and down his shaft to match Ryker's thrusts. "I'm going to come, so unless you want it in your hair..."

I put my lips back over the head, my tongue flicking his ring and my eyes stinging with tears as I sucked him hard.

"Paige! Oh, fuck! That's it, baby, just like thaaat!" He exploded in my mouth, the salty tang of his cum hitting the back of my throat as I swallowed.

I was pretty sure Garrett was up to four fingers, but it was hard to tell with how wet I was. All I knew was I wanted both of them inside me. I really wanted all three, but I'd need to Google that to see if it would ruin my vagina.

Ryker slowed to a languid thrust that felt so good yet so not what I wanted. I carefully removed my mouth from Luca and looked back over my shoulder. "Why'd you turn into Mr. Sloth?"

He smacked my ass and every single pussy muscle I had clenched. "Say it again."

"Yes, say it again," Garrett muttered, and then his tongue slid in alongside his fingers.

"Holy fuck." I was pretty sure my eyes were just as wide as Ryker's. "Keep moving, Mr. Sloth."

He hesitated just a moment before his hand slapped my other ass cheek. "You like that, don't you? I heard you like that pretty pink pussy smacked too."

"Yes," I whimpered, my legs shaking like they were about to give out. "Please, fuck me, Garrett. I can't take this anymore."

Garrett pulled away, leaving me feeling like something was missing, even though Ryker's cock was right there inside me. He got to his knees and offered his fingers to Luca. "Taste her."

If anything could make me come just from seeing it, it would be Luca sucking Garrett's fingers, his eyes locked on me.

"Are you okay with this, Paige?" Ryker was still thrusting leisurely, grinding when he was fully seated inside me before pulling almost all the way out. Over and over he repeated it, driving me nuts.

"Yes. What's taking so long? Get your cock in me, *Gary*." I wasn't sure of the logistics of what we were about to do but found I didn't really care when Garrett turned his head and gave me the most depraved look known to man. "You said I'd know when you were fucking me, but I have yet to be impressed."

I was provoking him, and it felt so good and so naughty that I couldn't wait for him to unleash whatever was under the cool exterior he always wore.

"Ryker." That was all Garrett had to say for Ryker to pull out of me.

I gasped at the emptiness, tears springing to my eyes. "What-"

Ryker grabbed me around the waist and pulled me backward and onto him, his cock filling me once more but this time with me lying on top of him. His arm locked around me and his other hand rested on my lower belly, just above my pubic bone.

Garrett walked between our legs on his knees. "Perfect. Now what was it you said?" He leaned down and kissed my inner thigh. "About being unimpressed?"

Ryker kissed along my shoulder. "Relax, Paige." I'd gone tense in anticipation, but it was hard not to.

"I don't feel you fucking me." My body was trembling and there was no way to stop it.

Garrett pressed the head of his cock at my opening and both me and Ryker groaned in unison. He pushed in slowly, his eyes burning into mine, his jaw clenched.

Luca was stroking his half-erect cock, his eyes locked on where Garrett disappeared inside me. "I bet that feels amazing on your cock, Ry."

"It does." Ryker's voice was all gravel. "Surprisingly."

I think I stopped breathing as Garrett bottomed out. He grabbed one of my legs, moving it to hook around his arm, and then the other. The stretch on my inner thighs was almost too much, but then he started moving and I forgot about anything else besides the feel of his cock sliding alongside Ryker's.

"Do you know yet?" Garrett slowly pulled out until just the tip was in.

I shook my head and he slammed into me. "Yes!"

I wasn't a hundred percent sure I was still alive as he pistoned in and out, making my toes curl and my stomach want to cave inward.

Ryker's arm tightened around me and his hand slid down to my clit. "Are you going to come all over us, baby? Are you going to scream for us?"

"Yes! Oh!" I was louder than I'd ever been, and my volume only increased when Ryker started rubbing my clit at the same pace as the thrusts. "It's too much!"

"This is exactly how... I wanted... to fuck you... since we met." Garrett was struggling to speak and beads of sweat dripped off his forehead and landed on his lip. "Hard." *Thrust.* "Fast." *Thrust.* "Full of cock." *Thrust, thrust.*

"Scream Garrett's name, Paige. Make him come all over my cock too." Ryker bit my earlobe at the same time he pinched my clit, and it was game over.

"Garrett!" His name fell from my lips as an orgasm unlike anything I'd ever experienced slammed into me. Pops of light danced across my vision, and I slammed my eyes shut, my body spasming with pleasure.

"That's it, ride it out. Fuck!" Ryker's hips moved up, burying himself even deeper.

With a strangled groan, Garrett buried himself to the hilt, his face a mask of pleasure as he came inside me right along with Ryker.

It was dirty. It was sexy. I wanted to do it again and again.

I couldn't feel my limbs and my clit throbbed with over stimulation as my body relaxed on top of Ryker's.

"Hey, don't cry." Luca dropped to his knees next to me, wiping away the stray tears I hadn't even realized had been falling. "Are you hurt?"

"No." I didn't know why I was crying, but I imagined it was sex hormone overload.

"Luca, can you go get some towels?" Garrett was still breathing heavily, but his voice had softened. He released my legs slowly and rubbed my thighs affectionately. "You were amazing, Paige."

I nodded, my head lolling to the side as exhaustion hit me like a ton of bricks. "I'm ruined."

Ryker chuckled. "Damn right."

Chapter 23

Enchanted

Luca

I could count the number of actual girlfriends I've had in my life on one hand. We all could, actually.

Sure, there had been plenty of hookups and dates, but not many made it past that threshold that turned more than casual and, even then, they were short-lived.

I'd always just assumed I was a perpetual bachelor, too focused on forging my own path with Ryker and Garrett to deal with everything that went with taking care of a woman the way she deserved.

But with Paige, it was different.

It didn't take long for me to rethink my bachelorhood and kick it to the curb. There was no hesitation, no list of pros and cons, no "dealing" with having a girlfriend.

Besides being smart and funny, she had this way about her that put me at ease. She showed her vulnerability but then pushed through it, emerging an even better version of herself.

I don't know what kind of asshole would cheat on such a woman, but he deserved to have his dick cut off and shoved down his throat.

It had been two weeks since we'd decided to give us a shot. Paige working with us only brought us that much closer; not just with her but with each other. I'd never realized how much we'd been in our own heads until I started thinking about someone else's needs.

"Luca, are you listening?" Ophelia, our executive accountant, had been going over two profit projections based on which route we took the business in the first quarter of the next year.

"Yes." I looked at the chart she'd projected on the large monitor over the small conference table in my office. "They're the same. How can that be possible?"

"I see you weren't listening." She sighed. "This is if you get the major client that Ryker has been after for the last few months. No difference in expected profit because they will replace the slower client acquisition moving forward."

We'd all mutually decided we needed to find a level of sustainability we could be happy with. Since both Garrett and Ryker were emotionally invested in the decision to pivot, I'd been tasked with making the final decision. On one side of the coin, I didn't necessarily need money and, on the other, I wanted Garrett and Ryker to earn the most possible without burning out.

"Well, that looks great." I crossed my arms over my chest. "I feel like you're about to give me a big but."

"And I cannot lie..." She cleared her throat, and I grinned. "Sorry. There is a projection without securing that client."

She clicked and a new graph appeared. My eyes widened at the difference. Millions of dollars difference.

"That's if we don't secure the client?" I knew there would be a drop in profit, but not that significant.

"It's a huge account with the potential for continued growth over the next several quarters without adding too many additional clients. That's what you want, correct?" She clicked to the next slide to show the entire year with the major client and without.

"Shit." I tapped my finger across my lips. "I mean, it won't break us if we don't secure them, but it will freak Ryker right the fuck out."

"It will open the doors for even bigger clients, which would allow you to take on less." She slid a folder across the table to me. "I printed all of the projections for you."

"Thanks." I flipped absentmindedly through the folder before looking up at Ophelia. "So, we need to secure that client."

"Correct." She closed her laptop and stood. "It's not like the company is going to go bankrupt if you don't."

"Right." But even though I'd reassured Ryker I'd always have his back, he wouldn't stand for that big of a decrease.

Part of the issue with the way we'd been securing clients, was that we were the draw. They wanted our hands on the projects, not just our employees. Several of our employees were more than capable of taking the reins, but the big clients got what the big clients wanted.

No wasn't in Ryker's vocabulary when it came to pleasing a client.

Ophelia left my office, and I took the folder to my desk, opening it to stare at the figures more closely. We would just have to nail negotiations when the time came.

My phone dinged with a message, and I swiped to open it, a grin spreading across my face. Sometimes it was worth the name-drop to get an appointment at an exclusive boutique that was booked months out.

I picked up my office phone and pressed the speed dial button to Paige's office.

"Paige speaking."

"Hi, beautiful. Want to take off early today and go shopping?" I shut down my laptop.

"Shopping? For what?"

"For a gown. Remember I mentioned the gala a few weeks ago? I got us an appointment at a really great boutique that I think you'll love." My cousins always went on and on about how much they loved Enchanting Silhouettes.

She was quiet. Way too quiet. Shouldn't she have been squealing in delight about leaving early on a Friday to go shopping?

"Paige? You there? Don't worry about your work. It can wait until Monday." I grabbed my bag, slipping my laptop into it.

"I... okay." She sounded so uncertain that my heart squeezed.

"Look. I'm your boss. You've worked your ass off the last few weeks. Ryker and Garrett aren't going to get mad. They aren't even here anyway. I'm coming to your office." I hung up the phone and grabbed my cellphone off my desk before leaving my office.

It would be nice doing something just one-on-one with Paige. Don't get me wrong, I loved how much time we'd all been spending together over the past few weeks, but I hadn't really had the chance to hang out with her by myself. With Ryker at his newly established Friday therapy appointment and Garrett at some hockey thing for his brother, it would just be the two of us for a few glorious hours. I couldn't wait to see her try on dresses and pick one that was perfect for her.

When I got to Paige's office, she had her laptop closed and was straightening some papers. Sue had been absolutely right about her being perfect for us. She was efficient, figured most things out on her own or with very few directions, and had even started slowly taking over Ryker's tasks. He might have been enamored with her, but he was still working through his fears of life imploding. Her working with us was a good push for him.

I leaned against her door frame, and she looked up. "Your office is really coming together." I gave her a smile as I took in the new desk accessories she must have just gotten. She'd also added a few plants and pictures to the surfaces making it not look as bare.

She blushed and looked away, opening her desk drawer and pulling out her purse. "Thanks."

Something was off, but I couldn't quite put my finger on what. "What's wrong? Do you not want to go?"

Her lips twisted to the side and then she sighed. "I like to shop alone."

"Oh. Well, I can wait in the car if that makes you feel more comfortable. I just thought it would be fun." I pushed off the door frame, walked to her desk, and tilted her chin up so she was looking at me. "You don't want me to see you looking all chic and sexy in different dresses?"

Her cheeks got even redder; more than I'd seen them even during sex. Maybe she wasn't blushing.

I put my hand against her cheek. "You're a little warm."

"I'm fine." She swatted my hand away and stood, reaching for her tote bag on the floor. "I'll go in and take a look, but they probably won't have anything I'll like."

"What? Paige, this is one of the best gown boutiques in the city according to my cousins. They always get their fancy shit from there." I was blocking her path to the door and didn't move even when she tried to push past me.

"It's a boutique." She stared at me as if that was enough of a reason why she seemed almost upset over it.

"Okay, do you want to go to Bloomingdale's or Nordstrom instead? I like supporting small businesses, but I'm okay with going wherever."

Her chin quivered and she bit down on her bottom lip. Ah, fuck. What did I say?

"Hey." I pulled her into a hug, her arms and tote bag trapped between us like a shield. "What's wrong, sweetheart?"

She sniffled, resting her forehead against my shoulder. "They won't have my size at a boutique. It's embarrassing to walk into a store and have to turn around and leave. Specialty stores are notoriously single-digit sized."

"Uh..." I rubbed her back soothingly. "One of my cousins is about the same size as you and she goes there."

"What size is that?"

An alarm went off in my head warning me to be careful with my words. "I'm not sure. Do you want me to call and ask the owner what sizes they have? Or look it up online? I'm sorry I didn't take that into consideration. Didn't think it mattered, honestly."

I vaguely understood that women had it way harder than men when it came to shopping but couldn't quite wrap my head around why. There's been so much in the media about body positivity and size inclusivity that I assumed stores had shifted to offering more mid-size and plus-size options.

She nodded against my chest. "Can you? I'm a size fourteen or sixteen depending on what it is. A lot of places stop at twelve or their fourteen is ridiculously small."

I pulled out my phone and moved around Paige to sit in her chair. "Sit." I patted my lap.

She placed her bags on the desk and sat on my lap, laying her head on my shoulder. "I'm also on my period so I don't know if today is the best day to dress shop. I'm a little bloated."

I didn't respond because nothing I wanted to say would have been the right thing. She didn't look bloated, but what did I know? Instead, I texted the owner, Seraphina, to ask what sizes they carried, and she responded immediately.

"They have dresses up to thirty. See, I told you it would be fine." I rubbed her lower back and she groaned. "Do you just want me to cancel? We can just go back to my place instead and figure out somewhere else to get a gown. I probably shouldn't have procrastinated on this."

"I'm just being stupid. Hormones are stupid. "She got off my lap and grabbed her bags. "I'm sorry."

"Don't apologize. Your uterus is currently waging a war with mass casualties." I stood and shook my head. "Forget I said that."

"You aren't entirely wrong." She grabbed a tissue and blew her nose. God, I loved how completely comfortable she was with us to do things like blow her nose and tell me she was bloated.

"Ready?" I offered her my arm and she hooked hers through mine. "If we get there and you change your mind, we'll just leave, okay?"

"Okay." She smiled at me, and fuck if my heart didn't skip a beat.

After a quick stop at Perky Squirrel Coffee for an afternoon pick-me-up, we arrived at the store. Paige seemed to be feeling better as she happily sipped her mocha blended coffee.

My driver parked in the drop-off zone and I got out, extending my hand to her as she slid across the seat. She took it with a smile, the tension in her face and shoulders now gone.

"Are you sure it's okay if I bring this in?" She shook her half-empty cup as I entwined our fingers.

"I'm sure they have somewhere you can put it. Why? Are you planning on spilling it?" I opened the door for her but pulled her to a stop against me.

She gasped, the straw of her drink nearly poking out my eye. "Luca!"

"In my head, this was a lot sexier." I leaned in and kissed the side of her mouth where a bit of whipped cream had been.

She groaned, her body not as close as I wanted it, as I took her mouth in a kiss. She tasted so delicious, and her cold mouth was giving me very bad ideas. Maybe we would just cancel the appointment and go home.

A throat cleared, and we broke apart to find a pixie of a woman standing with her hands on her hips and a teasing smile on her face. "We haven't even gotten her in any gowns yet and you're ready to pounce."

"I'm always ready to pounce." I put my hand on the small of Paige's back and guided her inside. "I take it you're Seraphina?"

"That would be me." She smiled warmly at Paige. "And you must be Paige."

"I am. Nice to meet you." Paige took her outstretched hand, which Seraphina clasped between both of hers.

"Let me just lock the door and we'll get started. I have

everything ready in the back. Right this way." After she locked the door, she led us through the small reception area and through thick black curtains to the back.

I'd texted Seraphina while we waited for our coffee, letting her know Paige's size so she'd have several dresses already pulled out and ready. I wanted Paige to walk in and not stress out about looking through rows and rows of gowns.

When I heard the word *boutique,* I thought of a small shop, but Enchanting Silhouettes was bigger than I expected. There was row after row of rolling racks filling most of the room and shelves filled with accessories and shoes along one wall.

Along the back wall was the fitting room area with a row of four changing rooms, their curtains pulled back. There were four pink velvet couches in front of each with a platform with chandeliers hanging over each.

"I pulled some things after Luca texted me your size to get us started. Are you looking for something specific? A certain color or style?" Seraphina sounded excited as we stopped in front of one of the changing areas.

Paige mixed her straw around in her drink. "I'm not really sure what I'm looking for. The last time I wore a gown was prom. Well, and..." She shook her head and stared down at her drink, her mood taking a downturn again. "Let's get this over with."

"We'll just try a few things and go from there, all right?" Seraphina's voice had softened, and she put her hand on Paige's arm. "Would you like music on or off?"

"On." Paige relaxed again a little and looked over her

shoulder, giving me the faintest smile. She wasn't into this at all, but I'd already told her to tell me and we'd go.

Seraphina picked up a tablet from a side table and handed it to me with a music app open. "Go ahead and pick some music for us and we'll get started."

"Trusting me with the music might not be such a good idea." I sat down on the sofa while the girls went into the changing room, sliding the curtain closed. I thought I'd get to be more hands-on with the process, but maybe it was better if I wasn't, considering Paige wasn't having the best day.

I could hear the girls talking but could only make out a few words as I scrolled through the music channels looking for something Paige might like. She had very eclectic music tastes and didn't seem to hate anything besides death metal.

When I heard the word wedding, my curiosity over what was going on behind the curtain got the best of me and I stood, tiptoeing over.

"That's tough, sweetie. I'm sorry," Seraphina said.

"Everything over the last few days has just been reminding me of it and now this." Paige sighed. "The gala is on the same night, and I can't just back out now."

"But maybe that's a good thing. You'll be on the arm of a handsome man instead of wallowing in a pint of Ben and Jerry's."

"I'm good at wallowing. Oh, this one is pretty. Really, they all are. I just hope they fit." There was still uncertainty in Paige's voice.

"They will and, if not, then I have the next size up and the next size down. We can alter any dress you choose to fit your body."

"Won't there be a wait for that? This thing is in two weeks... talk about last minute preparation. There was so much going on when Luca asked me to go that I completely forgot until he said something today."

"His family, extended family, and their friends are big clients of ours, so if it needs to be altered, we'll get it done in time." Seraphina made a sound of excitement. "Let's try this one first just to drive your boyfriend nuts."

I went back to my seat, pressing a random station, my mind on the first part of the conversation I'd overheard. Was she saying that her wedding would have been the twenty-eighth? We hadn't really talked much about her breakup or anything that went with it other than her fiancé cheated on her.

Even though their relationship was over, I was sure milestones and plans that never saw fruition hurt her. It was just a reminder of what he'd done and how he'd abused her heart.

I'd never do that to her, and if Ryker and Garrett ever did, they'd learn that all the jokes about cement blocks and sharks weren't so funny anymore.

The curtain opened just enough for Seraphina to step out. "You ready for the first dress?"

"I was born ready." I put the tablet down beside me and leaned forward with my arms on my knees. "Let's see."

She pulled open the curtain and Paige walked out; her

head held high with no signs that she'd just been talking about her canceled nuptials.

I was at a loss for words as I took in the flowing dress the color of wine. I hadn't the faintest clue what the fit was called, but all I knew was she looked breathtaking.

Was this what it felt like to fall in love?

Chapter 24

Stuck On Them

Paige

My life was starting to feel complete for the first time in a long time. I'd never realized what I'd been missing until Ryker, Luca, and Garrett crashed into my life. I found myself wanting to be around them all the time and I think they felt the same if their actions were any indication.

Things were unfolding between us so naturally it almost felt too good to be true. I'd expected there to be tension and disagreements between the three of them over time spent with me, but there wasn't. Unless I just didn't see or hear it.

Over the last three weeks, we'd spent every day together either as a group or individually. I'd only slept at my apartment twice and I didn't miss having my own space one bit. What I didn't enjoy was hopping from one place to the next, but hopefully in time that would change.

My phone buzzed with a text and I tore my gaze away from the passing scenery as Garrett drove the four of us east out of the city. They hadn't told me exactly where we were going, but I'd heard something about it taking a few hours when they thought I couldn't hear them.

Nora: *I miss your face. When can I come visit? Next weekend?*

Me: *The gala is next weekend...*

Nora: *Yes, but...*

Me: *I'm perfectly fine. I even made it through gown shopping without crying and that's a win because I was on my period.*

Nora: *Did you tell them?*

Me: *No and I'm not going to. They don't need to deal with my blubbering ass.*

Nora: *I bet they'd make you feel better.*

Me: *They do almost daily. My vagina is kind of a hussy for them.*

Nora: *I'm so jealous. Can you imagine me with three men?*

Me: *Would you be all domme with them?*

Nora: *Ma'am, do not threaten me with a good time. I'm actually quite meek in the bedroom.*

Me: **laughing emoji**

Nora: *What? I can be fierce on the ice and demure in the sheets. It's a nice change to be someone's good girl. I bet they call you good girl, don't they? You little slut.*

Me: *OMG stop. The guys are going to want to know why I'm laughing so hard.*

Nora: *Fine. How about I visit you as soon as you move out of that rat nest you're living in?*

Me: *The rat was someone's pet... I think. I hope. You'll be waiting a while. We've only been together for three weeks.*

Nora: *Technically you can count from when you met them. Now that we're old, time's a ticking.*

Me: *It's complicated with three of them.*

Nora: *But I bet you've thought about which of their places you'd want to live in the most. I bet it's Garrett's.*

I really needed to stop telling Nora everything about my love life. Now my mind was back on the complications that came with dating three men. I shouldn't have even been thinking about living with any of them, yet it was all I could think about whenever I was at one of their places.

"Are you guys going to tell me where we're going?" I both loved and hated surprises. I hadn't had to pack anything special besides warm clothing and a few nice outfits.

"Nope," Ryker said from next to me where he was typing away on his laptop. "It's a surprise, so don't try to figure it out."

"Why did you even bring that? It's Friday." I knew he was making progress toward calming his work schedule down, but it was a struggle for him.

"I'm working on sending out some project specifications to get bids and timelines back for the center. I'll be done by the time we get there." He looked over at me and smiled. "Don't worry."

"I guess the car blow job or even backseat sixty-nine is out of the question then." I shrugged, unable to hide my grin when Luca whipped his head around.

Garrett groaned. "Please don't. I won't be able to drive."

"You're insatiable." Ryker reached across the seat, and I took his hand. "You'll want to rest up that delicate bud of yours for later."

I burst out laughing. "Delicate bud?"

"It's a beautiful flower just waiting to give us its sweet nectar." He was typing one-handed, and I didn't know if he was writing smut or working.

"Well, I mean, your dick is the size of a bee's stinger so..." Luca turned back around, humor in his voice.

"That's not what Paige said last night." He kicked Luca's seat. "I believe her exact words were 'I want that big cock buried deep in my cunt, Ry.' Or did I hear her wrong?" Ryker squeezed my hand but then pulled away. "Shit. I wrote cock instead of cost."

"Exactly why you should put that away until next week," Garrett said.

Ryker sighed. "Next week is too busy with Badden Apparel coming for contract negotiations."

"I don't see why we can't just do it over video chat."

"They're here for the gala too so it just makes sense to meet in person. I heard they're pretty hands-on and like to meet people face to face before making big company decisions." Ryker stopped typing and looked over at me. "Remind me on Wednesday to go over the meeting agenda with you."

I gave him a salute. "Got it."

He raised an eyebrow and looked down at my phone on the seat between us. "You aren't going to put it on your calendar?"

"It's been on my calendar since the day they decided to choose LRG." I yawned and put my head against the window. "I need a nap."

"Scoot over here and you can use my shoulder as a pillow." Ryker patted the middle seat.

I moved my phone and switched seats, buckling up again before putting my head on his shoulder. It wasn't the most comfortable, but it was better than the shaking window.

~

When I woke up, it was dark, and we'd just turned into trees. I jumped thinking we were about to hit them but then the SUV straightened out and we were heading down a road lined with trees.

"You all right there?" Ryker had his arm around me and squeezed my waist.

"Yeah, the trees just surprised me." I rubbed my eyes. "Where are we?"

"We're at my Hampton's estate." Luca was on his phone and, up ahead, a gate swung open. "Well, I shouldn't say my. I co-own it with my brother. You'll meet him at the gala."

"We thought it would be nice to have a weekend away

from the city." Garrett pulled through the gate and up ahead a house was lit up.

As we got closer, my heart beat faster and faster. Luca's penthouse apartment in the tallest building in the city was impressive, but the house that came into full view was stunning.

Garrett pulled into a garage that Luca must have opened, and I tried to keep my excitement to a minimum. I'd never been in a mansion before, and I could tell from the large, finished garage with ceiling fans it was going to be an amazing weekend.

"Hope it's not too much." Luca unbuckled his seatbelt and looked back at me. "We decided driving would be a little less pretentious than taking a helicopter."

My eyes widened. "What?"

Luca laughed and shook his head. "Man, you should see your face. Like a deer caught in the headlights."

I reached forward and swatted his arm before unbuckling and getting out after Ryker. "It's way too much. How much does a place like this cost? Is that rude to ask?"

"Not at all." Luca shut his door and walked to the back of the SUV that was opening. "It was just under twenty, so about ten after me and Leo split the cost."

"Twenty million?" I looked down at the epoxy-covered floor and over at the two cars parked on the other side of the garage. "I can't wrap my mind around that much money."

"Just so you know, he donates just as much if not more than what he spends." Garrett helped Luca pull our bags out of the back. "A lot of the time anonymously."

"One of you needs to donate to my student loans." I wanted to hide the second it came out of my mouth. "Just kidding."

"Done." Ryker took my hand and pulled me toward the door into the house. "Give me your lender and the account number."

I stopped, his arm yanking me forward a little as he kept going. "I was joking."

"Well, I'm not. Give Luca and Garrett the other sticky notes I saw." He came back to stand in front of me, taking my face in his hands. "It can be an early Christmas present."

"I don't know what sticky notes you're talking about." I couldn't just let them pay off all my debt. Maybe if we had been dating for longer, I'd consider it.

"No big deal if you won't give us the information. I can get it." Luca winked as he went up the single step to the door and opened it.

Ryker searched my eyes and, when I didn't say anything else, he let me go, but not before kissing me. All I needed were their kisses, not their money. They were paying me enough as their assistant as it was.

"Come on. Wait until you see inside." Ryker took my hand again and I followed him inside, Garrett following with our bags.

We entered into a mudroom which opened into a wide hallway off the foyer. Already I felt at ease being away from the city.

The house was like something straight off of Zillow late-night searches. The living space was wide open with a large living room and a kitchen worthy of a Michelin-star chef.

Everything was white, cream, or beige with pops of blues and greens in the artwork and accessories throughout the space.

I ran my hand along the back of one of the couches and went to one of the floor-to-ceiling windows. The pool was lit up, with water jets shooting across it.

"It's heated." Luca came to stand next to me. "Or there's a jacuzzi."

I shook my head, looking at my reflection in the glass. I felt suddenly out of place with my jeans and t-shirt. This was a place where women probably wore their finest clothes, and when they weren't, they were wearing hundred-dollar yoga pants.

"You have that look on your face again." Luca was frowning at me in the glass.

"What look is that?" I turned toward him, wrapping my arms around his neck.

He raised a brow, tilting his head slightly. "I'm not falling for that."

"It just takes some getting used to." I leaned in and kissed him before pulling back.

"The sooner, the better so we can spoil you." He pushed my hair behind my ears. "You deserve the world."

My cheeks heated and I tried to look away, but he stopped me. "Don't." I had the sudden urge to flee.

I couldn't let myself get too attached to these men because who knew what tomorrow would bring? Eventually, the newness factor would wear off and, long term, did any of us really think it was going to work?

"What are you so afraid of?" Luca saw right through my walls and I wasn't sure I liked it.

I swallowed hard, meeting his gaze for a moment before dropping it to the floor. What were these men doing to me?

I stepped back, needing some distance. This kind of intensity was too much for me to handle.

Luca matched my retreating steps until I bumped into a strong chest and hands grabbed onto my arms.

"You're afraid of getting attached, I get it. But you're here with us now." Luca wrapped a possessive hand around the back of my neck. "Doesn't that tell you something? That maybe what we have could be more than fleeting? That it could be real?"

I nodded, not trusting myself to speak. I wanted to believe his words but wasn't sure I should. Words were just that: words. People threw them around all the time and didn't mean them.

Ryker rubbed my arms as if he were trying to warm up my cold heart. "We won't let you go if you don't want us to."

My traitorous heart thawed just a bit and I leaned back into Ryker. This week was hard. Hell, the past few months had been hard, but what was I going to miss by shutting them out?

This could be the best thing that had ever happened to me just as much as it could be the worst. Instead of one man holding my heart in the palm of his hand, there were three. Three opportunities for heartbreak. Three opportunities for a pain that I didn't know if I could recover from.

There was just as much at risk for them with their friendship and company. And yet, there they were, offering me something so different and beautiful that I couldn't turn away. They weren't going to let me run, that much was clear.

"I..." I closed my eyes as Garrett joined us, the three of them surrounding me like a protective forcefield. "Next Saturday was supposed to be my wedding day. It's hard to think past that."

"And that's okay. We'll be here." Garrett wiped a tear from my cheek.

The three of them wrapped themselves around me like this was right where I belonged, protected by the three of them.

I tried to keep my emotions bottled inside but they bubbled out of me in a sob so anguished that it nearly took me to my knees.

I didn't want them to see me like this or just how much it still affected me. But I couldn't hide it any longer.

Someone picked me up—not sure who—and carried me to the couch, sitting with me in their lap. The other two were there too, their hands smoothing my hair, my back, my arms and legs. They didn't sign up for the hot mess express, but here they were, picking up my pieces.

One by one, their lips found mine, melting away the pain and worry I'd been feeling. It was time I stopped giving in to my fears and accepted what was in front of me —three incredible men who wanted nothing more than for us to explore whatever this connection might be.

And that was exactly what I wanted too.

Chapter 25

Fun and Games

Ryker

Growing up, I never got to experience all the joys that holidays could bring. Even once Libby and I were taken in, there wasn't much joy when all I could think about was everything I'd lost in my life. It didn't help that I was a teenager and was too cool to be seen in public with the adults who were raising me.

So when Luca suggested we spend Saturday evening at an adult-only night at a fall festival and then rent the corn maze down the road after hours, I didn't have the faintest idea what was in store for me. I'd, of course, seen them on television and read about them, but I hadn't expected the sense of joy from the sounds, sights, and smells.

And I definitely didn't expect him to force me to wear a flannel that matched all of them.

"I can't believe I let you talk me into this." I climbed

onto the stool in the face painting booth, taking the laminated card from one of the four people doing face paint.

Paige giggled, sitting next to me and looking over at the card. "I already know what I want."

"You two are so adorable," the woman assigned to me gushed. "Most men don't get their face painted or match their... wife? Girlfriend?"

"Girlfriend." I took Paige's hand and held it against my thigh.

"He lost the corn cob eating challenge earlier." Paige squeezed my hand, her voice full of amusement. "So don't give him too much credit."

The woman laughed and pulled out her supplies. "What are we thinking of doing?"

Before I could answer, Paige spoke up again. "He should get a bee with a big stinger."

I looked over at her, raising my eyebrow with a smirk. "Really, Paige?"

"I'll get a flower with lots of nectar. It will be perfect." She winked and, fuck me, my heart did some weird flutter thing where I seriously wondered if I was about to have a heart attack.

Last night, I thought we'd somehow broken her. Had we pushed her too hard too fast when she'd just gotten out of a relationship?

Her anguished cries had made me feel sick and a little murderous. How someone could hurt her so deeply was unfathomable.

After she'd let out all the pain she'd been holding inside, she'd dried her tears and we'd enjoyed the rest of

Maya Nicole

the evening making dinner together and cuddling around the outdoor fire pit. It was domestic as fuck, and I loved every second of it.

I'd never been a cuddler until her. From that very first night, there had been this need to hold her close and never let go. It was scary and exciting to already feel so deeply for a woman, but there I was. There we all were.

Was this why none of us ever got into long-term relationships? Had we been waiting for someone like Paige to come along that we could love together?

"Do you want the bee on this cheek?" The face painter tapped my left cheek and broke the spell that thoughts of Paige had me under.

"What do you think, babe?" I brought Paige's hand to my lips and kissed our entwined fingers.

"I'll get the flower on the right so the bee can get its nectar later." She giggled as I bit one of her fingers.

A few minutes into our works of art, Garrett and Luca strolled up with sly grins on their faces. They'd made an excuse when we'd finished the hayride that they needed to go make a business phone call for our big meeting next week. Really, they'd been making sure everything was set for the corn maze.

"Oh, look, Britt. They're all matching!" The woman painting Paige's cheek looked between the four of us with curiosity.

Although polyamory was accepted more now than ever, it still gave me pause on how we should handle questions. But before any of us could think too hard on it, Paige spoke up.

"They're my boyfriends too," she said with a smile that showed no hesitation.

"Get it, girl." Britt's face turned beet red as she stepped back and grabbed a handheld mirror, holding it up for me. "Your bee is finished."

"Looks great." I pushed my tongue into my cheek, and it looked like it had too much nectar, which if I got my way, would be true in just a short while.

Garrett snapped a picture before I even realized his phone was out. "This is going in our company newsletter. The subject line will be 'Bee careful around Ryker.'"

I jumped up and he took off into the crowd, me hot on his heels. "Get back here!"

People jumped out of our way as we darted around in the crowd. It felt like we were back in college again, without a care in the world.

He made one wrong turn and found himself trapped between two tents that were up against a chain link fence. "Ah, shit." He raised his hands in surrender.

I put my hands on my thighs, a little out of breath. I needed to add sprints into my workouts if this was going to start up again.

He looked back behind him like he was thinking about hopping over the fence.

"Don't you dare, Gary Wilson Jr!" I strode toward him, cracking my knuckles. "You're cornered, now you must fight."

He crossed his arms over his chest, his phone clutched tightly in his hand. "We're in our thirties now, man. You can't do this. We have a girlfriend. If she saw or heard..."

I laughed, shaking out my hands. "May the best man win."

"I hate you!" He made a squealing noise as I lunged at him.

He ducked but didn't run since our rules were no running once caught.

His phone disappeared into his back pocket, and he got into a fighting stance. "I'm not holding back, Ry, and you know I'm the champ."

I grinned, bouncing on the balls of my feet like I was Rocky, ready to take down an opponent. "You got the title for a reason, Gary, but I've been holding back."

His first move was to go for the knees to tackle me, but I sidestepped him and caught him in an arm lock from behind, taking him to his knees.

"Should we break them apart?" Paige was standing next to Luca at the opening of our little alleyway.

"Nope." Luca grinned at me and Garrett as I struggled to take him down to the ground.

I tightened my hold. "Do you surrender?"

"Never!" Garrett twisted and broke free just enough and at the wrong angle to set him up for the perfect tackle.

I was on top of him in an instant and before he could get away, I reached between us and pinched his nipple.

"Ah! You fucker!"

"Surrender!" I was laughing my ass off as I started to twist.

"I surrender!" Garrett sighed in relief as I released him.

"Is this some kind of foreplay I don't know about?" Paige was standing right behind me.

"It can be anything you want it to be." I got off Garrett and stood up, extending my hand.

Garrett got to his feet, put a hand over his pec, and stuck out his bottom lip in a pout. "Paige, Ryker hurt my nipple. Can you kiss it and make it better?"

I shoved him as we all laughed. It was completely ridiculous and immature, but it made me feel like all the weight had been lifted from my shoulders.

Paige stepped forward and wrapped her arms around Garrett, planting a kiss on his chest where I had pinched him. "There. All better."

She turned to me, her eyes soft. "You can pinch me like that anytime you want if it makes you smile like that."

My heart flew into my throat, and I pulled her to me, burying my face against her neck. "You make me smile like this, Paige."

"Well, isn't this just as sweet as chocolate-dipped cannoli," Luca said in a high-pitched southern drawl.

"Excuse me. You four can't be back here." A security guard stood behind Luca, his hands on his hips. "Ma'am, are you all right?"

Paige pulled away from me and turned. "I'm fine. We were just lost."

"Sure you were," he muttered as we filed past him like scolded schoolchildren.

I took Paige's hand and Garrett took the other. Luca didn't seem to mind as he walked beside me, but that was just how Luca was. He and I were complete opposites but maybe that was why we remained friends despite our disagreements.

I'd been working through a lot in therapy. Having a session a week was intense, but it was what I needed if I wanted to move forward and be the best boyfriend and friend I could be. Letting go of control wasn't easy, but I was trying a little more each day and found myself happier.

"What are we going to do now?" Paige let go of my hand and pulled her phone from her purse. "They're closing down soon. Should we go?"

Luca looked at his watch. "We can. It will take a bit to get out of the parking lot."

"Seems like such a waste for our face paint." Paige looked up at me. "Your bee got a little smudged from play fighting with Gare."

"Yeah, the stinger looks like it was taken down to the right size. You can barely see it." Luca was lucky he'd fallen back into step beside Garrett.

"You just have stinger envy." I scratched my face with my middle finger.

When was the last time we'd all laughed so much together? Not for a long time, that was for damn sure, and it was all because I took a chance on a woman who joked about nipple hair.

Thirty minutes later we turned into the empty corn maze parking lot. Paige had been reading something Luca had sent her on her phone but looked up as the tires crunched on gravel. "Where are we?"

"We rented out the corn maze." Garrett parked the SUV and looked over at her in the passenger seat. "If you're interested."

She bit her lip and craned her neck to look out the front window at the dark maze. "But it's dark."

I grabbed one of the flashlights Luca had put on the seat between us and flipped it on, pointing it at him. "We have lights."

Paige turned around to look at me and then nearly jumped out of her seat when her eyes landed on Luca. He'd slipped on one of the Jason masks he'd brought and leaned forward to brush a lock of her hair from her face. "Do you want to play?"

"What the fuck!" She put her hand on her chest and turned a glare on me and then Garrett. "Do you both have masks too?"

"Yes." I reached down under the seat and pulled mine out. "You can say no."

"What exactly are you asking me?" She took the flashlight Luca offered her.

Garrett took her free hand. "Do you trust us?"

"Not anymore."

Luca snorted. "We propose a game of cat and mouse. You're the mouse."

"You want to chase me in a dark corn maze... with masks on?" She looked so cute as she processed the information and looked at our matching shirts. "And what happens when you catch me?"

"Whoever catches you gets the prize... you." Garrett

kissed her hand and then let it go. "But you won't know who it is... hopefully."

She sucked in a breath. "I can tell you apart even if you're matching."

Luca lowered his voice, sounding menacing. "When we're all together it's easy, but when you're running, your adrenaline pumping, your heart beating in your ears, your-"

"You don't scare me." She looked back out at the corn stalks rising up in front of us. "The corn does though... this is why I don't watch scary movies. Stupid people go into dark cornfields trying to scare each other and there turns out to be a real killer."

"This time there will be a pussy killer. Whoever finds you will destroy that sweet pussy of yours and the other two will get the consolation prize of watching." I put my mask on. "You know what word to scream if you want to stop. Ten... nine..."

Her eyes went comically wide, and she scrambled out of the SUV, running toward the open gate. I could see her flashlight like a beacon as she turned it on in the maze, the light dancing as she ran.

"Are we sure about this? I don't want to freak her out." Garrett grabbed her phone from where she'd dropped it on the floorboard and put it in the center console along with his.

"It's going to be fun. She wouldn't have gotten out of the car if she didn't want to do it." Luca got out, leaving his flashlight behind.

There was just enough light from the moon and the

perimeter lights to see, but I took mine just in case. It was a little chilly as we walked to the entrance of the maze, and I hoped Paige was warm enough.

I couldn't see her light anymore and I wondered if she'd turned it off or if she had made it far enough that we couldn't see it from where we were at.

"May the best man win." Luca adjusted his mask and then took off into the maze. "Paige! Here we come!"

"I feel like he's way too into this." Garrett put on his mask and followed Luca, leaving me at the rear.

My cock was already coming to life as I jogged into the dark field. I just hoped I found her first so I could claim her as my prize.

I wasn't very far in when I heard something to my left and then a masculine scream from even farther to my left. There was a soft giggle from somewhere in the corn stalks not too far away.

"That's not fair, Paige! You can't throw shit!" Luca yelled.

My eyes adjusted to the darkness, and I spotted a glimpse of white. I stood still, waiting for Luca to move on from where he was so I could make my move.

While they'd run ahead thinking she'd get far, she'd hidden out near the entrance. She was far too smart for this game.

Moving as quietly as possible, I crept forward, trying to control my breathing. She was lying flat on the ground and seemed to be focusing on whatever direction Luca was in, so she didn't notice me approaching.

I stopped again, listening to the soft rustle of the breeze

moving through the leaves. How was I going to get a hold of her with her in that position? This wasn't the WWE; I didn't want to dive onto her and potentially hurt her.

She started to move, getting onto her hands and knees, stopping to listen for any sounds. There was nothing to be heard, which meant if she even made a peep, they would know where she was if they were anywhere nearby.

Pushing to just her knees, she waited again, and that was when I made my move.

Chapter 26

Filthy

Paige

My heart had never pounded so hard. After running into the maze, I decided to hide rather than try to find my way through it. Luca had been loud, the other two I hadn't even seen or heard.

I couldn't resist the urge to throw an old ear of corn I'd found lying on the ground at Luca when he'd stopped just far enough from me that I could hide. It had been so easy to toss it in his direction and then drop to the ground. His scream was well worth the possibility of him catching me, but so far, he seemed to not figure out which direction it came from.

But now I couldn't hear a damn thing over the drumming in my ears, and I couldn't just lie on the ground all night. There were probably bugs just waiting to feast on my flesh, plus the ground was cold.

I carefully got to my hands and knees, listening for any noises first before sitting up on my knees. I started to wipe my hands on my jeans when a hand wrapped around the base of my ponytail and a hand went over my mouth.

I did what any sane woman would do if they were caught unaware; I screamed and tried to get away. But their grip was tight, and I could barely move at all with how far up his hold was on my hair. He at least knew what he was doing in that department.

He didn't speak so there was no way to tell who it was, but fear turned to excitement as he waited patiently for me to stop trying to waddle away on my knees. It was a good thing for him I hadn't been standing or I would have kicked him in the nuts.

He removed his hand from my mouth, and I heard the faint sound of his zipper being pulled down.

"Garrett?" I whispered, wanting so badly to know who was behind me. Garrett came to mind because he was into grabbing my hair the most.

He gave me nothing, no reaction. It made me clench my legs together knowing that I was about to be fucked and have no clue who it was.

I was preparing myself to be pushed back down to my hands when he walked around to the front of me, a flash-light turning on and shining right in my eyes.

My hand went up to shield myself, but he pushed it away before running the head of his cock against my lips. I squeezed my legs together, the tingle of desire making me ache for touch.

I didn't think it was Luca because as I opened my

mouth for him, there wasn't a ring. But he could have taken it out, couldn't he?

I moaned around the cock in my mouth, my hands going to the backs of his thighs to steady myself. They all had muscular thighs, so I still didn't know who he was.

His cock slid in and out, getting deeper each time. My eyes watered and tears squeezed out from my closed eyelids.

There was movement not too far away and my skin prickled with awareness. Were the other two watching? I couldn't see a damn thing since my eyes were shut.

His hands left my hair and then he was gone, the light disappearing with him. Two figures stood where the walkway met the corn, watching and possibly waiting for their turn.

A hand grabbed the back of my neck, and I yelped in surprise as he pushed me down, so I had to be on all fours.

"Oh my God." Was something wrong with me that I was so turned on by this? The risk of being caught. The anonymity. The watchful eyes.

Hands reached around me, undoing my jeans and pulling them along with my panties far enough down to bare my ass. He made a sound of approval and smoothed his hand over my round globe before he smacked it.

"Yes!" I pushed my ass back. "More."

He smacked the other side before pushing the tip of his cock between my legs. I was practically dripping for him, and he growled as he slid back and forth between my folds.

"Please, just fuck me. Don't you feel how ready I am

for you?" I spread my legs as wide as they could go in the confines of my jeans.

His hands gripped my hips, and then he pushed inside me in one smooth yet punishing thrust.

I cried out, my hands grasping at the ground. I didn't care that I'd have dirt caked under my nails for days or that debris was digging into my palms.

I'd never been fucked so hard before, and whoever it was behind me was not holding back. The once quiet field was filled with the sounds of our skin smacking together, my moans, and his grunts.

I needed him deeper and to free up a hand to rub my clit, so I lowered my chest to the ground, laying my cheek against the dirt. He groaned, his thrusts growing more intense and hitting me even deeper.

"That's it, fuck me into the ground, you filthy fucker." Surprised at my words I giggled, which was quickly cut short with a gasp when his hand came down on my ass again.

I could almost feel the other two men moving closer, their eyes watching us. Were they touching themselves? Did they plan on taking my fuck buddy's place once he finished?

God, I hoped so. I felt like I could go all night.

"Come on. You can go harder than that. Fuck me like you mean it." I pushed back against him as he thrust, practically seeing stars. "Fuck!"

I reached between my legs, and he batted my hand away before smacking my ass again. Every time he did it, my pussy clenched, and a zing went right to my clit.

His thrusts were unhinged and hit me in all the places that made my body burn. He buried himself one last time before grinding against me, his cum filling me, but not getting me to my peak.

I whimpered, needing to get off with an urgency I hadn't ever felt before. "Please. Touch me." There was no hiding the begging tone of my voice.

He pulled out, even though I wasn't quite sure he was done emptying himself yet, and flipped me over with a strength that surprised me. But then again, they were always surprising me.

He ducked in between my legs, which were still trapped in my pants, and placed them on his shoulders. He pulled me up until I was practically off the ground, my neck and head the only things still touching. He lifted his mask to the top of his head and then his lips wrapped around my clit.

It felt like he'd put a clit stimulator right over it and turned the setting to the max.

I screamed into the night, an orgasm so powerful exploding from every nerve ending between my legs. My legs squeezed around his neck, and I tried to grab at his hair, but the mask was on top of his head. I hadn't even been able to see the color of his hair or the shape of his face.

I moved against his mouth as he sucked and sucked until he pretty much siphoned my soul from my body. He switched to teasing licks before kissing each of my inner thighs.

Destroyed. That was the only word that crossed my

mind as he lowered his mask back on his face and set my legs on the ground.

I was shivering but wasn't sure if it was from the cold or the orgasm I'd just had. He wiggled his pants up and then offered me his hand, which I didn't take.

"Ryker?" I'd caught a flash of light-colored hair when he'd put his mask back down and his hands were a give-away. I'd never realized I knew their hands so well. Luca had tattoos that peaked out onto his and Garrett's had more veins than Ryker's.

"I didn't hurt you, did I?" He lifted his mask, his eyes unreadable in the darkness. "Jesus, Paige. I don't know what came over me."

"I loved every second of it." I lifted my ass off the ground and pulled up my pants, aware that dirt was everywhere.

"So did we." Garrett appeared right over me. "Especially when you said, 'fuck me into the ground, you filthy fucker.' You need to talk like that more often."

My cheeks heated and I reached my hand out to Ryker, who was still looking at me like he'd broken me. He pulled me to my feet, and I tilted my head up to kiss him.

He sighed and wrapped his arms around me, kissing me back with soft strokes of his tongue against mine.

"You threw an ear of corn at me." Luca was right next to us, practically right in our faces.

I jumped a little, breaking the kiss, which didn't last long before Luca pulled me into his arms, kissing me with so much heat I was going to be ready for round two.

Something wet hit my forehead and then my cheek. I

pulled away from Luca, confused for a moment until the sky seemed to open up above us.

"Ah, fuck!" Luca grabbed my hand and the four of us ran out into the maze. "Which way?"

"I'm not sure." Ryker spun around in a slow circle. "We could just cut through the corn until we get to the edge of it."

"Where's the fun in that?" Garrett spread his arms wide and tilted his face toward the sky.

"It's going to get muddy." Luca looked down at the already darkening dirt. "Let's just go this way." He pulled me down the walkway, but the turn was just a dead end.

"Let's just cut through." I pulled him back toward where Garrett was still standing with his face to the sky. "Garrett?"

"Hm?" He turned his head just a tad and opened his eyes. "Ah, fuck!" He didn't have his head tilted any longer and was rubbing at his eyes. "What the hell kind of rain is this?"

"Of course it's going to hurt when it's coming down this hard." Ryker took my other hand before leading us back in the direction we had fucked. "We weren't too far from the start of the maze."

"We should have checked the forecast," Luca muttered.

"It's fine. Rain never hurt anyone." My teeth were starting to chatter as the rain soaked through my clothes.

Ryker was right, and soon enough, we were piling into the SUV and blasting the heater. Garrett and Ryker had ended up in the back with me, Luca at the wheel.

Maya Nicole

"You're still shivering, sweetheart." Garrett turned and reached for the buttons on my flannel. "Let's get you out of these wet clothes."

I didn't protest because I was pretty cold and the air from the heater wasn't really making it through. Ryker took off his flannel and then shimmied out of his jeans.

"Are you three really stripping down naked in the backseat without me? We'll be home in like ten minutes."

"Focus on driving so you don't get pulled over." Ryker reached down and slipped off my shoes and socks, wrapping a hand around my foot. "Your feet are freezing."

My shoes were made of canvas, which wasn't very good for the rain. I lifted off the seat and had to practically peel my jeans off with how they clung to me. There was nothing worse than wet jeans.

"Come here." Ryker pulled me into his lap sideways facing Garrett and rebuckled the belt around both of us. It wasn't the safest thing to do, but neither was freezing.

"Well, isn't this just cozy?" I cuddled against Ryker's chest as Garrett took off his own pants and scooted to the middle seat, my legs across his lap.

"It's nice." Ryker kissed my shoulder and I shuddered. "Are you sure you're okay?"

I pulled away enough to cup his cheek and look him in the eyes. "It was perfect. Just what I needed." I kissed the cheek that didn't have a melting bee on it and then moved my lips to his ears. "I can still feel you between my legs."

"Did you know it was me?" He pushed some strands of loose hair behind my ear.

"Not until the end. You guys were right. I was too

amped up to pay attention to specifics. Plus, it was just dark enough that I couldn't see that much." I sighed happily as Garrett rubbed his hands up and down my legs. "I would love to be tied up and blindfolded."

Garrett's hands stopped for a moment before moving once more. "That takes a lot of trust."

"I can see it now... me blindfolding myself and lying on a hotel bed. Someone coming in but I don't know who. Eventually, all three of you would be there." I sighed and put my head against Ryker's chest.

They'd opened my eyes to entirely new ideas I'd never even thought I'd be into. Garrett was exactly right; it did take a lot of trust, and I trusted them more than I'd ever trusted anyone.

But that was exactly what happened when you truly loved someone. Or in my case, three someones.

Chapter 27

Office Rat

Paige

Working for LRG was one of the best things that could have happened to me. Not just because I worked closely with the three men I had very intense feelings for, but because it kept me on my toes and my mind occupied.

I'd thought I wanted a boring job that was the same thing day after day, but now that I was really in the swing of things, I couldn't imagine sitting at a desk all day doing data entry.

Things had been different between the four of us since our Hampton weekend trip. There was a closeness that had developed that wasn't there before and a happiness that I hadn't realized was missing not just from me but from the three of them.

There was no explanation for the intensity of feelings I

felt other than I'd met the ones I should spend the rest of my life with.

Of course with that came the doubt that they felt the same way and wondering how that would work. We wouldn't be able to get married and what would happen down the road when we wanted to have children? Did they even want children?

I finished writing my sticky notes to each of them and stuck them on the folders I'd prepared with an agenda and the proposed contract with the Badden brothers.

It seemed like a done deal with the country's leading sports equipment and apparel company, but things could always fall apart at the negotiating table. I'd seen it happen enough times to know that until the ink was dry on the page, anything could go wrong.

I couldn't find much about the Badden's legal counsel since they had their own team that worked in-house for them, just like LRG did.

The guys were already in the conference room preparing for their ten o'clock meeting. If things went to plan, they'd be done by late afternoon, but if not, negotiations might go into the evening.

I grabbed the folders I'd prepared, along with a bowl of treats, and walked down the hall to the main room. I knocked and when I heard a 'yeah' I entered. "Good morning."

I hadn't seen them since they'd left Luca's at the crack of dawn. We'd been rotating to each of their places every few days, except mine for obvious reasons. I hadn't stayed in my own place all week.

"Good morning, Paige. You look cute today." Garrett looked up from his laptop, a smile spreading across his handsome face. "Candy?"

"Yes, sir." I put the bowl of fun-sized candy in the middle of the table.

"Paige," Luca groaned. "Don't throw out 'yes, sirs' at work. I wouldn't want one of the clients to think I was popping a boner for him."

Ryker leaned back in his chair at the head of the table, folding his hands on his stomach. "I don't know, Luca. Alexander Badden was voted one of the hottest bachelors under twenty-five a few years ago. He might be looking hot today."

"Ethan is going to have a hard time taking meeting minutes when Paige goes on breaks." Garrett grabbed a piece of candy from the bowl. "This was a bad idea. I'm going to eat candy all day."

"Good. It will make you even sweeter." I smiled as I handed them each their folders, putting the others for the Baddens in front of empty seats. They had been sent digital copies of everything, but it was often easier to work with a paper copy.

"What's this?" Ryker took the sticky note off his folder.

"What's what?" I walked to the credenza against the far wall and opened the sliding door to grab water bottles for anyone who needed one.

"You dirty girl. I'm going to hold you to this." Ryker folded the pink note and put it in his jacket pocket.

I'd written them each a short note of encouragement

but also added congratulatory under-the-desk blow jobs were in store for them.

"This is the dream." Luca held his note to his chest before slipping his into his pocket.

"Can I get mine now? My pants are feeling a little tight in the crotch region." Garrett adjusted himself under the table.

I needed to ignore them and not spur them on. The last thing I wanted was to have to squeeze my thighs together the whole meeting thinking about dropping to my knees for them. "Is there anything else I need to get? They should be here any minute."

"Just your ass in this chair." Luca patted the seat next to him. He was sitting to the left of Ryker, and Garrett sat to the right.

"Are you going to be able to keep your hands to yourself?" I went to the door, needing to go get my laptop and coffee.

"I am the consummate professional, Ms. Harper. Hey! Don't kick me!"

I shook my head at Luca's ridiculousness and left the conference room, heading back to my office to grab my stuff. I really hoped the meeting went well for the guys because it would be one less strain on their relationship.

Ryker had been making tremendous efforts to not be so attached to work, and his relationships with his two best friends had improved right before my eyes. It helped that they also were working on the community project with Ryker and that brought him a level of peace over his past.

I unplugged my laptop, grabbed a notepad and sticky

notes, along with a pen, and turned to head back down the hall but stopped dead in my tracks.

My stomach dropped to the floor as I watched six people file into the conference room, one whose side profile I was very familiar with.

As if sensing someone was staring at him in horror, he turned his head, his smile sliding right off his face.

Daniel.

What the fuck was he doing in New York City, at my work, with clients that had their own legal counsel?

I darted out of the doorway so he couldn't see me anymore and slowly sat down in the chair across from my desk, my mind working so hard it was using all of my energy. It had to be a mistake. I was just seeing things.

I opened my laptop, had to type my password twice because my hands were shaking so badly, and pulled up the law firm I used to work at. Maybe they'd partnered with the Badden brothers. Thompson and Turner specialized in corporate law, so it could have been a possibility. This was such a big business deal, maybe the Baddens wanted more expertise.

Clicking on the associates tab, I sucked in a breath as I scrolled through the list of senior associates. He wasn't there. I quickly checked the partners' list, which was something Daniel had been striving for since he went to work at his father's law firm.

There was a knock on my open door and I jumped, knocking my stuff off the edge of my desk where it had been precariously perched.

"Damn, girl. You act like you've been caught watching porn." Ethan chuckled. "The meeting is ready to start."

I shut my laptop and picked up my spilled belongings. "Thanks. I was just checking something."

"Hey, are you okay?" Ethan came in and shut the door. "You look like you're about to pass out. Did you eat breakfast?"

I shut my eyes, begging for the tears to stay away. I didn't need this today and not just because it was an important meeting. Because it was the day before I would have promised myself to Daniel.

"Have they already been assholes to you? I'll kill them." Ethan squatted down in front of me. "Sweetie... talk to me so I can help."

"It's him." At Ethan's confusion, I shook my head in utter disbelief. "Daniel. My ex."

"I know it's going to be a hard weekend for you. Just try to keep your mind occupied, okay?" He patted my knee and stood. "Taking notes for that boring ass meeting is a good way to start."

I opened my mouth to tell him I meant Daniel was in the meeting but then closed it. The last thing I wanted was for Ethan to be involved. I could handle being in the same room with Daniel, couldn't I?

"Paige?" Ethan took my things from me. "Come on, I'll walk you there."

Numbly, I nodded and stood, smoothing a hand down the front of my blouse and adjusting my pants. I could just ask Ethan to go take meeting minutes for me. I could grab my phone from my desk and text the guys that you-know-who was right there. But then what?

If they knew he was *the* Daniel, they would ruin the meeting by beating the shit out of him.

I followed Ethan to the cracked-open conference room door where masculine voices were chatting animatedly. He handed me my things and put his hand on my arm. "Message me if you need a break, okay?"

I nodded. I could do this. I could walk into that meeting with my head held high, a smile on my face. I didn't in the slightest believe in manifestation, but just this once I willed the confidence I'd suddenly lost to come back and walked in.

"There she is!" Luca beamed at me and pulled out the seat next to him. "Gentlemen, this is our assistant, Paige Harper. She'll be here for whatever we need and will be taking minutes."

I plastered a smile on my face and walked around the table to my seat, horrified it was next to Daniel. I might have been okay had he been sitting anywhere else, but right next to me?

As I sat down, I could practically feel the tension radiating from him.

Ignore him. Do your job.

The meeting started with introductions, so I could put those in the notes, but then Daniel moved his foot right next to mine, nudging it.

I stiffened, my fingers pausing momentarily as I turned my chair slightly to adjust my legs.

Luca glanced over at me and then leaned into my ear. "You okay?"

I nodded and relaxed as his hand slid onto my thigh. It wasn't sexual in any way, at least to me, but it was comforting. I prayed no one would notice, but everyone was focused on Ryker.

Thirty minutes passed, then an hour, then two. I somehow managed to take notes while Daniel was speaking, and even laughed at one of Luca's cheeky comments.

Ethan knocked on the door around noon and poked his head in. "Lunch is here. Do you want me to bring it in or set it up in conference room B?"

"Conference room B would be good. Thanks, Ethan." Ryker shut his laptop. "Shall we break for lunch?"

"Thank fuck, I'm starving." Noah Badden was the first to get to his feet and his brother, Gabriel shot him a glare. "What? A man's gotta eat."

"I did appreciate the candy. Usually, during meetings, people put out nuts and seeds like we're birds."

Luca leaned in close, lowering his voice. "You want to have lunch in my office?"

I knew he didn't mean actual lunch, but the alternative was being social in a room with Daniel in it. "Sure. I'm going to run to the bathroom really quick. Grab mine for me?"

Before anyone else could stop me to talk, I was out the door and heading down the hall. The bathrooms were around the corner, and as soon as I was inside, my body relaxed.

I went into a stall, took care of my business, and when I

came out of the stall, I wasn't alone. "Daniel! What are you doing in here?" My voice was shaky, and I hoped he didn't notice.

He was standing right in the entryway, blocking my exit, his hands shoved in his pockets. "Why were they looking at you like that?"

"Who? You shouldn't be in here." I went to the sink and turned on the water to give myself something to do.

"Ryker, Garrett, and Luca." He said their names like they were beneath him, but that couldn't have been more inaccurate. "Luca had his hand on your thigh, Paige."

"I don't know what you're talking about." I washed my hands like I was about to perform a surgery.

"Bull shit, Paige." He moved from the doorway, and I could see him looking me up and down from the reflection in the mirror. "Have you fucked all of them? Is that why they all kept glancing at you the whole damn meeting like you hung the fucking moon?"

"You're delusional." I turned the water off, my jaw throbbing with tension.

"Look at me and tell me you haven't fucked at least one of them." Why was he doing this? Why did it matter?

I looked at him through the mirror but wasn't going to give him ammunition to be an asshole. "You don't work at Thompson and Turner anymore?"

He ran his hand over his hair, making a mess of the neatly styled brown strands. "My dad was pissed that *you* left so he fired me."

"You mean he was pissed that you cheated on me causing me to abruptly quit?" He wasn't about to gaslight me into thinking it was my fault his dad ousted him from the firm.

His jaw clenched and I could tell he was balling his fists in his pockets. "What will my new bosses think when they find out these guys are sexually harassing an employee?"

"You're so full of yourself. We're over. We've been over since you stuck your dick in someone else." I couldn't believe he was confronting me like this in a bathroom of all places.

He snorted and crossed his arms over his chest. "So, I'm right? You're sleeping with all three of them? They are taking advantage of you, Paige. This has lawsuit written all over it."

"I love them."

"You love them?" He threw his head back and laughed, the sound cutting me straight through my heart. "They're taking advantage of you, and I won't stand for it. You and I might not be together anymore, but I still care about you."

I was trying so hard not to cry, but the sting behind my eyes was getting harder and harder to stop. "They've done nothing wrong. I met them before I even worked here. You need to leave."

He stared at me in silence for longer than was comfortable before speaking again. "They'll get bored with the sick little game they're playing with you, and then what, Paige?"

Bile rose in my throat as he hit one of my biggest insecurities right on the fucking head. I swallowed it down but was unable to stop the tears from spilling over. "How did I ever think I actually loved you?"

He grabbed my arm as I tried to walk past him. "We were supposed to get married tomorrow."

"Let me go," I said through clenched teeth.

He let me go with a sigh, and I practically ran out of the bathroom, careening right into Ethan, who'd just been standing there. Oh my God. Had he been listening?

"Paige." The way he said my name sent a chill down my spine. He moved me out of the way as Daniel exited the bathroom, adjusting his tie.

He glanced between us, rolled his eyes, and then walked around the corner.

"All you have to say is the word and I'll get a shovel." Ethan enveloped me into a hug, and I bit down on my lip so hard to stop myself from breaking down that I drew blood. "Why didn't you say something?"

"You were listening?" I pulled away, wiping the tears that had escaped with the back of my hand.

"I saw him follow you in there and yeah... I cracked the door just enough to hear. I would have come in and punched the shit out of him, but I had been hoping you would."

I shook my head and wrapped my arms around my stomach. "I can't do this."

"Fuck. Okay. Do you want me to go get the guys?" He leaned back and peered around the corner.

"No. I... fuck. I told Luca we'd eat in his office. I can't go back over there like this... I don't want them to know,

Ethan. This could ruin their deal." I was starting to panic, my breaths coming faster and faster.

What if Daniel said something? What if one of my guys started a fight? What if. What if. What if.

"Hey. Shh." Ethan took my hands in his. "Here's what we're going to do. I'm going to go get your bag from your office and bring it to you so you can leave. Then I'll tell them that you were projecting out of both ends-"

"Ethan." I snorted a laugh despite everything.

"I'll take minutes for the meeting and try my best not to strangle this Daniel guy." He nodded his head like his plan was the best in the world. "Go wait by the elevator. Is your phone in your bag?"

"Yes." I squeezed his hands. "Thank you, Ethan."

"No problem. Don't let anyone ever tell you that me being nosy is a bad thing." He winked and let go of my hands. "Now go." He disappeared down the hall toward my office.

I walked toward the elevators, wanting nothing more than for the day—the whole weekend, honestly—to be over.

Chapter 28

Pastrami Made Me Do It

Paige

Pastrami Palace. Garrett had said it could cure a
bad day, and I was in need of that cure.

I don't know what led me to walk to the deli,
but as I stood in the long lunch line, the smell of pastrami
brought me comfort.

What didn't bring me comfort was the thought of
Daniel ruining the deal for LRG. Would he really stoop so
low to tell his bosses that I was sleeping with all three of
mine?

I pulled my phone out of my purse to a string of
messages in a group text.

Luca: *Did the thought of lunch with me make you
that ill?*

Garrett: *Shut up. Paige, are you okay?*

Luca: *I bet she's laughing into the porcelain bowl she's currently hugging.*

Garrett: *She probably isn't home yet.*

Ryker: *Please tell me you called our car service and are going to one of our places.*

Luca: *Do you want one of us to come take care of you? Say the word.*

Me: *I'm still a little queasy but think I'll be fine. What did Ethan tell you exactly?*

Ryker: *That you ran into the bathroom and then came out looking like you'd survived a whirlwind tour with your best friends Salma and Nella.*

Garrett: *What did you eat for breakfast? Maybe it was the coffee?*

Me: *It might have been the cream in the coffee. I had one of your breakfast burritos, but if you guys aren't sick...*

Luca: *That's what you get for not going to Perky Squirrel.*

Me: *Lesson learned. I'm sorry I'm missing the rest of the meeting.*

Ryker: *Don't worry about it. We just want you to feel better. We'll bring home stuff for Garrett to make soup.*

The guilt over lying to them about why I left was already gnawing at me like a rat who stole an Oreo.

I was finally at the counter and Jay's face lit up with recognition. I was surprised he'd remembered me since I'd only come in once with Garrett.

"No Garrett? Don't tell me he didn't treat you right."

Jay put his order pad on the top of the deli display, his hand poised to write down my order.

I smiled, feeling a twinge of sadness at the thought of Garrett breaking up with me. "He's treated me right. Just here for a bad day pastrami sandwich with extra mustard."

After paying, I managed to snag an empty table for two right next to the table me and Garrett had sat at. Maybe coming here for lunch wasn't such a good idea. I could always ask for my sandwich to go instead.

My phone buzzed and I took it out again. This time it was Ethan who said he'd update me on what was happening at the meeting.

Ethan: *Paige. His last name is Turner.*

Me: *I know you can't see me, but I'm rolling my eyes at you.*

Ethan: *That's red flag number one.*

Me: *He hasn't said anything about me yet, has he?*

Ethan: *No. They are all too busy stuffing their faces. Don't worry, I'm keeping my stank eye on him. Ready for red flag number two?*

Me: *I don't think I have a choice.*

Ethan: *You can tell me to stop. I just thought it would cheer you up hearing me rip apart all his flaws.*

Me: *Go for it.*

Ethan: *He's got a really long stray nose hair.*

I nearly spit out the sip of soda I'd just taken. It gave me great joy to know he'd missed a hair trimming.

"There's that smile that was missing when you

ordered." Jay set a tray with my sandwich in front of me. "Extra mustard, good day pastrami only."

"Thank you." I'd barely met this guy, yet he treated me like an old friend.

"Whatever might be the cause of your sadness, you did the right thing coming here. Nothing is more important than taking care of yourself." He knocked on the table and then left me to my lunch.

He was right. Taking care of myself was important and trying to sit through any more of that meeting with that asshole was only going to hurt me.

As I started eating, I started making my own red flag list. I'd ignored so much and just become complacent with a mediocre relationship. Now that I had three men who treated me like a queen, it made me realize how truly shitty Daniel treated me.

It wasn't that I couldn't see Daniel's reasoning behind me paying him rent and paying for some of the wedding, but to dump every single cent I had to my name? I'd done it because he'd said we were partners, and it wouldn't have mattered after we were married anyway. But we should have already been partners even before we were engaged.

He really didn't deserve any more space in my brain, but knowing he was back at LRG with my men and potentially ruining a big deal for them almost made my pastrami sandwich unpalatable.

Then he threw in my face that they'd get bored of me just like he did. And I'd just... ran. I ran away instead of telling him there was nothing boring about me. Maybe he'd been the problem all along.

I finished my sandwich and pulled out my phone.

Me: *Text me when the deal is signed. I'll be waiting on the sixty-ninth floor.*

Ethan: *I just got glared at for snort laughing about sixty-ninth. What are you going to be waiting for exactly?*

Me: *Don't you worry.*

Ethan: *Should I get some popcorn?*

Me: *No... I don't think.*

I had no clue what I was doing, but I knew that I needed to do something, or the weight of Daniel was going to continue to bring me down.

It didn't surprise me when Ethan texted me a little over an hour later that the contract had been signed. The negotiations in the morning had gone well since both parties had been prepared and willing to compromise.

I'd hung out in the breakroom, mostly keeping to myself. Most people knew me since an email had gone out when I'd come back. I couldn't help but wonder if anyone knew I was also in a relationship with my three bosses. But when I found myself thinking about if I cared, I didn't.

I used the stairs to get to the seventieth floor, not wanting to miss Daniel. My plan was pretty straightforward and was what I needed to do to finally let go.

Ethan was leaving the conference room as I approached, Fatima, the company's head lawyer following him out. His eyes widened at the sight of me. "You were actually serious about waiting?" He shut the door so no one could hear.

Fatima gave me a nod and headed for the elevators, her phone already to her ear. I was grateful she didn't stick around because the fewer people that knew about this the better.

"Yes, I was serious. Are they all still in there?" I had expected them to all be filing out and I could just pull Daniel to the side and say what needed to be said. The things I should have said to him in the bathroom.

"Yeah, they're talking about the gala. What do you need me to do?" He put his hand on my arm reassuringly. "I've got your back."

I handed him my purse and tote bag. "Put those in my office for me?"

"Um. I will but what are you doing? Are you going in there?" He looked uncertain but also excited.

"Do you have a better idea? I'll just ask to speak to him alone." It was bold to do in front of his bosses and my boyfriends, but the contract was signed and they'd see it anyway whether it was in the hall or the conference room.

"I'm going to need to see this." He slung the bags over his shoulder, shifting his laptop and notebook in his arms. "Should I make an announcement like the WWE? You can be known for your uncanny ability to deliver life-threatening paper cuts." He laughed at his own joke. "Get it?"

"You're ridiculous." I laughed. "No, it won't be violent."

He stepped out of the way just as the door opened

with Ryker on the other side. He looked confused at first and I didn't give him the chance to ask me what I was doing back.

I walked in, my eyes finding Daniel, who was busy putting his things into his bag. "Daniel, I'd like to speak to you. Alone."

The room went silent, like someone had pressed the pause button for everyone except Daniel. He zipped his bag and looked up at me, amusement on his smug face. I wanted to slap it off him.

"Paige, what's going on?" Ryker said under his breath.

Heads ping ponged between me and Daniel and my cheeks heated. No one was moving and I didn't necessarily want an audience. "We can just go to my office."

Garrett was staring intently at Daniel who was now leaning back in his chair with his arms across his chest. "Whatever you have to say, you can say it in front of everyone."

Luca suddenly stood, his chair flying back and hitting the credenza behind him. "No. Fucking. Way. You're *that* Daniel?"

I moved toward the conference table, bracing my hands on the back of an unoccupied chair. "Yes. I need to speak to him alone. Don't make this into a big deal."

"Maybe just wait until he goes to the bathroom and catch him unaware. It's only fair," Ethan said.

Gabriel looked at me. "He followed you into the restroom? Is that why you left?"

This was not going to plan—not that I had much of one in the first place. "Daniel is my ex-fiancé."

Daniel cleared his throat. "She's why I amicably parted ways with my father's firm. She was his executive assistant. I guess she decided to move up from the owner's son to the owners themselves."

The door shut loudly behind me. I could practically feel Ryker's anger radiating off of him, and I hoped none of it was directed at me. I hadn't been forthcoming with the bit of information about my employment status with Daniel's father.

Luca and Garrett both looked ready to throw punches, and the Badden brothers and their other lawyer were just along for the show.

Be strong.

"What you said in the bathroom wasn't true." I held up my hand when Garrett started to say something. "They aren't going to get bored with me because they care about me and there is nothing boring about what I have with them."

Daniel laughed mockingly. "They saw the perfect opportunity. You're desperate for attention, and they were willing to take advantage of that. Without a doubt, they'll break your heart and you'll come crying back to me. I can guarantee it."

The room was silent and thick with tension as my hands squeezed the chair in front of me. But I didn't look away from the man I'd thought loved me.

He had no idea what he was saying, but it didn't matter; his words would continue to do damage if I let them. "You don't know anything about Ryker, Garrett, or Luca... or me for that matter. You claim you cheated on me because I was boring in bed, but there has been nothing boring with them."

Daniel rolled his eyes. "Of course they aren't bored yet. You're their new shiny toy."

I ignored him and started counting off on my fingers. "Nothing boring in the gym, in front of the window, on the counter, with all three at once, in a dark cornfield-"

Ryker stepped behind me and put his hand on my hip, squeezing possessively. "Don't forget all the times you've made all three of us come at once."

Daniel's face morphed from smug to a mixture of anger and disbelief as he stood, his hands planted on the table. "What kind of men are you?" He looked over at Gabriel. "We can still void the contract. There's a forty-eight-hour cancellation clause with good reason, and this is a very good reason. You don't want to do business with people like this."

"You can't do that." I gave the brothers a pleading look, unable to get a read on how they were feeling.

They said nothing though. What must have been going through their minds to hear all of this?

"What kind of men are we?" Ryker stepped away from me and rounded the table, facing Daniel with a calm rage burning in his eyes. "We're men who love her. Now get the fuck out of our office."

The air around us vibrated as Ryker grabbed him by the arm and pushed him firmly toward the door. Luca and Garrett took up positions behind him, ready to join in if push came to shove.

I could do nothing but stare at Ryker. They loved me?

Daniel wrenched his arm away, going to the door that Ethan was holding open. "This is completely out of line. You can't kick me out because I called you out on sexually harassing your employee!"

Gabriel stood, buttoning his suit jacket and picking up Daniel's bag. He was kind of scary in the way his face was blank as he went to the door and shoved Daniel's bag into his chest. "You're fired. Now leave before security is called and you embarrass yourself further."

Daniel's face crumpled as he clutched onto his bag to keep it from falling. "What? But-"

"It was inevitable, Turner. I can't have someone working for me that corners their ex in a women's restroom and then acts like this." Gabriel returned to his seat, not an ounce of emotion showing.

Daniel stood there for a moment, mouth open in shock, before he finally turned and walked out.

I started to go after him, but Garrett grabbed my hand. "He doesn't deserve your sympathy, Paige."

"You're right, he doesn't, but I need to say one last thing... without an audience." I pulled my hand away and rushed to catch up with Daniel. "Daniel?"

He stopped at the elevators, stabbing the down button, but didn't turn around. "What?"

As much as he deserved everything he'd brought upon himself, I couldn't help but feel a little sorry and sad for him. "I know somewhere in your heart you know what you did was wrong."

He shook his head but didn't look back at me or speak.

"When you love someone, you cherish them. You don't

315

toss them aside like a piece of trash for a rat to eat. I just hope that one day you find someone who you want to cherish."

The elevator doors opened, and he stepped on, finally facing me with regret and defeat in his eyes. "Goodbye, Paige."

"Goodbye, Daniel."

The doors slid shut and for the first time in months, I felt like the past was finally behind me.

Chapter 29

All Ours

Luca

The very last thing I wanted to do was attend a gala where my mother was going to try to convince me that an arranged marriage was in everyone's best interests. Sure, it would mean more money for our family, but when was it going to be enough for her?

Before I met Paige, I would have seriously considered marrying for business if it was the right woman. Clara was not the right woman since she didn't even like men. Things would have been easier if I could have just told my mother that, but it wasn't my place.

And how would Paige feel? Going to the gala on what would have been her wedding night was one thing, but having to hear my mother go on and on about marrying me off? It made me a little sick to think about.

She'd been through so much in the past few months with it all coming to a head at the business meeting the day before. We'd had no clue she was sitting right next to her ex for half the day. An ex that showed his true colors in front of us all.

Had we been a little upset she didn't say something about him being there or about working with him and his father? Maybe a little, but it was mostly because we didn't want to see her in pain.

"I'm surprised you're the first one ready." Garrett walked down the hall, his shiny black shoes clicking on the stone floor. "Usually, we have to wait on you."

I turned from where I'd been staring out at Central Park, nursing a glass of scotch. "The sooner we go, the sooner we can come home."

Garrett grabbed one of the three glasses I'd poured and came to join me at the window. "Paige still wants to go, otherwise I'd say let's just skip it."

"My mother would never make me cannoli again if I missed this. Not just because she wants to try to marry me off but because it's in our hotel." I sighed and took a sip of my drink. "There are just some things in life I'm not willing to go without, and cannoli are one of those things."

Garrett chuckled. "You and fucking cannoli."

"Okay, Mr. Life Changing Pastrami." I looked over my shoulder as Ryker entered the room. For once he didn't look uncomfortable in his tuxedo. "And Mr. Where's My Cardigan."

"Maybe you should try a cardigan sometime, you might like it." Ryker grabbed his glass. "How am I the last one ready to go?"

I shrugged. "It doesn't take much when you're already good-looking."

Garrett laughed, shaking his head. "You willing to tell Paige that when she's ready?"

He had me there, so I raised my glass to my two best friends for a toast. "To a long-lasting friendship that has been through some tough times but come out the other side stronger."

We clinked our glasses together and all turned to look out the window. I took another sip of my scotch, the feeling of warmth spreading throughout my body. I wasn't sure if I'd finally had enough scotch or if it was because everything was falling into place.

For a while, I hadn't been sure our friendship would make it. We'd really been starting to struggle; fighting more and not wanting to be around each other. But now I couldn't think of any better way to spend my time than with Garrett, Ryker, and Paige.

As if on cue, Paige's heels clicked on the floor, and we all turned.

My breath caught in my throat as I took her in. The curve of her hips and the swell of her breasts made my pulse race. She hadn't shown me the dress she'd ended up going with, and now I was glad because I would have ripped it right off of her in the dressing room.

She radiated confidence as she walked across the room, the burgundy material parting to show her right leg every time she stepped forward.

"What do you think?" She stopped in front of us and

spun around, giving us a full view of how stunningly beautiful she was.

"Hot damn." I threw back the rest of my scotch.

Garrett grabbed her around the waist, pulling her to him. "I think you have some mustard right here." He kissed right at the V in her neckline, and she giggled, swatting at him.

"You look beautiful." Ryker took her into his arms next, pushing her perfectly curled hair away from her neck and kissing her there.

I moved in behind her, kissing her exposed shoulder blade. There was something so sexy about having a V in the back of the dress too. It wasn't too far down, but just enough to expose the elegance of her upper back and shoulders. Was I getting hard over her shoulders? Yes. Yes, I was.

"You guys need to stop, or we'll be late." She sighed as Garrett took her arm and peppered kisses from her wrist all the way to her shoulder.

"Are you really ours?" Garrett murmured against her skin.

"Yes." She breathed her reply, swaying a bit on her feet.

Ryker groaned against her ear. "We should stop."

She made a noncommittal noise in her throat and leaned back against me, her ass connecting with my ever-hardening dick.

That seemed to bring her back down and she pulled away from us, giving us a stern look. "You three need to behave."

"You're the one who picked this dress." I wanted to kneel down and put her leg over my shoulder to explore under the slit. "It is missing something, though."

She looked down at herself, running her hands over the chiffon and lace. "It is?"

"Mm." I reached into my jacket pocket and pulled out a black velvet box we'd picked out earlier in the day. "It will go perfectly with the beading at your waist."

Her eyes widened and then filled with tears as I opened it to reveal a platinum and diamond pendant necklace that was one larger heart with three small ones linked in the middle of it.

"It's gorgeous." She took it from me with shaking hands and ran her fingers over the diamonds on the bigger heart. She freed the necklace and handed it to Ryker. "Put it on for me?"

"Gladly." He secured it around her neck, and it hung perfectly where her cleavage started.

"It's perfect. Thank you." Her smile warmed me more than any amount of scotch could. "We should get going before we never leave."

I wasn't opposed to never leaving, but tonight was as good a night as ever to show not just my mother, but everyone in attendance that Luca Caponetti, Ryker St. James, and Garrett Wilson were no longer single.

Even I had to admit, the gala was one of the more impressive fundraising events I'd been to, and I'd been to a lot.

There was a dinner followed by an evening of entertainment, presentations, and silent auctions which all benefited an arts foundation that brought art education to schools across the city. It wasn't just that, though; it was a networking dream.

With so many people to talk to, I'd managed to avoid my mother since she'd arrived with my father shortly before dinner. Since I'd added Paige as my plus one, they'd moved us to a table to accommodate the four of us.

But my luck had run out as we chatted with the Badden brothers about potential sponsorships with Ryker's new community project.

"Luca." My mom slid in next to me, looping her arm through mine. "It's so nice to see my oldest son finally."

I looked over at her and smiled before kissing both of her cheeks. "Mamma, you look lovely as usual. I'm sorry I haven't been around; you know how busy I am."

"Leonardo is just as busy as you are, and he finds time to see me." She looked over just as my brother slid into place next to her. Who knew where my dad was.

I heard a giggle and looked over at Paige across our small group. She was chatting with Noah Badden and had her hand covering her mouth as she stared back at me, her eyes widening as if I should know what she was laughing about.

"Good. You're both here. I have someone I want you to meet." I reached out my hand to Paige and she placed her hand in mine, coming to stand at my side. "This is my girl-friend, Paige."

My mother's eyes nearly bugged out of her head. "Girl-friend? This is news to me."

"It's nice to meet you, ma'am." Paige extended her hand, and my mom thankfully took it. "I've heard a lot about your fabulous cannoli."

"I see Luca has already taught you how to get in my good graces." She took Paige's hand between hers. "It's lovely to meet you."

I looked over my mother's head at my brother, who looked just as surprised as I was that our mother wasn't throwing a conniption fit over me having a girlfriend.

"Leo, where's your date?" I gave him a smug look because the last thing any of us wanted to do was bring up our love lives around Mom.

He shot me a glare and then looked at Paige who was giggling again. She'd had a few glasses of champagne, but not enough to giggle over nothing.

"What's so funny?" I pulled her into my side, my mouth at her ear.

"Nothing..." She giggled again as my mom turned to my brother. "It's just... your brother's name is Leonardo."

"So?" I didn't quite know where she was going with how his name was funny.

Ryker kissed Paige's cheek, taking her hand. "Ninja Turtles."

"I'm not going to marry Clara, Mother. Luca isn't even engaged yet and look!" He gestured wildly toward us.

Ah, shit.

My mother turned and her eyes widened comically at me holding Paige close on one side and Ryker holding her hand on the other.

"Yeah so..." I looked over at Ryker and he shrugged. "Paige is my girlfriend but she's also Ryker's and Garrett's."

"Oh, my." My mother put her hand over her heart. "Luca Michelangelo Caponetti."

Paige absolutely lost it at hearing my full name and turned into Ryker's chest. I'd really give her something to laugh about later.

"Neither of us is going to marry Clara, Mother. She's a perfectly lovely woman and will make someone very happy, but not us." I was pretty sure my brother knew about Clara as well.

"I need to go speak with your father. If you'll excuse me." My mom kissed me and then my brother on our cheeks and then walked away like a fire was lit under her ass.

"Jesus Christ, Luca. Warn me next time you plan on ripping apart Mom's carefully orchestrated plans." Leo moved next to me and clapped me on the shoulder. "So, you're a sharing man now?"

I rolled my eyes. "Sharing insinuates we divide her up. This is a joint relationship."

Paige finally got herself together and turned back to us. "Sorry about that. Champagne really loosens me up."

"Does it now?" Leo smirked and I elbowed him in the side. "Ow. Fuck. Don't tell me you weren't thinking the same thing, asshole."

"She's my girlfriend. Go find your own before Mom finds one for you," I teased.

He sighed. "I'm not done sowing my oats yet." He looked over at Ryker. "So, I heard that you're starting a non-profit and building a community center?"

While Ryker and my brother fell into conversation about planning and donors and how my brother could help fast-track everything, I pulled Paige out onto the dance floor.

"Your mom seemed nice. You made her sound like she was going to force you into marrying Clara." Paige wrapped her arms around my neck as we swayed to the music from the live band.

"She's just very business minded. Even more so than my dad is, which is saying a lot. They were in an arranged marriage, and it's worked out for them pretty well. I guess with me being thirty-one and Leo being almost thirty and both unattached, she is getting anxious." I rested one hand on the small of Paige's back and pulled one of her hands into mine.

"Well now you're attached, and she can stop worrying." Paige pulled her bottom lip between her teeth. "Right?"

I kissed her fingers before holding her hand against my chest. "Right."

Garrett joined us on the dance floor, drawing lots of curious stares as he moved behind Paige. At first, he just had his hands on her hips like he was at some middle school dance, but it didn't take him long to wrap one arm around her waist.

"Everyone is staring," Paige whispered as we pressed in even closer to her. "And I can feel both of you."

"Let them stare." Garrett rested his head against hers. "Luca, your brother is quite impressive."

"Wait. Are we talking about your dicks?" Paige started laughing.

"No, goofball." I pressed a little closer so she could really feel me. "At least, I don't think we are."

Garrett kissed her shoulder and groaned in frustration. "I was ignoring the comment because I'm barely holding myself back."

"It's difficult when she's looking as delectable as she is, isn't it? And that slit showing off her leg? I haven't stopped thinking about pulling it to the side and burying my face between your thighs." I brought our hands back to my mouth and bit one of her knuckles gently.

Her swaying faltered a bit and the hand wrapped around my neck dug into my hair. "Don't tease me."

Garrett cleared his throat. "As I was saying. Leo's already pretty much convinced Ryker to let him be the executive director. They're already talking about a gala."

That made me smile. "That would be good for him. They both have the same workaholic personalities and have always gotten along." My brother had been a little lost lately and running a charity might be just what he needed.

"I didn't understand a word either of you just spoke with your dicks pressed against me instead of inside me." Paige wiggled ever so slightly between us.

"Fuck me." Garrett grabbed her hand and pulled her off the dance floor.

I laughed, following them to where Ryker and Leo had just parted from shaking hands. "Leo, we need to steal Ryker."

"I'm not even going to ask." He walked away laughing and shaking his head.

"What's going on? Need me for a dance? Not sure how three of us will work out there." Ryker rubbed his chin in contemplation. "We could make a triangle around her I guess."

"Let's go home." Paige led us back to our table where Paige had left her shawl and clutch.

Ryker cocked an eyebrow at us, and while Paige was preoccupied, Garrett and I melted back into the crowd. After all, it was only fitting since we were at the place where it all began that we have a little fun.

Chapter 30

Circle of Love (and Orgasms)

Garrett

Luca and I waited in a small alcove just past the VIP security desk for Paige and Ryker to go to the private elevators. It felt a bit surreal that we were back there again, but this time my head and my heart were in the right place.

"What is taking them so long?" Luca checked his phone for the millionth time, making sure nothing had changed.

"It's barely been a minute. Calm your ass down." I peeked around the corner. "See, they're coming."

I had to wonder what was going through her mind as Ryker led her through the doors and to the elevators. He was supposed to tell her there was a private after-party in an exclusive club on the top floor so she'd have no clue what was in store for her.

We waited for the door to close and then came out of

hiding to follow.

The security guard smirked at us and looked at his computer screen, which showed him which floors the elevators were currently on. "It will be a second. One is coming down right now."

"Thanks, man." Luca handed him a hundred as a couple came up behind us.

"Not a problem." He opened the door for us and stopped the couple from following us through.

The same elevator started to close just as we approached. We had perfect timing and walked right in. And just like before, Ryker had Paige up against the wall, his lips devouring hers.

Her right leg was hiked up around his hip, exposing almost her whole leg.

"What floor do you need?" Luca didn't bother pressing the floor before.

Ryker broke their kiss. "Forty."

Paige shuddered, her inhale of breath loud in the quiet elevator. "I thought-"

Ryker silenced her with his mouth, his hand running up and down her thigh. Fuck. Why hadn't I told him I wanted to do this?

Luca and I took our positions across the elevator, watching as Ryker kissed down her neck. Her eyes met mine and then moved to Luca's before closing as she tilted her head back against the wall.

Unfortunately for us, her dress wasn't the same stretchy material as last time, so watching Ryker take her nipple into his mouth was something we'd just have to wait for.

The elevator arrived at our destination and Ryker released her, taking her hand. "Grab her bag and shawl."

He led her off the elevator and I picked up her things. None of us spoke as Ryker got to the room and opened the door. Things were different this time, and we followed Ryker into the dimly lit hotel room.

Paige was already at the window, looking out at the view. She was so absolutely perfect for the three of us and she'd accepted us, flaws and all.

Before Ryker could even lock the door, she turned back toward us, a soft smile on her face. She lifted her arm, sliding down the zipper of her dress.

None of us moved, transfixed by the vision in front of us as she let the sleeves of her dress fall off her shoulders and the dress hit the ground. She kicked it to the side, her body only clad in lace that matched her dress and heels.

Her hands hung at her sides, not making any move to take off anything else. "Crawl to me."

Ryker sucked in a breath and lowered to his knees. I couldn't help but smile at how she was turning the tables on the three of us.

"All of you."

"Fuck me," Luca groaned, dropping down and following Ryker across the room.

"Garrett." God, I loved the way she sighed my name as Ryker ran his hand up her leg. "Come here."

"Make me." I did my best to hide my amusement when her eyes widened. I'd crawl to her eventually, but I wanted to see what she was going to do.

Ryker and Luca removed her heels and then both took their time kissing up her legs. Her eyes closed and her fingers clutched at their hair. Luca pulled her panties down her legs, looking up at her the whole time. I just knew she was dripping wet for us from the lust-filled expression across her face.

Before either of them could even have a taste, she pulled them to their feet with a few tugs of their hair. Luca kissed her, and Ryker unclasped her bra, taking a nipple in his mouth. She moaned against Luca's lips and then broke away before slowly lowering to her knees, her eyes on me the entire time.

"Undress for me." She sat back on her heels and waited as they took off their shoes and tuxedos.

I toed off my shoes as I loosened my bow tie and unbuttoned my vest and shirt, but didn't undress completely. Her eyes moved between all of us, her hands resting on her thighs. I wanted her to touch herself; to roll her nipples between her fingers.

"Perfect." She got back to her knees and a hand went on each one of their ass cheeks, pulling them closer to her.

I couldn't see a damn thing she was doing but I heard the distinct sound of sucking. Was she trying to suck both of them at once? If she did that, she would only be able to fit the tips.

"Garrett?" her sweet voice called out. "Are you ready to crawl?"

"What do I get if I do?" I took off my clothes the rest of the way, tossing them on the table.

"You can have my pussy first."

Well, I guess I was crawling sooner than I thought.

I lowered to my knees and crawled to her, watching her peeking around Luca's tattooed leg. Her eyes twinkled with mischief, at least until I crawled around her, pushed her legs farther apart, and lay on the ground under her.

"Why does he get a reward for... oh, fuck, Paige." I could see everything she was doing from underneath her as she flicked her tongue over his piercing.

I pulled Paige down onto my face, burying my tongue in her slick heat. Her moan turned muffled, but I didn't stop to see who had silenced her with their cock. I wanted her all over my face and ready for us.

She was trembling above me, her body ready for more if there had been only one of us. But there wasn't just one of us.

I plunged two fingers in, groaning against her clit at how hot and wet she was. I could be a greedy bastard and take her first like she said, but I wanted us all to enjoy her at once. I wanted her to feel so full that she'd never be okay with any other men touching her.

Sucking her clit, I slid my two fingers back to her ass, and she stiffened. We'd been getting her ready for this moment slowly over the past week, but she still seemed unsure of it.

"Relax, baby. You're doing so good," Ryker reassured her with a softness that was still taking some getting used to. "Keep sucking us while he gets you ready to take us."

"You going to take all three of us at once, beautiful?" Luca ended on a groan. "Your mouth almost feels as good as your pussy."

She made noises of approval, and I pushed one of my fingers into her ass, my dick throbbing at how tight and hot it was. As soon as I was past the ring of muscle, she relaxed some, which made it a whole hell of a lot easier to slide my finger in and out.

With my other hand, I returned to her pussy, pushing three fingers inside. Things quickly escalated to her not being able to suck cock, but I didn't stop adding fingers until she had two plunging inside her ass and three spread wide in her cunt.

"Garrett!" Her scream as she came all over my face was loud and completely unabashed.

She was more than ready for us as Ryker lifted her from my face and carried her to the bed. Luca threw a wet washcloth onto my chest with a smirk and turned to the bed where Ryker was already sitting on the edge of the bed with her standing between his legs while he squirted lube all over his dick.

He threw the bottle onto the bed behind him and grabbed her hips, backing her up. "Sit."

She made a strangled moaning sound as she slowly lowered her ass down onto his cock.

"Look at you taking his cock in your ass." Luca moved away from me and toward the bed as I cleaned up my hands and face. "How does he feel?"

She whimpered, and for a second, I wondered if I hadn't prepped her enough for him. But then she moaned. "Good."

"Let us know when you're ready for another cock." Luca knelt in front of them and spread her legs, so they were over Ryker's. "You look so good taking his cock like this."

Tossing the washcloth onto the table, I stood, my cock pointed straight out in front of me at its intended target. She'd only ever had two us at a time inside her like this, but the idea of all three of us practically made me come just from the air hitting my cock.

"I'm... ready," she panted, stilling on top of Ryker.

Luca lifted her left leg and placed it on his shoulder as he moved in to position, his cock at her entrance. "Breathe." He slowly pushed in, and Ryker and Paige both groaned.

I slowly stroked my cock, watching as Luca worked up his speed. There was just no way the position we'd thought would work would be comfortable for any of us.

"Luca, lie on the bed so Paige can ride your cock. This position isn't going to work." I couldn't tell you how many times we'd tried positions with a pillow trying to figure out how the puzzle pieces were going to go together.

Luca pulled out and Paige whimpered at the loss of his cock. I tilted her chin up to look at me and kissed her as Luca got himself situated in the middle of the bed.

"We want to make this good for you," I murmured against her lips.

"It's so good." She groaned as I helped her off Ryker's cock and turned her toward the bed.

She climbed on, sinking onto him with an ease that showed she was more than ready for my cock.

Excitement tingled down my spine as I crawled in behind her, pushing the head of my dick against her entrance. I slid in slowly, feeling her stretch to accommodate two cocks.

"You ready, baby?" I smoothed my hand down her back and gave her ass a light smack.

"I think so." She didn't sound one hundred percent sure, but once she had all three of us inside her, I thought her uncertainty would change.

I leaned back some as Ryker stood on the bed and put himself between me and Paige. One of the reasons we'd wanted to at least try the other position first was because of the leg strength his position took hovering over her while he fucked her ass and the fact that I'd have a front row seat to his ass in my face.

At least he had a nice ass.

I leaned back as he slowly pushed into her. And fuck, was it an amazing feeling. I felt like my cock was in a vice grip with Luca's cock against mine and Ryker's with the thin wall between us.

This was how it should have always been with us, but it just took the right woman to bring it out in us.

"I... can't... oh... my..." Paige could barely talk, and her pussy squeezed around me and Luca. "Oh my God!" she cried out, even though none of us were moving yet.

"You just have to say your word if you want us to stop." Ryker was shaking as he held still in front of me in a partially squatting position.

"Don't stop." She wiggled a bit and we all groaned. None of us were going to last long. "Please. Fuck me."

As soon as Ryker started to pull back, so did I. Now

that we were in the positions we were, I quite liked seeing our cocks come out of her.

We thrust back in at the same time, and she cried out in pleasure, her walls gripping me like she didn't want to let me go. It didn't take long for us to find a groove and for Luca to join in from underneath.

His piercing rubbing against me added a whole other element to the mix, and my entire body tingled as my balls tightened. I didn't want to be the first to go, but I was.

"Fuck!" I buried myself as far as I could go, my cum shooting out of me in the most extreme orgasm I had ever experienced.

"Garrett!" Paige clamped down on our dicks, another orgasm, rocketing through her.

"Holy mother of cannoli!" Luca shouted, the warmth of his release wrapping around me.

Ryker pistoned in and out of her, chasing his release before one last thrust sent him over the cliff. His ass clenched tight as he circled his hips, getting every last drop out of his cock.

While this was definitely not an everyday activity, I couldn't wait to do it again and again. I felt closer to my best friends than I'd ever been, and that was saying a lot.

After what felt like an hour but was more like two minutes, I poked Ryker's ass cheek. "I'm sliding out and getting a towel. Don't move."

We all needed a shower after that, but housekeeping probably wasn't going to be happy with a trail of dripping cum across the hotel floor. I returned with a few towels and handed them out, holding one between Paige's legs as they each pulled out.

"So beautiful..." I kissed her lower back since she was still lying on top of Luca.

"The cum dripping out of every hole or me?" Paige giggled and sighed in satisfaction.

"Both." I grabbed a second towel. "Let's get showered."

After a shower that was oddly tame considering all four of us were in there at once, we peeled the comforter off the bed and climbed in.

"When can we do this again?" Paige hooked a leg over mine, which gave Luca enough space to slide between her legs, his head resting on her lower abdomen.

"Whenever you want." Ryker was propped up on one elbow, trailing his fingers up and down her side. "Tomorrow, the day after that, and the day after that."

Luca pulled the sheet up, situating it so it bypassed his head and Paige could cover her upper body. I was burning up from all the skin-to-skin contact, so I didn't mind the cool air hitting me.

"We've come full circle, haven't we?" I played with some of Paige's damp hair.

"Hm." Paige yawned. "It's like the circle of life but with orgasms."

"Circle of love." I sat up, looking down at her. "I love you. I know it's crazy in such a short amount of time, but it feels like you're it for us."

"I think I loved you from the moment you sat down next to me." Ryker nuzzled his face against her neck.

"I loved you when I realized how much life you

brought back to Ryker." Luca traced a circle on her hip. "It's funny how we just... knew."

Her eyes filled with tears, and she sniffled. "I almost moved back, but now I'm glad I stuck around."

"Yeah?" I ran my knuckles along the side of her breast. "Because you just got railed by three of us at once?"

She giggled and swatted at me. "Because, somehow, you three put my heart back together and I not only fell in love with three amazing men, but with myself."

Epilogue

Paige

"Happy groundbreaking day!" I threw my arms around Ryker as he stared out the windows overlooking the city.

He turned, a smile lighting up his face before he leaned in and kissed me. "Good morning, beautiful."

Ryker tucked me under his arm and turned us to face the window. It was quiet moments like these, staring out as the city came to life, that filled me with so much happiness.

The past ten months with my partners had been nothing short of amazing. Not long after the gala, we'd decided to move in together since it was starting to become a pain in the ass to rotate to a different person's place every few days, and my short-term lease was up.

They'd ultimately left the decision of where we'd call home up to me, and it just made sense to move into the biggest place where we could still have our own spaces. As much as I loved Garrett's place, it just was too small for me to keep my sanity with three men.

Luca's penthouse had plenty of space for the four of us, and since Luca hadn't done much in the way of decorating, we all decided together how to make it all of ours. We each had our own rooms—which we rarely slept in—plus the primary suite where we'd ordered the biggest bed known to man.

Living together was comfortable and surprisingly easy. We, of course, had little squabbles about the level of cleanliness we were each willing to accept, but we agreed from the get-go to communicate instead of keeping our feelings bottled up inside.

"Why couldn't we have planned this thing for the afternoon?" Luca grumbled as he walked into the kitchen with Garrett and opened the cabinet with the cups.

"Shouldn't have stayed up so late last night." Garrett reached around Luca, who was staring blankly at the shelf of coffee mugs. "Your mug is in the dishwasher."

"Are the dishes clean?" Luca sounded so confused I had to laugh. He was not a morning person until he had his coffee, and then it was like his brain fully turned on.

"They're dirty." Garrett grabbed a second mug and filled them both. "You'll survive drinking out of this one."

"You know, Luca's morning grumpiness is really good practice for when we have kids."

Apparently, I needed coffee too.

"We're having kids?" Luca's voice cracked like he was going through puberty. "Holy shit! Are you pregnant?"

"No." I laughed, putting my hand on my stomach. "I

said when. We really should get a coffee maker for the bedroom, or maybe an IV drip."

"Back up a second." Ryker turned me to face him. "So, you do want children? With us?"

I shrugged. "I could go either way. Probably a conversation we need to have soon. To make sure we're all on the same *page*." I suppressed a giggle. I hated when other people made a joke out of my name, but it was fair game for myself.

"We all want kids." Ryker kissed my cheek. "We were thinking three."

My eyes widened. "You guys talked about this without me?"

Panic crossed Ryker's face, and I put my hand on his arm. It wasn't that it upset me, it was just surprising.

Garrett sighed and leaned against the kitchen island. "We did. It's a serious conversation, and with three potential fathers, we didn't want it to turn into a mess. And he's joking about three. We can have however many you want."

"What if I wanted ten?"

"Uh. Ten?" Luca shuffled over to where Ryker and I were. "I mean... why not make it eleven so they can be their own soccer team?"

"Lacrosse has ten." Garrett looked at me, his eyes filled with love. "We should get started on that right away."

I laughed. "I will not be having ten children."

"We'll be happy no matter what." Ryker looked at his watch. "We should get going so we're not late."

"I'm so excited and proud of all you three have done." I

looked between the three of them, still not believing they were all mine.

"Couldn't have done it without you." Ryker kissed my temple. "Now, let's go before someone decides to take their clothes off."

He wasn't wrong in his warning; it had happened far too many times to count.

My heart nearly exploded as I watched Ryker and his sister share a shovel to break ground on the St. James Foundation's community center. The other major phase one donors, which included Garrett, Luca, Leo, and the Badden brothers, all took part, wearing hard hats as cameras captured the moment.

After all of the initial fundraising and a metric ton of paperwork, Ryker was finally able to see his vision begin to come to life. A name for the center hadn't been decided yet but the first hurdle was conquered, and now construction and phase two fundraising could begin.

The crowd came to life as the ceremony came to a close. Ryker, Libby, and Leo were kept behind by the foundation's photographer as the donors dispersed into the crowd.

"What's going on there?" I nudged Ethan and nodded my chin toward Ryker's sister shooting daggers at Luca's brother as the photographer put him on the other side of her.

"That's a good question." He shoved his hands in his

pockets, a concerned expression taking the place of his usual carefree one. "Libby doesn't usually show her venom towards anyone."

"Libby has venom?" I laughed because that girl was the sweetest human being I'd ever met and had become an instant friend. She was quiet, but only around people she didn't know.

"Well, clearly, she does. Jesus, I feel my nuts shriveling a bit on Leo's behalf." Ethan hadn't looked away from them and his eyes narrowed as if he could read their minds.

Leo tried to put his hand on her lower back as they took the photo, and she moved her body to indicate she would cut off his hand if he touched her.

I wasn't sure if anyone who didn't know them would see the tension bouncing between them, but to me, it was very clear. "Kind of looks like they are having a lovers' quarrel."

"She wouldn't have," Ethan said in horror. "Fuckboys are not her type."

"You never know." I looked up at him since he was so damn tall and was wearing boots with a slight heel to make him even taller. "Do *you* like Leo?"

"Ew. That man's penis has been in way too many orifices." He shook his head, and I swore his cheeks pinkened, but it was getting a bit warm in the sun. "He would destroy Libby."

"You mean destroy her pus-" I gasped as tattooed-covered arms wrapped around me in a bear hug and picked me up off the ground.

Ethan rolled his eyes dramatically and took off to

where the photographer was now talking to Libby and Ryker, Leo nowhere to be seen.

"Were you just about to say something about a pussy being destroyed?" Luca nipped at my ear. "Ethan has already seen and heard enough, don't you think?"

"Not my fault he didn't knock." I squirmed in his hold and spun around, looping my arms around his neck. "You looked sexy in that hard hat. I think we might need to get you one."

He snorted. "Do you want me to dance around naked singing the YMCA song for you?"

"That would really get me going if I'm being honest." I felt someone behind me and then caught a hint of Garrett's cologne. "Garrett too. We need to be safe with all the nailing, hammering, and screwing going on."

Garrett groaned as he wrapped an arm around my shoulders and kissed the side of my head. "Good thing you're cute. Want to go help us convince people to support the foundation?"

We made our rounds through the throng of attendees over the next hour, Ryker joining us not long after we began chatting with potential donors. Phase two was all about securing donations to run the center for the first year of operation. The first phase donations went toward building the center and employing a small staff which included Leo and would eventually include Libby when she moved into Ryker's currently vacant condo in the coming weeks.

With things finally winding down, I stood with Garrett and Luca, waiting as Ryker checked in with Leo one last time. He was still working on not micromanaging every single little thing, but it was a work in progress. His trust in Leo as the executive director of the foundation grew every day.

Ryker walked over to us, waiting on the sidewalk. "Everything seems to be handled for clean up, so we can head home."

"I was thinking." Garrett took my hand as we walked to the waiting SUV. "Let's go to Pastrami Palace for lunch."

"All of us?" Luca opened the back door for us.

"Yeah. It will make a great day even better." Garrett slid in and across the seat.

"That sounds-" I squealed as a giant rat ran across the street with what looked an awful lot like an Oreo in its mouth. "It's Splinter!"

Ryker laughed, ushering me into the back seat before getting in next to me. "You know, maybe that rat is actually good luck. He brought us together."

I buckled my seatbelt and sighed. "Maybe he was here making more magic happen for other people."

"Why not for us?" Garrett rested his hand on my thigh.

"We have all the magic we need."

Also by Maya Nicole

Check out my website for an up to date list of books.

www.mayanicole.com

Printed in Great Britain
by Amazon

43679733R00195